Single All the Way

Single Dads of Dragonfly Lake

Amy Knupp

Chapter One

Ben

Being a single dad of two little girls was not for the weak.

Balancing the single dad gig with a thriving veterinary practice? I'd been trying to do it for several years, and most days all I could do was hold on and get through the day, hoping everyone's needs were met.

Take today, for example.

This chilly, rainy Sunday morning four days before Thanksgiving had started with an emergency call just before five a.m. from Bill Gibbons, a family friend since my childhood. His mare was in labor and needed help. I'd been waiting for my coffee to brew, preparing for my morning chores, planning to wake up the girls for feeding time as usual—our animals', not the girls'—when the call had come in.

When a mare experienced dystocia, there was no time to waste—both her and the foal's lives were in danger.

I'd woken the girls as my mind spun through options for

childcare. I didn't want to call Grandma Berty, because she'd stayed with Evelyn and Ruby last night until nearly midnight while I went to my weekly single dads' night. At seventy-four, my grandmother needed her sleep.

Normally I'd call one of my techs, but Kat was sick, and Brad was out of town, so I'd had no choice but to grab a box of granola bars and some juice boxes and pile the girls into the truck with me.

"Daddy, I want to get a baby in Freckles's tummy," Ruby, my six-year-old, said from the backseat as I drove us home from what thankfully had ended up a successful birth.

My girls had hung out with Alice, Bill's wife, during the tense birth, but they'd been able to witness the newborn foal standing for its first time just before we left. They'd been happily chattering nonstop ever since, still riding the high of that enchanting miracle.

I couldn't help but be moved by it myself, even though I'd seen it dozens of times. I'd also experienced tragic results in similar situations, so I was all too aware we'd been lucky today.

"Freckles can't have babies. He's a gelding," Evelyn, nine, told Ruby in her older-sister-knows-all voice.

"Bay Leaf then," Ruby persisted. "She's a girl."

"A mare," Evelyn corrected.

"A mare is a girl, and she can have baby horses," Ruby said. "Please, Daddy?"

A laugh burst out of me, but instead of *hell no*, I said, "No baby horses for us for the foreseeable future, Ruby Tuesday. We've got our hands full already."

"Grandma Berty said we shouldn'ta got the llamas." Evelyn was wise beyond her years, an old-soul type, but she didn't hesitate to keep me abreast of all my dear grandmother's opinions. Which was good and bad.

In this case, the logical part of me acknowledged Grandma Berty could be right, but the animal-loving sucker in me would never give those llamas up. Not even escape artist Esmerelda.

"Betty and Esmerelda are part of the family," I reassured my girls.

"So their last name is Holloway?" Ruby asked, pulling another grin from me.

"Of course it is," I confirmed.

"I'm hungry," Ruby said, flipping mental channels at the speed of a first-grader.

"We'll get a real breakfast as soon as we feed the animals. How about pancakes?" I watched my younger daughter's brown eyes light up in the rearview mirror.

"Yes!" Ruby said.

"I bet the chickens are even hungrier," Evelyn said. The hens—all eight of ours and Emerson's six—and Gordon, the rooster, were her responsibility, and she took it seriously.

"Maybe after we feed everyone and I get cleaned up, we'll go to the diner for brunch," I said, thinking it'd be nice to have Monty's crew at the Dragonfly Diner cook for us. The birth had been touch and go. Getting the foal into the right position had been a challenge, and the adrenaline had finally receded, leaving me exhausted.

"We can't go to the diner," Evelyn said. "Miss Emerson is moving in today."

"Shit!" I looked at the dash clock.

"You said a bad word, Daddy," Ruby informed me.

"We're late," I muttered, only half-present in the conversation, my mind jumping to Emerson and her kids

3

and how long they'd been waiting for us. "Which doesn't make bad words okay," I dutifully said to Ruby.

"We're almost home," Evelyn said.

I was, in fact, about to turn into our driveway.

As I pulled in, I noted the clinic parking lot was empty. That wasn't always the case, even when it was closed, as people brought ill or injured animals in at all hours.

Next, out of habit, my gaze veered to the pasture, where the horses and llamas spent their days, to ensure that Esmerelda hadn't escaped. Of course, none of them were out of the barn. I hadn't had a chance to feed them or put them outside. It looked like an indoor day for them anyway due to the incessant cold drizzle.

As soon as I could see past the house to the driveway, I spotted Emerson's SUV. I could tell it was running, as the windows were steamy, and the back wiper swished across every few seconds.

Damn.

At least they'd waited.

I pulled up next to the SUV and turned off the engine. Emerson looked my way, and I mouthed the word *sorry*, but I wasn't sure she could see me through the steam and rain.

"Evel—"

"I got the chickens, Dad," my older daughter said before I could.

"Go in *front* of Miss Emerson's car," I said as she let herself out the back passenger door.

She didn't answer, so I watched to be sure she did as I said. Without a glance at Emerson or her kids, Evelyn walked to the front of the vehicles, her mind fully on the birds, I would bet, then ran toward the chicken coop to do her morning chores.

"Let's go, Ruby."

I got out and opened my daughter's door so she could climb down. She raced around to the passenger side of Emerson's vehicle, likely looking for Xavier.

"Around the front, Ruby!" I called out. "We don't go behind cars, remember?"

"Sorry, Daddy!"

Luckily Emerson wasn't going anywhere, but I wondered how many times a parent needed to repeat the same thing for a kid to finally hear it and follow it. Three or four thousand was my guess.

I made it to Emerson's door without her getting out. When I got there, I saw why. Her four-year-old daughter, Skyler, was curled up in Emerson's lap, her head tucked into Emerson's shoulder.

I heard the door on the other side open, and Ruby and Xavier, who were thick as thieves whenever they were together, ran toward the house, wrapped up in their conversation. Emerson's dog, Nugget, raced after them, around them, in between them, tail wagging, excited to be free of the car.

Finally Emerson opened the door and flashed a smile that was not at all real. Her makeup-free green eyes were tired and concerned. She wore her toffee-colored hair in a messy bun on her head.

"Hey, Ben."

"I'm sorry I wasn't here at eight thirty. I got an emergency call on a distressed mare in labor."

"It's totally fine. We were late too. Everything okay with the mare?"

I couldn't help smiling. "She and her foal are doing well. Everything okay with you?"

As Emerson slid down from the driver's seat, Skyler clung to her like she was never going to let go. Supporting her daughter with one arm, Emerson reached in and picked up a kid-sized backpack.

"Hi, Skyler," I said to the back of her head. "Welcome."

Emerson frowned over her daughter's head. "She's sad to leave Kizzy's house. It's the only home she remembers having."

"That's rough," I said sympathetically. "I think you'll like staying here, Sky. It's like living in the middle of a petting zoo."

She turned her head to look at me, staying glued to Emerson.

"You like animals, right?" I asked.

She nodded, her eyes wide.

"And you get to share a room with Evelyn. It'll be like a sleepover every night."

"I wanna sleep with Mommy," Skyler said and turned her dark-blond head away from me.

Emerson and I exchanged a look as she said, "We'll see, baby girl."

"Let's get in out of the drizzle. I still need to feed the animals, and I promised my girls pancakes after that."

Skyler flipped her head back to face me.

"Do you like pancakes?" I asked her.

She nodded. "With lots of maple syrup."

"We've got lots of maple syrup." I made a mental note that food won out over animals with this little one.

I led them to the house. Once inside, we were swarmed by all three dogs. Fortunately our two knew Emerson's and got along with her. My two cats, Pixie and Jett, however, were untested. I was sure we'd know soon enough how that would go down, but I didn't have time to search for the felines right now.

"Let's go upstairs so you can see the room where you're

staying," I said to Skyler, wanting to do something, anything, to help Emerson out.

Moving was a lot. Moving right before Thanksgiving had to be extra chaotic.

Emerson's mother-in-law had put her in a difficult spot by moving to Las Vegas unexpectedly then selling her house, where Emerson and her kids had lived for four years, suddenly. I suspected Emerson would've bought it from her mother-in-law had it not been in the Heights, which translated to high dollar. I got the impression the military had taken care of Blake's widow sufficiently but not at a level where she could afford the bougiest neighborhood in town.

Emerson claimed to be fine with it all and happy for Kizzy, who'd eloped with an old friend, but I wondered how the woman could justify displacing her son's widow and her grandkids like this.

Our arrangement was temporary, just until the end of the year while Emerson searched for a house, so she and her kids would be somewhat unsettled for the next six weeks. That'd be a challenge for anyone, but for a single parent...

"I wanna sleep with Mommy," Skyler said again.

Emerson closed her eyes for an almost indiscernible moment, just long enough for me to see she wasn't as cool and unbothered as she seemed on the surface. "Come on, sweetie. Let's go check it out and unpack Waylon. He'll want to get comfortable, won't he?" She bent over and slid her daughter to her feet, then handed her the backpack.

Waylon? My brows went up. Was there a critter I hadn't accounted for? I was a chronic rescuer, but even I could admit we were nearing max occupancy at the Holloway homestead.

"Her plush elephant," Emerson explained, grinning. "He doesn't eat much."

I let out my breath and smiled back at her. "Plush elephants we can handle. So...laundry's in that bathroom." I pointed into the room off the kitchen. "Use it whenever you want."

Emerson had been to my house before. She and her kids had lived in town since Blake's death. We sometimes watched each other's kids, but she hadn't spent a lot of time here. I wanted her and Skyler and Xavier to feel completely at home. Blake and I had been friends since we were three, and it was a no-brainer for me to help Emerson out whenever she needed me—or my house.

From the kitchen, we went into the dining room to access the stairs. Skyler walked over to my bedroom doorway.

"That's my room," I told her. "Everyone else's is upstairs."

"It's off the dining room?" Emerson asked.

"Welcome to the early 1900s," I said. "The layout is awkward. My efforts went into building the clinic first. I was hoping to tackle house updates before now, but I haven't had time to think about it."

"I get that. Life is...a lot. This place has a certain charm the way it is though."

"There's lots of room upstairs. Come on up."

We went upstairs, where I could hear Ruby and Xavier in her room. All three dogs followed us up and joined us on our three-minute tour.

"I've got you in here," I told Emerson. I opened the door and let her precede me into the small but cozy room with a ceiling that angled in on both sides.

"This is adorable." Emerson tilted her head at me. "Did you do it up just for me?"

"I've been meaning to make it into a guest room anyway," I said, which was the truth.

"It's very feminine. Do you have a lot of female guests?" she teased.

"Just one."

Her smile disappeared, which made mine grow.

"Her name is Grandma Berty. She doesn't normally sleep here though. She drives home even on nights like last night, when I don't get back till midnight. I don't like her out that late. So eventually, this will be hers when she needs it."

I showed them the bathroom, Ruby's room, where Xavier was making himself at home, having lugged in his suitcase from the car, and finally Evelyn and Skyler's room.

"You two get the biggest room," I told Skyler.

Emerson went in and sat on the floor, pulling her daughter to her lap and making a production of unpacking Waylon.

"Sorry to desert you, but I've got hungry horses and llamas," I said, noticing it was nearly ten a.m.

"Go. We're fine."

"Evelyn will be done with the chickens in a few minutes. She can show you around in more detail."

"We'll grab our suitcases in a few." Emerson checked her watch. "I have to meet the movers at noon."

I headed downstairs with Nugget following me. Pixie, our gray former runt who now weighed seventeen pounds, was at the foot of the stairs, probably wondering what all the commotion was. When she saw that the dog wasn't one of our approved family members, she went into a defensive stance and hissed.

The dog, who'd probably not met a cat before, went

right up to Pixie and sniffed, which got her a swipe across the nose before the cat hightailed it into my bedroom.

I patted the dog, who looked up at me in confusion, wondering why she couldn't be friends with every living thing. Then I closed my bedroom door, hoping both cats were in there and that they wouldn't need the litter box for the next hour.

When I stepped outside, the cold rain had intensified, but I didn't care. I walked out into it and breathed in the relative silence. I loved my daughters more than anything in the world, but life with them—and all our animals—was loud. Sometimes I craved quiet more than a Meat-astic Pizza from Humble's.

The light in the chicken house was on, telling me Evelyn was still doing her chores. With full confidence she was okay, I entered the barn and inhaled the smell, a mix of animal, wood, humidity, and yes, manure, and my shoulders loosened. The barn was my sanctuary, feeding the horses and llamas my meditation. The aroma had the power to lower my stress level instantly.

"Hey, Smoky." I rubbed the black quarter horse's sleek neck. "I know you're hungry, boy. I'm on it."

Freckles and Bay Leaf, in the next stalls, were also impatient for their breakfast, so I made quick work of getting all three of them fed and watered. Next I took care of Betty and Esmerelda, making sure everyone had enough feed and water for the day.

My friends gave me shit for adopting so many animals, calling me a sucker and saying one more adoption would put me over the edge. I had a lot on my plate for sure, and I could cop to having a tried-and-true soft spot for creatures in need of a home, but I never took in someone on a whim.

At least I hadn't until I'd invited Emerson and her kids to stay with us.

We'd been at the grand opening for Earthly Charm when she'd taken the call from Kizzy and learned Kizzy had an incredible preemptive, time-sensitive offer on her home in the Heights. Emerson had graciously, in my opinion, told her mother-in-law to accept. When she'd ended the call, I'd seen reality start to settle in as she realized what a tight spot that put her in, so of course I'd offered them a place to stay. How could I not?

I'd been too busy to really think about the implications in the two and a half weeks since, aside from figuring out who would sleep where. Until now, it'd all been logistics.

Now I was realizing how much I'd bitten off—three more personalities to weave into our daily life...plus a dog. We'd already moved her six hens in with our brood. Our family's schedule could be irregular due to my unpredictable work. Today was a perfect example.

Which reminded me, there were five people in my house waiting for pancakes. As I finished up with the outside animals, I shoved down the fatigue and ignored that depleted, post-adrenaline-crash feeling. The day was young, and resting was a myth.

I bent down and scratched two of the barn cats between the ears, told the horses and llamas goodbye, and headed to the house, wondering what kind of chaos I'd walk into.

As I opened the door to the kitchen, the first things I registered were the smell of bacon and the sizzle of food on the stove. I froze and took in the scene.

Emerson was at the stove, flipping bacon in a skillet and eyeing the griddle, where golden pancakes were fluffing up. Skyler was in the adjoining dining room, setting the table. My mouth fell open as I leaned against the door behind me.

"You're incredible," I said, stunned and so fucking grateful.

She turned and smiled as she met my gaze with her pretty eyes.

I realized I should've said *This is incredible* instead. That was slightly less personal. Because for the next six weeks, I'd be living with my late best friend's wife, who I'd had feelings for a lifetime ago.

"You seem to be having a crazy day," Emerson said, "and part of that's because you're taking us in. This is the least I could do."

I made a point of turning my attention to the food. "Better be careful. I could get used to this."

I said it as a joke, but truer words had never been spoken.

I needed to be cautious, and I needed to *not* get used to any of this.

Chapter Two

Emerson

Why was it that, when you were so exhausted you thought you might collapse, you couldn't sleep once you finally went to bed?

Today had been crazy. Of course it'd been crazy. We'd had movers helping us for hours. Thank God for movers and for Kizzy's generosity in paying for all of it, because there'd been a lot of moving parts.

First they'd moved the kids' beds and some clothing and toys to Ben's house for us to use for the next few weeks. Then they'd taken the rest of the kids' and my belongings to one storage unit and anything that was left, which belonged to Kizzy, to a separate unit for her to deal with later.

After that circus, we'd picked up a couple of carryout pizzas from Humble's and eaten a late dinner with Ben and his kids. Then everyone had gone to bed. Tomorrow was a school day and a workday for Ben. Though my hair salon was closed on Mondays, I usually went in to take care of the business and paperwork that piled up, like bills and payroll.

And here I was, wide-awake.

After some time at the salon, I planned to organize the kids' stuff and figure out how to keep their detritus out of the way at Ben's. He'd been so kind to invite us into his home, and I didn't want to wear out our welcome before I found a place of our own. I'd done my best to teach my kids to pick up after themselves, but they were seven and four. Tidying was a constant battle.

On top of all the chaos and upheaval, I hadn't slept much last night—or the past hundred nights or maybe a thousand. Ten thousand? I'd been perpetually sleep-deprived for years. I figured I could catch up when the kids were grown.

Now I lay in the double bed in Ben's guest room with Skyler cuddled up beside me. When she'd first wandered in, lugging Waylon, I'd welcomed her. As tired as I was, I knew she was struggling hard with our family's unsettled state. I just wanted to hug away her anxiety. Honestly I'd appreciated the contact too, content to pull her into me under the warm blankets and try to get used to the night noises of a different house.

That was nearly two hours ago. Skyler had fallen asleep almost immediately, but now my mind was spinning with all the things: Would any new real estate listings pop up tomorrow? What was that periodic clicking in the walls? Would my employees at Posh stay healthy for the upcoming holiday season, a.k.a. our busiest four weeks of the year? How awkward would Christmas at Ben's house be? Was he really okay with Kizzy and her new wife joining us for the holiday as planned?

Shut up, brain. It's almost midnight, and I need sleep!

I was no closer to slumber, with the exception of my arm, which was going numb. Very carefully, I pulled away from my daughter, holding my breath to make sure she didn't stir. Then I lay there on my back, staring up at the ceiling, wondering what the light shining in from outside was. A barn light? Porch light? Full moon?

Did it matter?

Of course not, but my brain was not my friend right now.

Irritated, I inched away from Skyler, then rolled out of bed and tiptoed to the door, pausing to make sure she stayed asleep. I closed it without a sound and crept down the stairs. Halfway down, just after I stepped on a creaky step, I realized there was a dim light coming from the kitchen.

Before I could take another step, Ben stuck his head around the kitchen doorway and looked straight up at me. So much for sneaking back to my room.

I glanced at myself to make sure I was decent enough and realized I made quite a sight. I wore calf-high fuzzy slipper socks, boy shorts because I hated pants on my legs under the blankets, and a long-sleeve thermal pajama shirt that outlined my torso. I'd never been so conscious of the ten or fifteen pounds I'd failed to lose after Skyler was born.

"Oh, it's you," he whispered.

"I didn't know you were up. I was just going to make a cup of bedtime tea."

He gestured me into the kitchen with his head, so I descended the rest of the steps, my arms over my chest.

"What is this magical bedtime tea you speak of?" he asked as I came around the corner.

I didn't immediately answer because I was too busy taking in the scene. Ben wore gray sweatpants and a long-sleeve tee that stretched over a nicely sculpted chest and intriguing biceps I hadn't noticed before. His feet were bare and must have been cold on the old, wood-plank floor.

Though I was sure he'd gone to bed when the rest of us did, he didn't look at all mussed, just his usual competent, put-together, good-looking self.

The counter, which had been cleared and cleaned after dinner, was covered with loaves of bread and a large mixing bowl.

"What are you doing?" I asked.

"Thanksgiving prep," he said with a noticeable amount of enthusiasm in his tone.

"At midnight? Four days out? I thought you went to bed."

"I realized I forgot to take the bird out of the freezer. I bought a big one this year since you three will be here. It needs to thaw."

There was indeed a frozen turkey taking up two-thirds of the generous farmhouse sink.

"I'm sorry to butt in on your family's holiday."

If we had any other options, I'd make alternate plans. I'd considered taking the kids to a restaurant, but I knew Ben well enough to understand that would never fly. He'd be hurt or offended, and that was the last thing I wanted. I had my tribe of girlfriends in town, but they had their families or other plans I didn't want to shoe-horn my kids into.

"Emerson," he said sternly. "Stop it. You and your kids are like family. And you're living here. We're looking forward to having you with us."

He returned to doing something at the counter with his back to me, as if the case was closed, and I supposed it was.

"I'm not really a holiday person, I guess," I said, trying to keep my tone light. "What are you doing now?"

I went to the cupboard he'd shown me earlier for my tea storage and took out the box of lavender and chamomile, then tried to remember where the mugs were.

Ben pointed to the mug cabinet. "Cubing the bread and setting it out to dry for stuffing."

"You make it from scratch?"

"I do. I go all out with Thanksgiving dinner. It'll be even more fun with more people to feed this year."

"Want some?" I held up a second mug.

"I'll try it," he said, his attention on the bread.

It occurred to me I should offer to help with the meal. Not tonight, but on Thursday. Wednesday? Whenever he'd be doing the work. I didn't know because Kizzy and I had kept it simple every year since it was only the four of us and sometimes one or both of her other sons. Precooked ham, side dishes from the Country Market, pies from Sugar.

"What's on the menu?" I asked as I put the mugs in the microwave and started it.

"Turkey with stuffing, green-bean casserole, mashed potatoes and gravy, cranberry sauce, corn casserole, pie... What else would you like? Am I missing any favorites?"

"You're going to make all that?"

"I can alter the menu if you guys have any traditions or there's something the kids are used to."

I stood there with my mouth gaping open for a few seconds as I tried to comprehend the trouble he was going to for one meal that would be devoured in less than an hour. I sensed him switching his gaze from the bread to me, waiting for an answer.

"We don't have any traditions," I said. In truth, I'd never had a big, homemade feast for Thanksgiving in my life.

"What kind of pie do you like?"

With a chuckle, I said, "I like all the pie. Not picky."

"What's your favorite though? Pumpkin? Apple?"

"French silk. Chocolate pecan. Oreo."

He laughed. "Still with the chocolate after all these years, huh?"

I gave him a scandalized look. "That's not something a girl grows out of."

"I remember you brought a candy bar with you to biology lab nearly every day."

"You have a good memory." Those were the days when chocolate didn't go straight to my ass.

"You really don't have any traditions?"

"Thanksgiving's never been big for me. When I was growing up, my mom and grandma were always so tired from working that we went for easy. There were a few years my mom and I did frozen pizza because Grams had to work on the holiday."

It had always been just the three of us. My grandma was widowed before I was born. My dad had never been in the picture. A fling with a tourist, my mom had always told me, and she hadn't been able to track him down.

"What about with Blake?"

"We had a grand total of two Thanksgivings together once we were married." Most years he'd been overseas working. We'd tried not to let it bother us. We were young and had our whole lives ahead of us, or so we'd thought.

I swallowed down those thoughts and noticed Ben was watching me, as if gauging how hard the subject of my husband was.

Flashing him a subdued smile, I said, "I'm okay. The upside of that is that Thanksgiving doesn't bring a lot of hard memories, you know?"

He nodded and looked somber as he glanced back at the bread.

"What about you and Leeann?"

He was quiet for several long seconds. "Holidays were...

tricky with Leeann. Some of them were good. Others... drama filled, you could say."

I knew now his late wife, who'd been raised in foster homes, had been plagued with mental health issues and had taken her own life when Ruby was a baby. Apparently postpartum depression, added to her other challenges, had been too much for the poor woman. I was beyond sympathetic, but I didn't have much insight about Ben and Leeann's life together. I'd lived across the country on base.

Though Blake and I had spent a lot of time with Ben in high school, our connection had weakened after graduation, when Blake and I married and moved away. After my mom died and then a few years later my grandma, I'd become even more disconnected from the goings-on in Dragonfly Lake. By the time Ben met Leeann, when he was close to finishing vet school, we were lucky to see him once a year if we had a chance to make it home.

"I'm sorry to hear that," I said, not wanting to pry and bring up hard memories.

"Now I go overboard to make holidays special for my kids." He chuckled. "Let's just say we've started some traditions, especially since moving out here to the country. They don't have many memories of their mother, good or bad. They were too young. Maybe I try to overcompensate."

"I get that."

Though holidays were barely on my radar, I could relate to trying to love my kids enough for two parents.

My mother-in-law, Kizzy, had been so good for Xavier and Skyler, loving them like a grandmother yet never hesitating to guide them or discipline them when they needed it. She was exactly what we'd needed after Blake's death. She'd sacrificed a lot for us to be able to live with her—her privacy and peace, for starters. That was why I didn't begrudge her her freedom and happiness now. She deserved all the bliss and love she could find with Shannon.

It was past time I stood on my own two legs anyway. God knows I'd had it hammered into my head—and my heart—that loss was inevitable. The more people I got close to, the more I risked losing.

"What kind of traditions have you started?" I asked, more to make conversation than out of true interest. I had a grand total of zero excitement about Turkey Day. My focus was on securing the future for my kiddos by finding us a place to settle, hopefully for the rest of their childhood and beyond.

With a quiet laugh, he said, "Nothing too out there. We all pitch in to make the meal. Before we eat, we go around, and each person tells what we're most thankful for. After dinner, we go on a long walk in the woods to burn off some of the calories and get fresh air. Then we come back and have pie and play board games. In the evening, we hit the tree-lighting ceremony on the square."

The microwave dinged, so I took the mugs out, added the tea bags, and let them steep as what he said soaked in.

"That's a lot," I said, trying to keep my voice neutral.

Inside, I was thinking I wasn't entirely comfortable with any of it. My introverted self would rather hole up with my kids and watch a movie, maybe even drift off during it. We'd still be together as a family that way.

"That's the point," Ben said as he opened the final package of bread and started ripping it up. "It's family time overload in a good way. Memory making. It's turned out to be a special day the past couple years."

I nodded.

"The kids love it," he added, "and hopefully you will too."

I made myself smile, and my brows rose as I looked at him. "We'll see."

"A skeptic, huh? Challenge accepted. We're going to do whatever we can so you and Xavier and Skyler have the best holiday ever."

"I'm terrified." I made it sound light and funny, but I couldn't deny the truth in that. I wasn't in a holly-jolly mood. Never had been. Holidays were a hassle more than anything. Ben was a dear friend, was my husband's best friend for most of their childhood, but that didn't mean I was up for deepening the friendship. We both had too much on our plates to focus on anything but our kids and businesses.

What had I gotten myself into by moving in here for the next six weeks?

Chapter Three

Emerson

I felt like I'd only been asleep for a few minutes when I was jolted awake by an awful noise. It sounded like a shrill, coarse woman's laughter outside in the distance.

Skyler rolled into my side and ducked her head under the covers. "Mommy, what *is* that?" she asked in a high, small voice.

The sound came again. "The rooster," I realized. "That's awful."

Skyler didn't stir from being glued to me.

"He's outside, sweetie. Just doing his wakeup call." *From hell,* I added in my head.

"I don't like him."

I wasn't sure I did either. Was that how we were going to wake up every day for the next month and a half? God, save my sanity.

I kissed my daughter on the head, then rolled out of bed, my eyes burning from lack of sleep. The air was chilly outside of the blankets. I went to the small dormer window and peered outside.

The sun wasn't up yet. I could see the chicken house beyond the garage, and the birds were still locked up for the night. Wasn't a rooster supposed to wait for sunrise to do his cock-a-doodle-death sounds?

I went back to the nightstand and picked up my phone. The time was ten after five.

"I'm going to the bathroom, Sky. Be back in a few."

When I entered the hall, I was met with way too much activity for this time of day. I nearly ran into Ben, leaning against the doorjamb of Ruby and Xavier's room.

"Oh," I said, startled, though I shouldn't be. He'd warned me they started early around here in order to fit in the morning chores.

"Good morning." He was dressed in jeans and a thick hoodie, looking wide awake as he smiled down at me.

"Morning," I mumbled. "Need the restr— Ah. After Evelyn." His daughter went in before I could.

"Hi, Mom!" Xavier, my blond cutie, bounced into my sight beyond Ben, fully dressed as well, excitement lighting up his eyes.

"Hey, kiddo. How'd you sleep?"

"Good! I'm gonna help Dr. Ben and Ruby with the animals."

I glanced at Ben to check his reaction. He nodded and smiled. "It's what we do around here."

"I don't want him to be more work for you."

"He won't be at all. He can help Ruby with the horses today."

"Should I— Can Skyler and I do something to help?" If it was what they did around here, we should probably all contribute.

With a chuckle, he shook his head and said, "No. It's dirty work, and we've got it covered."

Today I wasn't going to argue, but maybe there was something Sky and I could handle in the future to earn our keep, so to speak. "If you're sure..."

"I'm surprised you're up. You had a long day yesterday."

"So did you," I said, recalling the tale of the horse emergency.

"Used to it, but I'm betting you're not."

"Does the rooster do that every day?"

He grimaced. "He does. Same time every morning and several times throughout the day. You get used to it."

"I don't hardly notice Gordon's wakeup call anymore," Ruby sang out as she pulled on knee-high socks with horses on them.

"Gordon," I repeated, wondering how Gordon would taste.

"Gordon Ramsay is his full name," Ben said.

"Oh, my God. Your hens..." His chickens had names like Cinnamon and Pepper and Ginger...all eight of them.

"Spices," he confirmed.

My hair fell over my face when I looked down at Ben's wool-socked feet and grinned slightly.

"Your room is closest to the chicken house," Ben said. "Sorry about that."

When I lifted my gaze to meet his, he brushed my hair back behind my shoulder with one finger. The tenderness and familiarity of the gesture startled me, but I hid any reaction. I didn't hate it, just didn't expect it.

"Front row seats to the crazy cock," I said. "He sounds like a woman laughing."

"A disturbed woman laughing," he agreed. "We might need to get you a white noise machine while you're here."

Evelyn came out of the bathroom before I could answer.

"Anyone need the bathroom?" I asked.

"It's yours," Ben said. "If you think you can go back to sleep, feel free. The kids and I will be doing chores for an hour or so. I've got Xav."

Both our gazes went to my son, who was stuffing his feet into tennis shoes.

"Might want to get him some work boots if his interest in morning chores persists," Ben said.

I nodded as I hurried off to the bathroom.

After I relieved myself, I washed my hands, thinking I'd go ahead and shower as soon as Ben and the three kids went outside.

When I'd agreed to take Ben up on his offer for us to stay here, I hadn't stopped to think about the logistics of the six of us sharing two bathrooms. Hadn't stopped to think about many of the details at all of sharing a house with him and his family. I'd mostly been relieved one tricky detail was figured out as I'd busted my butt to pack an entire four-bedroom house—one Kizzy had lived in for fortyish years and had the *stuff* to prove it—in less than three weeks.

I glanced in the large mirror behind the sink as I turned off the water and gasped when I caught sight of myself.

My hair was a tangled mess from tossing and turning, my eyes looked puffy, and my nipples were sticking out through my sleep shirt like beacons of light in a dark storm for anyone to notice.

And I'd just stood a foot away from Ben and talked to him for five minutes without a thought to pulling a heavy sweatshirt on.

Super.

I could hear Ben herding Evelyn, Ruby, and Xavier

downstairs, leaving me privacy to get back to my room and check on Sky.

Even though I was alone, I crossed my arms over my chest as I hurried back to Skyler. The outside door slammed beneath my room, and the house went quiet.

Enough light shone in from the hall that I could instantly see Skyler had fallen back asleep, bless her sweet heart. It was early, and she'd had a restless night too. I'd let her sleep while I showered.

Forty-five minutes later, I was showered and dressed with my hair and makeup done. I woke up Skyler, took her and Waylon into the room she was supposed to share with Evelyn, and encouraged her to get dressed and meet me in the kitchen. I planned to get breakfast going for everyone. It was the least I could do.

As I went down to the kitchen, I vowed I'd work on getting her to sleep in her own bed.

By the time Ben and the other three kids tromped in, I had a big skillet full of scrambled eggs and another with sausage nearly ready to serve. The four-slot toaster popped up, and I slid over to add the golden-brown slices to the plate of toast, buttering each one.

"Emerson, you don't have to do this," Ben said at the doorway as he took his work gloves off and tucked them in a cubby in the mudroom.

I shook my head. "Sure. I'll just let you do all the chores while I sleep, and then you can feed me too." I shook my head at him with a *you're crazy* expression. "I need to pay you for groceries."

"We'll split the next grocery run," he said, not seeming concerned at all.

I *was* concerned. I was already epically aware of how

much we were imposing on him and his family. I'd do whatever I could to pull my weight by helping with the animals and kids as well as paying our fair share for food.

I'd find a way later to even things out. Right now, I had three chattering kids and a large man to feed.

As I turned the burners off and dished up the food, Evelyn and Ruby set plates and silverware around the dining room table as if they did it every day. I suspected they did.

My kids helped out whenever I asked them, but we had a long way to go to get to Holloway standards.

"What can Xavier do?" I asked Ben, who was pouring himself a mug of coffee. I'd found the pot already brewed when I got downstairs, so he must've started it before waking the kids.

He glanced toward the table in the other room. "Juice cups." He took down colorful cups and handed the stack to my son. "Then you can get the jug of orange juice out of the fridge and put it on the table," he said to Xavier.

My son did as he was told, which wasn't always how it went with him.

"How do you do this?" I asked Ben quietly as I stuck a serving spoon into the bowl of eggs.

"Do what?"

I laughed dryly because pretty much his whole lifestyle confounded me. "Let's see, get the kids up before the sun, get them to help with chores and set the table without asking, no arguments along the way..."

I couldn't even get Skyler to sleep in her own bed, let alone help with chores. To be fair, she wasn't herself at all. This temporary move was messing with her in ways I hadn't expected.

"Llamas are cool," Ben joked. "Who wouldn't want to get up at five a.m. to help with them?"

I made a face and laughed. "I can think of things I'd rather do."

"You're not under ten."

"Your household is so organized. Remind me to never let you into mine...when I have one."

He inched closer and said in a low voice, "I made a deal with the kids when we got the horses and chickens. We could only get them if they helped me every day."

"That was a couple of years ago, right?"

"Going on three. Then we added the llamas earlier this year. Same deal applies."

"They help *without you asking*," I repeated. "Are there special pills for that?"

He laughed. "It's not always as seamless as today. They're excited to have your kids here and show them how it's done."

I nodded as we loaded our arms with the food and headed to the table.

"And one of mine isn't even dressed yet." I set the eggs and toast on the table, then went to the foot of the stairs and called up, "Skyler, you need to hurry. We're eating breakfast."

I heard a door squeak upstairs, then the bathroom door close. I'd check on her in a few minutes. She wasn't the fastest riser in the morning, but this was slow even for her.

The rest of us had filled our plates when Skyler appeared, still in her nightgown. She looked on the verge of crying, then dashed over to me and buried her face in my side.

Ben caught my gaze with a concerned look that matched the feeling in my gut.

"What's going on, sweetie?" I asked her, pulling her into me.

"I don't wanna go to school," she said, her little voice muffled by my sweater.

I made eye contact with Ben again without thought, even though this wasn't his problem.

"You have to go to school," Evelyn said.

"You're doing Thanksgiving projects this week, Sky," I said. "Remember?"

My daughter only burrowed deeper into me, twisting my heart. This wasn't normal. Skyler liked school.

I wasn't going to get answers with an audience, so I pushed back from the table, eyeing my hot food with a flash of longing. I had a feeling it would be cold by the time I saw to this challenge, but Skyler was more important.

Hoisting her up in my arms even though she was getting heavy, I told Xavier, "Get your tummy full and help with cleanup if I'm not back."

He nodded, likely sensing I needed his cooperation more than usual.

I took Skyler up to her room, hoping to get her dressed and ready to go as we talked.

My hope would be throttled over the next ten minutes, during which Skyler mostly cried and gave me no specific reasons for her sudden refusal to go to preschool. I peppered her with questions, trying to ensure nothing bad had happened last week that was causing her reluctance, but it just made her cry harder.

I was almost certain it was nothing to do with school and everything to do with change. My heart went out to her. Change was hard. Our family had been through a lot, but Skyler was too young to remember most of it. She'd been quieter and quicker to cry since Kizzy went away to visit her college friend and ended up eloping with her and moving to Nevada. It didn't matter that we FaceTimed with her grandmother several times a week and only marginally calmed her when I reminded her of her nana's upcoming holiday visit.

"Okay," I finally said, feeling defeated, because there was no way around a hundred more changes and six more weeks of being unsettled, minimum. My optimism that I could find a good house for sale within my budget and in the Dragonfly Lake school district by then was dwindling. I leaned down and forced eye contact with her, holding her hand. "I'll make a deal with you. You can stay home today if you promise me you'll go tomorrow and Wednesday. Then it's Thanksgiving, and you'll go back on Monday."

Her lower lip protruded, and she inhaled shakily as I held my breath, hoping this would indeed solve this particular problem. Obviously there was a much bigger issue here, but all I could handle was one step at a time.

Peering at me with her big green eyes, she nodded slowly. "Okay, Mommy."

"Okay?" I repeated. "You promise you'll go to school tomorrow to see your friends and do Thanksgiving art?"

She looked about to cry, but she nodded again.

I exhaled as I pulled her in close. "We still have to take Xavier to school, so let's get you dressed."

When we returned to the dining room, all the places except mine and Skyler's were cleared, and Xavier was in the kitchen with Ben and his kids, putting plates in the dishwasher. The serving bowls were still on the table, so I loaded up my daughter's plate.

"Okay, you three. Thanks for your help," Ben said. "Upstairs, brush your teeth, use the bathroom, get your school stuff."

Xavier and Ruby raced through the dining room to the stairs.

"Hi, Mom! Hi, Skyler!" my son said before he stomped up the stairs with his best friend.

Evelyn came through more slowly, sedately. "Is Skyler okay?"

That was the question of the hour, but to the little girl, I smiled and reassured her, "Skyler's just fine. You're sweet for asking."

Evelyn eyed Sky with skepticism but made her way up the stairs.

Before sitting down to my cold breakfast, I went into the kitchen.

"Thank you," I said quietly as I sidled up alongside Ben at the counter. "For keeping Xavier on track. I owe you."

"You don't owe me a thing," he said in that low, private voice.

I laughed at that. "Let's see, you're putting us up in your home *during* the holidays, letting my kid help with the animals, keeping him in line while I handle Skyler... I don't know how I'll repay you. Can I at least pick your kids up after school and drive them home for you?"

"No need. They take the bus. Grandma Berty will be waiting when they get here."

"The bus. Of course they take the bus. Mornings too?"

"Mornings too. It'll be here in"—he looked at his watch —"eight minutes."

"I'll call the school today and sign up Xavier for morning bus."

"Afternoons too," Ben said.

"He comes to the salon with me."

"He can come here. Grandma Berty stays with Ruby and Evelyn. She loves kids."

I shook my head. "No. No way am I taking advantage of your generosity in yet another way."

"She's here every day. She's good with them."

"I'm sure she is, but I'm not going to throw two more kids at her."

"I need to get my two out the door and to the bus, then get ready for work."

He went to the stairs and hollered up at his kids to get moving, and I went back to the table with Skyler and finally sat down to eat.

As Skyler tore into her eggs, Ben turned toward me and said, "We'll discuss childcare later."

With a bite of cold eggs in my mouth, I shook my head. As soon as I swallowed the bite, I said, "Waste of time. You're already doing too much for me."

Ben came up to the edge of the table on the opposite side, leaned his hands on it, looked me in the eye, and said, "For the next six weeks or however long you're here, Emerson, we're in this together. We help each other."

His eyes were intense as he stared into mine. It got to me. The thought of having someone at my side, a partner in all the chaos, had as much allure as a restorative, full-service spa getaway. In that moment, I couldn't help noticing how good-looking Ben was with his empathetic, handsome eyes and his just-right beard on an angled, masculine jaw.

I shook my head at myself, because that was a random and pointless thought. As tempting as it was to lean on someone, I couldn't let myself. The kids and I would be moving on soon enough, and then I'd have to readjust to handling everything on my own. It'd be better to never let myself get used to it in the first place.

Peering back at him, I said, "Your kids are going to be late for the bus."

He swore silently, straightened, and bellowed out to his kids just as they thundered down the stairs. I counted it as a win for me, even if only temporary.

Chapter Four

Ben

"What the heck did you do?" I asked as I walked into exam room one for my first appointment of the day.

My buddy Max Dawson was crouched in front of the two chairs where most of my human clients sat, trying to urge someone out.

"Come on, Mahomes," he said to whatever was under the chairs. Felines, according to my tech Kat's notes.

As he reached farther under to grab Mahomes, a fluffy gray kitten wandered out from the other side of the cabinet and looked up at me.

"Who is this?" I bent down and held out my hand, wiggling my fingers.

"That," Max said as he stood up holding a orange kitten about the same size, "is Monet."

The little beast looked at my fingers half-cross-eyed and couldn't resist pouncing toward them. When he got close enough, I scooped him up.

"Aren't you a cute one?" I held the critter at eye level in one hand.

He looked to be about ten to twelve weeks old and had curious eyes that didn't miss anything—and razor-sharp claws that could put holes in a guy.

"Mahomes and Monet. I get the football connection, but French Impressionism?" I asked.

"Harper named that one. She likes the way it sounds with Mahomes, plus art representation."

"You don't have to work today?"

"This is my planning period. I've got about forty minutes left."

"Let's not waste time then." I looked at Monet's underside and confirmed he was a male, then took him to the exam table and started a routine kitten exam. "Saturday night at Chance's, you didn't mention adopting kittens," I said.

"Saturday night at Chance's, I didn't have any intention of adopting kittens," Max countered. "Then yesterday, some asshat abandoned these two in a cardboard box at the edge of my yard."

I clenched my jaw and shook my head at the callousness of people. "So you're keeping them?"

Max chuckled. "Between Harper and Danny, I didn't stand a chance. When I called your office at seven thirty, Colby said she could work us in before your first appointment. I thought you should check them over, make sure they're healthy."

"They look pretty good on the outside, like someone's been taking care of them."

"We gave them a bath last night. They were a little ragged, but their appetites are voracious. They like tuna."

"Human tuna?" I asked.

35

"It's all we had. I'll pick up cat food today."

"We sell it here. Save yourself a trip. I don't suppose the asshats left a note saying whether these two were vaccinated?"

Max scoffed and shook his head.

"We'll give them full dosages to be sure. I'll also do a blood test to rule out the bad stuff. I don't see any fleas, so they must've been kept inside."

Max stood on the other side of the table, up against it. He tried to hold Mahomes still on the surface, but the orange kitten insisted on climbing Max's sweatshirt and perching on his shoulder.

"Danny must be in kitten bliss." I knew exactly the spot Max had found himself in with baby animals thrown in his lap and a toddler's instant love. It would do my friend some good to have these two feline menaces running the household.

"I've never heard so much infectious giggling." Big, tough football coach Max had a goofy, happy grin on his face.

I wouldn't say he hadn't smiled before Harper, but his grins were wider now and made his eyes light up. He'd loved Danny from the start but had been uptight. From where I stood, it seemed like Harper had lightened Max up good.

"Kittens'll do that," I said, laughing at the big-eyed look Monet gave me as I palpated his abdomen.

"How'd move-in day go?"

"It was sheer chaos, but we got it done. Or rather the movers got it done."

Max shook his head. "I still can't believe you sponta-neously offered to take in four more souls in need." He'd been giving me shit about my "rescue syndrome" since I adopted the llamas.

"I could say the same to you." I held up the kitten in a cheers-type salute, then gestured for him to trade cats with me so I could check out Mahomes.

"I guess your point is valid," he allowed. "To think two years ago, I lived alone in a quiet house..."

I laughed. "This is better though, right?"

"This is so much fucking better." He grinned like a man infatuated with both his boy and his fiancée. I had a feeling he was halfway there with these kittens too. "You should try it."

My traitorous brain flashed to Emerson, but I shut it down immediately, just as I'd done last night after our talk in the kitchen. Instead I forced a laugh. "My life is full to overflowing, man. You just said so yourself."

"Your responsibilities are full to overflowing. Not the same thing."

I went quiet while I listened to Mahomes's heart, acting too focused to respond.

"Don't you want a partner in life? A woman to love?" Max persisted. "Emerson's good-looking. Any attraction there?"

I shook my head, but there was *so much* damn attraction. I couldn't admit it out loud. It was bad enough I'd let those thoughts climb into my head, making it that much harder to shut out Emerson's allure.

I needed to slam down on it with a vengeance. Hell, it was day two of her staying with me, and I'd already slipped up and brushed her hair back this morning in an intimate way that didn't exist between us. *Couldn't* exist between us.

"You sure about that?" he asked.

"Just friends. We've known each other forever."

"She's living in your house. You're sharing meals, kids, animals, even holidays. That's a lot of togetherness. Lots of chances for some off-script."

Didn't I know it. I was the dumbest ass alive to have taken her and her kids in, yet if I had to make the decision again, I wouldn't change it.

"Emerson's important to me," I said. "Blake and I were friends from the age of three. She was his wife."

That I'd been attracted to her first, before Blake had ever asked her out, didn't matter.

Though I'd known Emerson in a surface way since grade school, I hadn't gotten to know her on a deeper level until sophomore year in high school.

We'd been assigned as biology lab partners for the semester. She was outgoing and popular. I wasn't an outsider, but I wasn't as social as Blake or the others in that circle. Shy, serious, and studious was probably how someone would've described me even though I did play basketball and run cross-country.

Emerson had been social, friendly, the kind of girl who always had a smile. I don't know why it took being her lab partner for me to notice how pretty that smile was. Maybe it was because I got to know her beyond the surface. The better I'd gotten to know her, the more I'd liked her.

I'd been a late bloomer, more interested in grades and science than girls. She was my first crush.

Back then, I hadn't been overflowing with confidence. I'd kept my feelings to myself, looking forward to fourth-period biology in a way I never would've guessed or admitted to anyone. I started to care more about lab days and what Emerson and I might talk about than the biology lesson itself as we extracted DNA from a banana or dissected a frog, and that was saying something for a kid like me.

In hindsight, not confessing my feelings to Blake had possibly changed the course of my life—and his and hers. Oblivious to my interest in her, Blake had asked Emerson to homecoming that year. They'd started dating, stayed together throughout high school, and the rest was history.

I'd never stood a chance.

Our lives had gone in different directions, with Blake enlisting after graduation, them getting married soon after and moving away, and me heading off to college.

Max was studying me as I examined Mahomes's ears and eyes, then checked in his mouth for teeth. There were a couple breaking through, confirming my guess on his age.

"I knew Blake from sports," Max said. "He seemed like a decent guy—the type who'd want Emerson to be happy if something happened to him."

I nodded, pretending not to understand what he was hinting at.

Blake and I had been inseparable as kids. His grandma had lived next door to me, so whenever he visited her, which was several times a week, we got together. We played T-ball together, hung out in my treehouse, played video games in person and online.

In the four years Emerson had been back in Dragonfly Lake, she'd been grieving and raising her kids, much like I had. There was nothing deeper between us, just platonic support that went both ways, mostly where our kids were concerned. Only since she'd moved into my house had those adolescent sparks of attraction been reignited.

It felt wrong to think of her in any way but as a friend.

"Emerson's holding her own during a challenging time," I said. "Her little girl's having a hard time. Slept with

Emerson last night instead of in Ev's room. She didn't want to go to preschool today, so Emerson kept her home."

"Kizzy threw them into a mess, didn't she?"

"Sold the house out from under them. I'd be pissed, but Emerson says her mother-in-law deserves whatever happiness she can find. I think she's genuinely happy for the woman."

"She's a better person than me then. I'd be hot too," Max said, stretching to catch Monet before he skittered from Max's shoulder down his back.

"It could be a tough few weeks for them—or longer— before Emerson finds a house. I can't change the real estate market or the lack of housing, but I can help in other ways."

Max's brows shot up suggestively. "I can think of a few ways."

"Quit acting twelve," I told him, laughing. "I'll just be there for her. Someone to pour her a glass of wine when the kids are making her nuts. She's a single mom, but she's had Kizzy's help since moving back. Now she doesn't."

"Parenthood is sure as hell a little less difficult when you have a partner."

"That's what I'm thinking." I didn't hate the idea of teaming up while the Esteses were staying with us. "We're including them in our Thanksgiving in every way, with all the trimmings and traditions."

"The kids will love it. Emerson too."

"They've had a rough few months. It'll be a while before they get settled somewhere."

"Lucky thing they just moved in with a knight-in-shining-armor type," Max quipped.

"I can't fix their housing problem, but I can spread Christmas spirit around like glitter."

"So...what? You're going to Christmas the crap out of them?"

As I scratched Mahomes between the ears and got his purr motor revved up, I nodded. It was an easy call. "Yep. Like it or not, Emerson and her kids are about to experience Christmas the Holloway way. It'll be life-changing," I joked.

"For them?" Max asked, looking smug, "or you?"

"Them." I made my voice strong with conviction, but as I walked out after telling him Kat would be in for the blood-work, I felt a hell of a lot less sure.

Christmas spirit I could handle. A crushed heart... No, thank you very much. I'd just have to keep a tight rein on myself.

Chapter Five

Emerson

As I walked with my little girl from A Novel Place to Sugar, I held her hand, half listening to her talk about her new books and half-ensconced in a storm of worries.

I hated that this was so hard for her. She'd been increasingly anxious the past two weeks as the stacks of boxes had grown and our belongings had disappeared into them, but I'd hoped once we got to Ben's and unpacked her most-loved things, she'd settle in and worry less. I thought maybe she'd get carried away with the novelty of having Ben's kids around and sharing a room with Evelyn.

So far, she'd withdrawn more and clung to me. I didn't know how to help her other than what I was doing today.

I'd taken her to the salon with me, where she'd colored pictures and worked through an activity book while I hurried through the admin stuff that couldn't wait. Then we'd gone to the Dragonfly Diner for a special mommy-daughter lunch of Dragonfly Dust Waffles.

Next we'd hit Earthly Charm, where Harper Ellison had shown us pictures of her new kittens and helped Sky pick out a labradorite stone she said helps with courage and bravery during difficult times. I don't know if Skyler chose it for its alleged powers or because of the shiny rainbow iridescence in it.

After that we'd hit the bookstore, where my friend Maeve worked. While Maeve and I caught up, Sky had painstakingly picked out a book after reviewing a dozen. Maeve had shown us a handful of kids' books about moving, and I'd let Skyler pick two. I'd grabbed a cozy mystery for myself, and now here we were, heading for more sweets.

I hoped the mother-daughter time would help my girl feel more grounded. We couldn't do this every day, but though I'd left a lot of work untouched at the salon, this was so much more important.

Times like this made me wish for a partner in parenting, someone with another perspective that could maybe help our kids. Someone else who could spend one-on-one time with them and love them as much as I did. Blake had loved them with all his heart, but being in the military didn't allow him the chance for much hands-on time. Tragically our kids didn't know their father. Xavier had been three when he'd been killed and Skyler only a month old. I'd made most of the parenting decisions alone since they'd been born.

Parenting was the hardest thing a person could do, in my opinion. Doing it solo? Some days I wasn't sure I'd get through the next twenty-four hours, never mind twenty years.

When we walked into Sugar, Skyler ran to the counter, where my friend Olivia was working. The only customers in the place turned out to be Chloe Henry and her daughter,

Sutton; Hayden North and her son, Harrison; and Sierra North. I'd graduated with Chloe and Olivia and knew Hayden from her family's restaurant. Sierra was a more recent acquaintance because of her marriage into the North clan, which was now entwined with the Henry family.

"Hey, Emerson," Hayden greeted with a smile.

"Hi, guys," I said, veering toward their table before joining my daughter, knowing Olivia was chatting with her already.

"Look at your adorable little outfit," I said to ten-month-old Sutton, who grinned up at me from her mom's lap. "Rainbow dragons and ripped jeans? You dress better than me, cutie pie."

"Faye loves to buy little-girl clothes," Chloe said of her stepmother-in-law. "It doesn't suck."

"Don't kid yourself," Hayden said. "Faye also loves to buy little-boy clothes. She's behind this jean jacket." She tugged at the sweatshirt-material hood of her son's jacket. "Right? Mimi got you this, didn't she?"

Harrison's mouth appeared to be full of cookie, and he nodded.

"Mommy!" Skyler called from the counter.

"We need to get treats," I said to my friends as I headed toward my daughter.

"We'll pull up two chairs," Sierra said.

"Hi, Olivia. Sorry about that," I said as I joined my daughter.

"No worries. Sky and I've been going over today's specials. Haven't we, hon?"

"I want the sprinkles, Mommy. They're my favorite."

"Sprinkles are your favorite?" Olivia asked, her voice animated.

Skyler nodded importantly.

"You know who else's favorite is sprinkles?" Olivia continued.

Skyler shook her head and glanced up at me.

"Esmerelda the llama," Olivia said. "She sometimes escapes her enclosure and comes all the way to this bakery hoping for a frosted sugar cookie with sprinkles."

"We live with the llama now," Skyler told her.

"That's what I heard," Olivia said. "Esmerelda's owner, Dr. Holloway, buys her cookies every week."

"You've got to be kidding me," I said. I'd read about the llama's love of cookies on the Tattler, the town app, but I found it hard to believe Ben indulged it. "Mr. Health Food himself?"

Olivia grinned. "Our veterinarian has a big, fat soft spot for animals."

"That's no lie," I said. Ben had always been quiet and reserved...until it came to animals. "We're living in a zoo, aren't we, kiddo?"

"He hasn't been in for a few days to replenish Esmerelda's cookie supply," Olivia said. "I can send some with you if you want."

"I could do that. If he does it anyway, I could save him the trip. Not that a trip to Sugar is a hardship."

"Right?" Olivia took out a cookie for Skyler, then raised her brows at me. "What would you like today?"

"Do you have my favorites?" I asked as I perused the display case.

"Of course. I've got two-dozen fresh-baked chocolate cherry bombs. How many?"

"Just one, please. We had waffles for lunch."

"Sugar makes the world go round," Olivia said matter-of-factly as she rang up our cookies, bottled waters, and a dozen extras for the household and...the llamas.

"Amen." I paid her and directed Skyler to the girls, who'd pushed two bistro tables together. "You can sit next to Harrison," I told my daughter, then helped her get situated between me and Hayden's two-year-old, who mostly stared at Skyler as he chewed his cookie, his face an adorable mess of frosting.

"Chloe said you moved in with Ben Holloway," Hayden said before I could even sit down.

"The kids and I are staying there for a few weeks," I said to emphasize that it was temporary. I explained about Kizzy spreading her wings and finding love and selling the house and how I was looking for something to buy.

"It's a tough time of year for that," Hayden said empathetically. "Nice of Ben to take you in though."

"He apparently likes to rescue people," I joked after swallowing a heavenly bite.

Olivia pulled up a chair to join us while there were no other customers.

"You two must be close," Sierra said. She was Hayden's best friend and lived in Nashville, so she wouldn't know any of our history.

"He was Blake's best friend growing up. We all went to school together."

"He's the veterinarian," Chloe added. "Single dad of two, right?"

"His wife passed away too," Hayden said. "Sadly something you two have in common."

"He's really awesome to open his home to us," I said carefully, "but I'm not going to lie. It bothers me more than I expected to depend on someone's generosity so much."

"Ben's got a big heart," Olivia said. "I don't think he would've offered if he didn't mean it."

I frowned, knowing she was probably right, but still... "I'm not good at needing help."

"Oh, do I get that," Chloe said, her brown eyes sympathetic.

"And at the holidays? I feel like such an imposition." I broke off another bite and popped it in my mouth.

I glanced at Skyler to make sure she wasn't paying attention, even though she wouldn't understand everything we said. She was being goofy with Harrison, each of them taking exaggerated bites of their cookie then giggling.

"I've been trying to think of how I could pay him back and make it worth his while to uproot his whole household for weeks," I continued.

"I can think of one way." Olivia's brows crawled up her forehead suggestively, drawing laughter, even from me.

"A BJ here and there?" Hayden added. "Makes all the difference in the world for a guy."

"You guys are terrible!" I said, again checking the kids, who of course had no idea what we were talking about.

"She's my most inappropriate friend," Sierra declared proudly.

"She's not wrong though," Chloe added.

"Ladies!" I said as if I was scandalized, not letting my mind go where they were suggesting, even for a moment.

Harrison climbed down from his chair and nearly darted off. Hayden caught his hand and wiped him clean. "You can go look at the books now," she told him, pointing at the kids' corner, where there was a rack of well-loved board books and wooden puzzles that had been there for as long as I could remember.

"Why don't you help Harrison find a book," I said to Skyler as she inhaled her last bite. She loved being the older kid for a while since she was the baby of our family and now the youngest at Ben's. I wiped her hands, and she pranced off.

"On a serious note," Olivia said, "are there feelings between you two?"

"Ben and me?" My mind flashed to this morning when he'd brushed my hair back so intimately. "No," I said automatically.

"He's nice to look at," Hayden said.

"Caring, compassionate, kind…" Olivia added.

"He sounds like he'd be a catch," Sierra said, and I laughed.

"You guys are so transparent." I'd known going into this roommate situation that people would talk, but I didn't worry about it, as long as nothing harmed my kids.

"Sierra's right," Olivia said.

"Do you want me to set you up with him?" I teased her. In the back of my mind, however, I thought Olivia and Ben wouldn't be right together. She was too extroverted for him.

Olivia wrinkled her nose. "I don't think I'd do well with farm life or instant momhood. But you, Emerson… You've got the mom thing down."

"Mom thing, maybe, but farm life?" I told them how Gordon the rooster had scared the crap out of Skyler and me this morning.

"So many cock jokes, I can't decide which one to say," Hayden said.

"Cocks can be scary," Olivia said.

"Or magical," Hayden shot back, sending us into fits of laughter.

"Not sure I'll look at my brother-in-law the same ever again," Chloe said about Hayden's husband, Zane.

"Maybe the handsome Dr. Holloway has a magical cock," Olivia said, her attention back on me.

After the laughter died down, they looked at me as if there was a serious suggestion somewhere in there that I needed to put to rest.

I gazed down at my cookie, ran my finger over a large chunk of dried cherry. "I haven't gone there with anyone since Blake died."

The mood went somber in an instant, and I hated that.

"That's understandable," Hayden said, her voice teeming with compassion. "I can't imagine what you've been through."

Attempting to lighten the mood a little, I said, "I'm doing okay. I'll always miss my husband, but it was four years in September. I've done a lot of healing. Just...dating?" I cringed. "I don't know how single moms manage that on top of kids."

"That'd be tricky," Chloe agreed. "I just have the one, and between her and work, my days are overfull. And that's with Holden's help." She kissed the top of her daughter's head.

"Single moms are badass bosses for sure," Hayden said.

"That's the truth." Olivia leaned closer and lowered her voice. "But I just wanted to point out nobody but you mentioned anything about *dating*. You've got yourself a built-in way to take care of your lady needs. No dating required."

I was taking a drink and nearly spit my water out.

"Lady needs are important," Sierra said, grinning.

"Indeed," Hayden said.

"You can take care of lady needs yourself, but I'm a big

fan of getting help when there's a suitable helper available."
Chloe bounced Sutton on her knee and winked.

After our laughs died down, I said, "When I get to that point, it will be weird."

"Probably so," Olivia said with an empathetic frown.

"So maybe that's where your very fine host comes in," Hayden said. "You trust him, right? He could help you get back on the bicycle. Friends-with-benefits scenario."

Again with the traitorous mind flashes, this time to how Ben had looked last night in those low-slung sweatpants and the bicep-hugging shirt.

I shook my head, not letting the image get too vivid.

"I'm not ready, not with anyone but especially not with him. He's my friend, and I don't want to mess that up."

That was only one of a dozen reasons I wouldn't give in to the convenient circumstances with Ben, but it was a big one.

"I understand that," Chloe said. "Holden and I went through that. I was terrified to lose his friendship."

"But look how well it worked out," Hayden said, turning her attention to Sutton. "We're happy it did, aren't we, sweet pea?"

The little girl gave her aunt a big grin.

"We just want you to be happy," Hayden said. "Whatever it takes to get there. Sorry if we're pushing."

"It's okay," I said, meaning it.

These women were some of my best friends in the world. I'd made close friends on the base when we'd lived there, but I'd lost touch with most of them since I moved home to Dragonfly Lake. The girls I'd known since childhood were still here and had welcomed me back into the fold.

I knew what Hayden said was true. They did want me

to be happy. They couldn't help it if they were overzealously championing something I couldn't let happen.

As much as I longed for a parenting partner when life or the kids got tricky, I knew better. Life had taught me loud and clear that I needed to be self-sufficient and able to handle it all on my own. Better to do that than to depend on someone, then lose them.

Chapter Six

Ben

My commute from the office was my sanity time, if there was such a thing for a single dad.

The quarter-of-a-mile walk from my clinic to my front door was an opportunity to transition from the fast-paced chaos of my thriving veterinary practice to the chaos of home. It was five minutes of serenity, five minutes of relative quiet in the countryside. A chance to breathe.

Today had been particularly hectic as we'd stuffed in a few extra appointments to make up for closing at noon tomorrow, the day before Thanksgiving. I liked to give my staff extra time for the holidays when I could, even if someone was always on call in case I needed assistance with an emergency.

I stepped out into the brisk, post-rain air, locked up behind me, and headed across the parking lot and down the paved driveway. Like always, I scanned my land, noting that the animals were secure in the barn where I'd left them this morning and nothing was out of place.

Lights burned in all the windows on this side of the house, telling me the inside was likely alive with noise and commotion. As I drew closer and could see beyond it, I noted Grandma Berty's car in the driveway and wondered if Emerson's was tucked into the garage.

I might be a crazy man, but the extra people in my house had a kernel of anticipation unraveling inside me.

As an introvert, I'd always sought out quiet and calm. Being a single dad was the literal opposite of quiet and calm, but kids changed a guy. Rearranged his priorities. Walking in that door and getting hugs was a highlight of my day. Seeing Emerson in my home was a new treat. It affected me whether I wanted it to or not.

The instant I walked inside, the aroma of Berty's spaghetti sauce hit me. Seconds later, my younger daughter ran into my legs with an enthusiastic hug, Xavier right on her tail. Three dogs and one of the cats were next.

After I hugged both of the kids, patted each animal, and kissed Grandma Berty on the top of her wispy white-haired head, I turned and noticed Emerson at the dining table with Skyler. She was still wearing her work clothes—black leggings, black boots to her knees, and a fine-knit plum sweater that reached her midthighs. Her hair was pulled back in a loose, wavy ponytail at the middle of her head, a few dark strands draping around her face. Yep, that sight was definitely a treat, but I wouldn't let myself get caught up in it.

Even after a long day on her feet at her salon, she looked pretty and put together. When she glanced up at me and smiled, though, I could see shadows of fatigue and worry in her eyes.

"Welcome home," she said.

"Thanks. How'd it go today?" I nodded toward her daughter.

"Can you tell Dr. Ben about your day?" she said to Skyler.

"We made turkeys with our names on the feathers." She held up a paper plate with paper feathers glued to it along with googly eyes and a beak. "And me and Grandma Berty made hearts until the big kids came home."

"Your grandma is too good to be true," Emerson said.

"I heard that," Berty called out from the stove, where she was fiddling with the spices in her red sauce.

"It's true," I said back.

Yesterday when Emerson had shown up with her kids after school, she and my grandmother had apparently come to an agreement about whether Berty would watch Skyler and Xavier every day. I'd expected a battle between them, but Emerson told me later, in private, that Berty had won her over easily—too easily, in Emerson's opinion—by explaining how the kids were the number one purpose and love in her life. She thrived on staying with them every day and said they kept her active and young. If Emerson didn't see fit to entrust her babies to Berty, she'd be depriving my grandmother of the thing that meant the most to her: lively, happy children.

I had to hand it to Berty because it had worked, though I knew it was also the truth.

"Daddy, it's cookie day!" Ruby galloped around me. "The llamas get their cookies tonight."

I bit back a curse. "Bad news, Ruby Tuesday," I said. "I forgot to buy cookies."

"Miss Emerson got them," my daughter said, hopping from one foot to the other.

I met Emerson's gaze, and she nodded.

"Olivia said you hadn't been in for your usual half dozen yesterday, so I bought a full dozen, knowing some humans would want to participate." She stood and went into the kitchen. "They're in the cabinet by the tea. I was afraid I might eat them if I could see them." She took the bakery box out and handed it to me.

"You're a lifesaver," I said quietly.

"I could say the same," she replied with a ghost of a grin. "We're not remotely close to even."

Evelyn entered the kitchen and said, "Hi, Dad!" She gave me a drive-by hug. "Can Xavier help me with the chickens again?" She walked to the mudroom to get her boots.

Xavier had asked if he could go with her this morning. I'd gone out with them to make sure Gordon didn't have a problem with someone new in the chicken house. The rooster had behaved himself—he was actually a pretty good rooster once you got past his awful crowing—and Xavier had taken to the chore like a true farm kid.

"You want to help Evelyn again?" I asked him.

"Yes!" He jumped up with his fist in the air.

"As long as you go in calmly and do what Evelyn says."

"Yes, sir," he said more sedately.

"Your mom and Skyler and Ruby and I will be in the barn, feeding the llamas and horses."

"Okay!" He rushed to join Evelyn in putting on shoes and a jacket.

As the two went out the door, Evelyn was already instructing him like a future boss lady, making me smile.

"You're coming for cookie day, aren't you?" I asked Emerson.

"I...guess so?"

"You might want to change into something less nice."

"I'll just watch from a distance."

"Okay. Give me three minutes to change, and we'll have cookie time."

"Do we get cookies too, Mommy?" Skyler asked.

"We'll save them for after our dinner," I answered when Emerson looked to me.

I changed into barn clothes, and when I came downstairs, Ruby, Emerson, and Skyler had their jackets on.

"How long?" I asked Berty about dinner.

"Thirty minutes."

"Let's go," I said.

Ruby took Skyler's hand, and the two girls preceded Emerson and me out the door.

Emerson was quiet as we walked toward the barn.

"You okay?" I asked her, matching my pace to hers.

She took in a deep breath and looked up at the sky. "Fresh air seems...fresher out here."

I noticed she hadn't answered my question but let it go. "I can't imagine moving back to town."

"Do you ever take time to enjoy the peace out here?"

"As often as possible," I said.

"Which I'm betting isn't very often with two kids and your clinic."

"I take it in little bits whenever I can. Walking to and from work. Feeding the animals. Sometimes when the weather's nice, I sit out on the porch after the kids go to bed."

She nodded but went quiet as we entered the barn. I was beginning to suspect she was afraid of either the horses or the llamas.

Smoky snorted, knowing it was time for his dinner. Bay stuck her nose eagerly over the gate of her stall.

"Hey, guys," I said as we walked past the three horses. "Cookies first. You know the routine."

Ahead of us, Skyler stopped, and Ruby kept going toward the llamas. Skyler's eyes were wide as she gaped at the llamas, who were peeking out over their stall walls.

"They're big, but they're friendly," I told her. "Especially when there're cookies."

Emerson came up behind her daughter and rubbed her head affectionately, looking uncertain herself.

Ruby already stood in front of Betty's stall, her neck craning up at the gentle spotted animal. "Betty, we got the cookies!"

As I approached, Esmerelda hummed at me, or rather, at the treats I bore.

"Hey, ladies," I said. "Yes, it's cookie time."

I realized Emerson and Skyler hadn't moved any closer. I gestured for them to join me. Emerson ushered her daughter forward about three steps, and they stopped again.

"Come here, Sky. They won't hurt you," I promised. "I'd never put you in any kind of danger. You know that, right?"

She nodded silently.

"You want to help Dr. Ben?" Emerson asked.

As Ruby chattered to both the llamas, I bent down and coaxed Skyler to come to me. She finally let go of her mom's hand and dashed over. I picked her up and handed her one of the cookies.

"This one's for Esmerelda," I said.

Skyler shook her head and ducked it into my neck.

"You want me to give it to her?"

She nodded.

"She won't hurt us," I repeated as I stepped to the stall.

Skyler hid her face against me.

"I'm about to hold it out to her. She'll take it fast, so you have to watch if you don't want to miss it."

As soon as Skyler turned her head toward Esmerelda, I stretched my arm out to the white, long-haired princess. The llama took the cookie with her big teeth, then Skyler ducked into me again.

"Can I do Betty, Daddy?" Ruby asked.

"Here you go." I handed her the second cookie, concerned about Skyler's reaction and ongoing fear. I was confident Ruby knew what to do since she'd done it countless times. Betty was always gentle with my girls.

I turned to look at Emerson and realized she hadn't moved since urging Skyler toward me. Like mother, like daughter?

I motioned with my head for her to come closer.

"I'm good," Emerson said. "Don't want to get my work clothes dirty."

"You girls know llamas are really gentle and friendly, right?" I asked as I took Skyler back to her.

"Yes," Emerson said. "They're just..."

"Scary looking," Skyler said.

"They're not scary; they're funny-looking and beautiful at the same time," my daughter proclaimed as she pranced up to my side.

The llamas had downed their treats in no time.

"I wanna go to Mommy," Skyler said, so I set her down. She rushed to her mom's side.

Emerson bent down. "You okay, Sky?"

Her daughter nodded but looked about to cry. Emerson hugged her.

"Horses are next," Ruby explained. "You want to see the horses, don't you, Skyler?"

Skyler looked toward the horse side of the barn and

nodded, looking somewhat relieved. Ruby again took her hand, and they marched toward Smoky's stall. Skyler glanced over her shoulder one more time at the llamas, as if to ensure they weren't coming after her.

"They're locked in their stalls, sweetie," I said. "They know they have to wait for the horses to get fed before they get their dinner."

"More cookies?" Skyler asked in a small voice.

With a chuckle, I said, "Just like people, they have to eat mostly healthy food. They only get two cookies a week."

"On Tuesdays and Saturdays," Ruby said.

"Are you afraid of horses too?" I asked Emerson in a low voice. I wasn't throwing her shade. It was obvious her unease was real and something I hoped to help her work through soon, as, well, she was living with llamas for the next few weeks.

"Not afraid," she said, her gaze taking in Smoky, who was a big guy but gentle. "Just...intimidated? They're big and strong."

"When I adopted these guys"—I swept an arm out in an encompassing gesture—"all of them, my priority was that they had a gentle disposition. My kids are around them every day, so I needed to trust any animal I brought home."

She tilted her head. "They're animals. Animals are unpredictable."

"They can be, and you always have to remember that. But first you start with animals who have a gentle disposition. Some horses are projects. They've had a rough life or gone through poor treatment. Those need homes too, but that's not what I wanted with Ruby and Evelyn around. Second thing is to build a trusting relationship with each of them, just as you would with a human."

"Do you trust Esmerelda not to break out and head to

the bakery anymore?" she asked, her lips twitching toward a grin.

"We're working on that," I said with a laugh. "That's part of the reason I broke down and started buying her cookies—in moderation. There's usually a reason for animal behaviors, just like there is for people. It just might be harder to figure out because they don't answer questions."

Ruby and Skyler had stopped a few feet in front of Smoky's stall, my daughter sensing Skyler wasn't ready to get closer.

I held my hand out toward the horses and raised my brows at Emerson. She hesitated only a second, then nodded and stepped toward her daughter. I fell in beside her and, without thinking, put a hand at her waist to comfort her.

Comfort was not the word I'd use for what shot through me at the feel of her curves beneath my fingers.

Dammit. I needed to be cautious and keep myself in check. That was tricky though, because Emerson was so familiar.

I'd known her for most of my life. Moving her and her kids into my house had been a no-brainer, a gut instinct, because I cared about her. Keeping attraction out of the equation, when Blake had fallen in love with her and eventually married her, she'd become important to me in a different but deep way, as the person who made my best friend happy.

I let go of her, reminding myself I needed to be more mindful of boundaries when we were together. She was a house guest. A good friend, yes. But also my best friend's partner.

Skyler had stepped closer to Smoky, with Ruby at her side. Not close enough to touch, but her interest was clear.

This was night-and-day from how she'd acted with the llamas, and I got it. Llamas looked odd, and that could frighten a child. Or a woman, apparently.

"Would you like to meet Smoky?" I asked Skyler.

With her neck craned to look up at the horse, she nodded slowly.

I picked her up and approached Smoky carefully, talking in a low voice, introducing Skyler and her mother. Eventually Skyler worked up the courage to pet Smoky on the neck. She giggled, then told her mom about her bravery even though Emerson could see everything. She too had come closer.

I eventually set Skyler down, and Ruby and I fed the five large animals and the barn cats, with the Estes ladies looking on.

When we exited the barn, the girls were animated, Skyler's mood the opposite of when we'd entered. She'd met all three horses, though briefly. It was a first step. The llamas would be more of a process.

Emerson and I walked side by side toward the house. The temperature was nearing the freezing point, the air crisp but fresh.

"Sky did well with the horses," I said.

Emerson nodded. "I'm proud of her. She'll want to ride them before long, just wait. The llamas though... That's a different story."

I let several seconds pass before I spoke. "She can read your fear of them, you know."

"You think?"

"I know. The best way to help her overcome her fear is to conquer yours."

She narrowed her eyes at me. "I don't want to get spit on."

"The odds of getting spit on are tiny. Llamas spit when they're threatened. We're their friends, the people who feed them."

"And give them cookies."

"Exactly."

"So I can't just stay out of the barn for the next month?" she asked, a lightness in her tone suggesting she wasn't serious.

I shook my head. "In fact, the best thing to do would be to put on some old clothes and help me feed them in the morning. Once you get to know Betty and Esmerelda, I think you'll like them."

"I'd rather cook breakfast for everyone."

"We can cook together. It'll go fast."

"I'll...think about it."

"It would help your daughter," I said.

"You don't play fair."

"Never claimed to." I grinned as we reached the house. "Getting your daughter used to the animals will help her settle in overall, don't you think?"

"You're right."

"First step is you. We got this," I told her. "Everything'll be okay."

Chapter Seven

Emerson

"That man would forget his balls if they weren't attached," Kona Powers said, making me laugh as I fastened a cape around her.

"Men," I said sympathetically. "They have their strengths, but sometimes remembering things isn't on the list."

I'd been cutting Kona's hair since I opened my salon just over three years ago. Her husband, Abraham, was the sweetest man, but he'd apparently forgotten to buy a fresh turkey when he'd picked up groceries the other day.

"Bless his damn heart," she said with a grin and a shake of her head.

She was my last client of the day, as we were closing early because of the holiday tomorrow. Kids didn't have school today, and two of my five stylists had already left town to visit relatives. Everyone was in a festive mood, and Gustie had insisted on playing Christmas music throughout the salon. I knew that's how it would be for the next four weeks, so I basically braced myself for the crazy ride and the repetitive music. When you ran a business in a small town, the last thing you could be was a Christmas Scrooge.

"What are we doing to your gorgeous locks today?" I asked her as I pointed her at the mirror.

Before she could answer, my cell phone rang. I didn't get many calls, especially while I was at work, because everyone knew not to bother me. Text messages were different. I could catch up on those later.

I took my phone out and saw Ben's name as Kona explained the change in hairstyle she was hoping for.

Odd. Ben usually texted me instead of calling, usually about kids or logistics. I'd call him back as soon as I finished with Kona.

The call went to voicemail, but before I could put my phone back in my pocket, it rang again, and my heart lurched with the thought that something must be wrong.

"You need to answer that, hon?" Kona asked just as I was about to excuse myself.

"I'll be right back," I told her.

I connected the call as I headed into the back room. "Hey, Ben."

"Emerson, you need to come home. We can't find Skyler."

My blood froze in my veins, and my heart stopped. "She l-likes to hide," I stuttered out as I stepped out of the back and waved frantically at Willow, one of my stylists. "Did you look in the closets? Under her bed?"

"We searched the house up and down, and I just checked the garage, the barn, and the chicken house. Her coat is gone, so I'm pretty sure she's outside somewhere."

"Oh, my God. Should I call nine one one?" My terror made it impossible to think straight.

Willow grasped my hand as I spun around trying to figure out what I needed to do to get out of here and go find my daughter.

"Not yet. Let's look around the house, on the property. Berty knows she was still in the house twenty minutes ago, so she can't be far."

"What if someone took her, Ben?" I clung to Willow as I swayed.

"Berty's ninety percent sure the doors were locked. I think she ran off." His breaths were getting heavier, telling me he was actively searching as we spoke. "Come home. Have somebody drive you if you need to. We're going to find her, Em."

"On my way." I ended the call.

I wasn't sure whether I was breathing or how I was functioning. My mind had shut down on everything except my baby girl.

"Skyler?" Willow asked, apparently having heard Ben through the phone.

"She's missing." My throat closed up as I said it. "I have to go."

"Let one of us drive you."

Nobody would get me there fast enough. "I can drive. I'm going now." I halted. "Kona."

"We'll tell her what's going on, and one of us will take care of her if she'll let us. You go...if you're sure you're okay to drive."

I nodded, and she shoved my coat and purse into my hands.

"Where are your keys?" she asked.

"In here." I opened my purse and dug till I found them, my mouth desert dry with fear.

Willow ushered me to the door. "Be careful. Call as

soon as you know something. Call if you need help. What-ever you need, Emerson..."

I nodded, barely hearing her as I ran to my car, got in, and started it.

My heart was racing hard enough I might stroke out, but until I did, I had to do whatever I could to find my baby girl.

Minutes later, I squealed into Ben's driveway, scanning for Skyler as I forced myself to slow down in case she popped out in front of my car. I was out of the driver's seat the second I braked.

"Skyler!" I yelled, leaving my coat and purse on the passenger seat. "Skyler!"

My phone, which I'd apparently thought to shove back in my pocket, rang. It was Ben.

"Did you find her?" I said.

"Not yet, but I found footprints her size in the mud heading into the woods." He described where he'd seen them and where he'd gone into the trees. Running in that direction, I scanned the area for Ben but didn't see him.

"I'm coming," I said.

"You loop out to the main road and go right. Walk along the shoulder and scan the trees from there. I'm following the paths. I don't think she'd veer too far from the trail. It's pretty thick in here."

My heart was pounding so hard I couldn't get a breath in, but I diverted myself and jogged toward the road as best I could in the worst possible shoes. I couldn't take the time to change into something better than booties with heels.

"Skyler!" I called, then realized I'd yelled into the phone that was still connected to Ben's ear. "Where are the others?" I asked him.

"Berty's staying at the house in case she comes back. I

sent the other three to walk along the east fence. Told them to hold hands and not split up no matter what. Evelyn knows what to do, and I trust her to keep the other two close." His breath was coming fast, telling me he was covering ground. "Call me if you see anything," he said, then disconnected.

I kept my phone out and my eyes on the dim woods as I skirted the outside of them, calling Skyler every few seconds, trying to shut down the awful thoughts racing through my head. Failing.

"Please, Skyler, come back. Be okay," I pleaded quietly, desperately. Then I yelled her name again. Each time, I listened carefully, hoping to hear something in return, but there was no response. I could hear Ben calling out in the distance from time to time, but no little-girl answer.

My pleas turned to prayers to God, begging for her to be okay.

The day was cloudy but dry, so at least she wasn't getting wet, but it was chilly, in the forties. It got dark early this time of year. The sun would set in another hour or so. If we hadn't found her by then, I was calling in every law enforcement team I could think of.

Maybe I should call them now? Wouldn't it be better to get them searching *before* it got dark?

I reached the county road and turned right, hurrying along the outside of the trees, nausea rising, hysteria making me want to scream things besides my daughter's name, but I held it in because it wouldn't help us find her.

I didn't know exactly where Ben's land ended, but I didn't figure it mattered. I just kept going, futilely calling for Skyler, my panic growing with every minute that passed. I wouldn't stop until we had her back.

A while later—I wasn't sure how much time had gone

by—I spotted the next cross street in the distance. I had probably a quarter of a mile to get there, but this was doing no good. Skyler wasn't popping out of the woods or calling out for her mommy. I'd never felt so utterly helpless in my life.

I lifted my phone to call Ben and figure out a better way. It rang, and his name appeared before I could press Call myself. My heart took off at a sprint again.

"Did you find her—"

"I've got her," he said. "She's okay."

"Oh, my God. Thank God. Where?"

"Meet me back at the house, and we'll talk. Let's get her inside."

"You're sure she's okay?"

"Say hi to your mommy," I heard him say, his voice farther away.

"Hi, Mommy," Skyler said in a quiet voice.

"Skyler! Are you okay?"

"Yes." Her voice was tiny, as if she was scared or exhausted or both.

"We're heading to the house," came Ben's voice. "Skyler's no worse for wear, but are you okay?"

"I will be as soon as I hug her." Dozens of questions circled my mind, but I swallowed them down. "See you as soon as I can get there."

I ended the call and took off running, or more like hobbling in the awful shoes that were likely ruined. I didn't care. I considered throwing them into the woods, but that would slow me down, and I needed to get to my girl.

When I burst into the kitchen, gasping for air from running who knew how far and being terrified for the past hour, three dogs circled and sniffed me, but I sought out my daughter.

Skyler climbed down from Berty's lap in the dining room, ran up to me, and threw her arms around my legs. I picked her up and squeezed her tight, breathing in her little-girl smell, tears gushing down my face.

"Baby girl, what were you doing? You scared me to death."

Skyler buried her head in my neck and wailed.

My son rushed to us and put his arms around my waist, telling me he was shaken up too. I bent down to hold both my children close. Through my tears, I saw Evelyn hanging on to Ben's side, and Ruby had crawled into her grandma's lap.

I met Ben's gaze as he hovered a couple feet away.

"She said she wanted to go *home*," he said gently, breaking my heart.

I squeezed my eyes shut. "Baby, this is our home right now. This is where our family is: you, me, and Xavier. That's home. Sometimes the place has to change, but we're all together, right?"

"I wanna live with Nana," she said through her tears.

My poor, darling girl. We'd talked a dozen times about Kizzy falling in love and getting married and having to move away so she could be with her new wife. I'd explained how Nana still loved her to the moon and back and always would. The three of us had discussed finding a new house where we could live happily ever after and that it would take some time for me to find the right place.

"She'll be here for a visit in three weeks, remember?"

Skyler's eyes lit up, and Xavier cheered.

"Nana loves you both so much," I said now. "She would be so scared if she knew you went outside by yourself. You know that?"

She nodded slowly, her face still hidden. "I don't want to live with the llamas."

My gaze popped up to Ben's again. With Evelyn still glued to his side, he stepped toward us and rubbed Skyler's back. "Their house is out in the barn, sweetie. They can't get in here. Even if they could, they don't want to hurt people."

"Their teeth are scary," Skyler said.

"That's fair," Ben said. "Llama teeth are sort of ugly, aren't they?"

Sky nodded into my shoulder.

"It wouldn't be a good idea to put our fingers in their mouth, but those teeth aren't nearly as sharp as Nugget's or Milo's or Sprocket's. Are you scared of the dogs' teeth?"

She nodded again.

"But you're not scared of the dogs, are you?" he asked.

Nugget wandered into the kitchen as if she'd heard her name. Xavier turned his attention to the dog, hugging her as if she too had been concerned about our girl.

Skyler lifted her head to watch Nugget, interest sparking in her eyes. "No, Nugget loves me."

"The llamas will love you too as soon as they get to know you," Ben said.

"I don't want to," Sky told him.

"That's okay too," he said. "Whatever it takes to make you feel safe here. We'd never let anything happen to you."

I slammed my brain down on the thought that something so easily *could've* happened to her this afternoon, pulling her in closer still.

"I'm hungry, Mommy," Skyler said.

My laughter was semihysterical, the laughter of release. My little girl had flipped from life emergency to status quo in the blink of an eye.

Grandma Berty came in with the other kids in tow. "How about some hot cocoa for everyone?"

Skyler perked up instantly. "Can we have lots and lots of marshmallows?"

"We might be able to have a few extra marshmallows," Berty said, winking at me.

Skyler wiggled to get down, then jumped up and down as if it was just another day and she hadn't scared me to within an inch of my life less than an hour ago. Thank God for the resilience of kids. It would take me a little longer to recover.

Berty involved all four kids in cocoa making, with Skyler in charge of the marshmallows.

Ben and I stood out of the way, watching the controlled chaos.

"Hot cocoa makes everything better," he said, and the kids all heartily agreed.

Though I was relieved the kids seemed to be bouncing back from the situation, I had to force my smile.

Hot cocoa couldn't begin to make me feel better. Not even if I added a double shot of liquor to it.

Chapter Eight

Emerson

On the surface, things were back to normal—whatever normal was—when we put the kids to bed. They seemed to have forgotten about the earlier trauma of Skyler taking off.

I hadn't, of course.

I'd put on my happy face for the rest of the evening, but this afternoon had taken a toll on me. Bone-tired didn't begin to cover it, and my limbs weighed a hundred pounds each.

Evelyn had had the brilliant idea of pushing her bed and Skyler's together so Sky wouldn't feel alone. I hoped it would be enough to keep my daughter in their room tonight, as I needed real, deep sleep—the kind you couldn't get with a four-year-old hogging your space. It'd be a while before I could test the theory though.

I'd told Ben I'd help him bake pies for tomorrow, so after kissing my babies good night, I went down to the kitchen. My holiday spirit was in the negative numbers, but the least

I could do was put on a brave face and not ruin Ben's excitement.

"Sous baker, reporting for duty," I said as I entered the kitchen, mustering up as much cheer as I could fake. There was a heavenly aroma permeating the main floor. The oven was on, and I suspected something was already baking.

Ben turned from the counter and focused all his attention on me as I washed my hands. "Hey." His voice was low and caring, in contrast to my loud bluster. "How are you holding up?"

"I'm good," I lied, fighting to keep up my nonchalance. It was that, or...I didn't know what. Tears? Breaking down? Blubbering all over him? "Evelyn's got a heart of gold."

"She's a pint-sized mother hen," he said, his affection audible. "Bossy on the surface, but that little girl cares deeply about her sister and your kids. She was all business during the search and had Xavier and Ruby marching from one end of the east property line to the other and back, right at her sides. The three of them came running when I told them I had Skyler."

My nonchalance shattered as I imagined Ben returning to the house with my precious girl, the other kids rushing to them to dole out hugs. "Thank you," I managed, my voice only cracking a little.

I pressed my lips together and closed my eyes, fighting for control over my emotions. I hadn't had a moment to myself yet, by design. I just needed to make it another hour or however long pies took. Then I could disappear to my room, close my door, and sob into my pillow until I fell asleep.

Except Ben slid his arm around me from the side and squeezed my shoulders, his large palm strong and gentle at once.

It'd been a long, long time since I'd felt that kind of masculine touch from anyone, the kind that infused strength and support, that said, *you're not alone*. Not romantic, not sexual, though it'd been just as long since I'd experienced those. They weren't what I needed right now.

I hadn't thought I needed anything from a man, as I had a tight circle of strong women in my life, the most supportive girlfriends I could ask for. But something about Ben's quiet strength and his unselfish offering had tears plummeting over the rims of my eyes and down my cheeks. I wiped them away, slid my arm around his waist from the side, and allowed myself to lean into his shoulder for a few seconds.

"I don't think Skyler will ever try running away again," he said. "She was scared out there, so scared she wouldn't come to me when I called at first."

My heart squeezed even harder for my little girl. "She was hiding?"

"Behind an old, thick tree trunk."

"How'd you get her to come out?" I asked.

"Promised her a cookie."

An emotional laugh burst out of me. "Brilliant."

"It was the first thing she asked for when we walked in the door. She devoured it before you got here."

I couldn't help a slight smile in spite of all the fear and sadness circling my head. "You know her well already." I swallowed hard, determined to get the pie making over with so we could both go to bed. "Thank you doesn't seem sufficient, but it's all I've got."

He pulled me closer into his side for a moment. "No thanks necessary, Emerson. She's as close to being my own kid as she could be. Blake and your kids are basically family, even more so now that you're staying here."

I sniffled a final time and wiped away any remaining tears, still determined to wait until I was alone to unleash my fear, relief, and worry. After a deep, leveling breath, I stepped away and turned my attention to baking. "What needs to be done here? Where do we start?"

"The pies are finished," Ben said, snapping back into kitchen mode. "Pumpkin's baking and french silk's in the refrigerator."

"What? We're supposed to do pies after the kids go to bed." The aroma coming from the oven finally registered in my brain. Cinnamon, cloves, and pumpkin.

"You're exhausted. I got them done while you were reading to the kids."

"Wow. You're fast and sneaky. What else do we need to get ready?"

"Thanksgiving dinner is locked and loaded. Nothing else to do tonight. I just have to finish cleaning my mess."

Gratitude rose in every one of my cells. I'd thought I knew Ben through and through, but living with him temporarily, I was seeing yet another side of him. An amazing one. A guy who could cook? Who could make french silk pie? Who could sense when I was about to collapse and shorten my to-do list accordingly?

"You are rare, Ben Holloway." I let out my breath and nearly wilted with relief that my bedtime was considerably closer than I'd thought. "Thank you for that too. My debt load increases even more." I kept my voice light for the last bit, not wanting to incite yet another debate of whether I owed him or not. I did. No question. "I'm helping you clean though. You need to sleep too."

"If you insist." He turned on the sink and poured in dish soap. "The pans need to be hand-washed. I'll wash; you dry?"

"Deal."

As he stacked pans and mixing bowls by the sink, I wiped down the counter. "You really think Sky won't run off again?"

"I'd put today in the not-a-good-experience category for her. I really don't think she will."

She'd been extra clingy and full of hugs this evening, which I didn't mind at all. I'd needed them as much as she had.

"Tomorrow's Thanksgiving. It's going to be special," he said.

I held in a groan.

Ben glanced over at me and chuckled. "It is. You'll see. My kids love it, and I think yours will too. Then we'll go to the tree-lighting ceremony in the evening."

My kids did love the ceremony, but I hadn't even thought about going yet. We'd had too much happening for me to be able to plan more than one day at a time. "Yeah," I said on an exhalation. "Good idea."

"That kicks off the holiday season. We'll keep the kids so Christmased up, Skyler won't have time to think about her worries."

"Ugh." The word slipped out before I could stop it.

"I know you're not feeling it," he said as he rinsed a saucepan. "I understand that more than you know."

That made me laugh. "Okay, Ghost of Christmas Present." I took the pan from him and dried it.

Instead of grinning, he went serious. "After Leeann died, the last thing I was up for was Christmas cheer. For years."

I nodded. Blake's death had definitely had that effect on me, but that was only a fraction of why I wasn't busting out the red and green.

"When I bought this place, I very deliberately decided to make the holidays a magical time for my kids, even though I wasn't feeling it."

I eyed him sideways because I had a suspicion his "not feeling it" was different from mine.

"Really," he insisted. "My heart was still heavy from Leeann's death. My parents started their tradition of cruising over the holidays. I was overwhelmed from moving out here, being a single dad, building the clinic, all the things."

"All the things," I repeated, grasping on to something I felt in my soul. "Yes. What did you do? How'd you make yourself be holly jolly?"

"Faked it."

I shot him another skeptical look as I put a pan in the cabinet.

"I made a list of holiday activities. Tree ceremony on the square. Cutting our own tree down and decorating it. Christmas concert at the high school. Cookies and candy making. Letters to Santa. Gingerbread houses."

The thought of adding even half of those to my to-do list made me want to curl up in a ball and weep. During this time of year, making sure my kids had a reasonably nutritional dinner was almost more than I could handle. To me, the holidays meant a filled-to-the-brim schedule at the salon, requisite holiday parties and dinners, school programs, and gift buying. This year I'd be managing it all for the first time without Kizzy's help.

I kept my concerns to myself and tried to put a lid on my bone-deep dread. "That's a big list. Obviously you made it through." I forced lightness into my voice.

"A weird thing happened. About halfway through, I

didn't have to fake it anymore. Seeing my kids' joy?" He shook his head and chuckled. "There's nothing better."

"How do you handle all of that on top of your clinic? And, you know, feeding them and getting them to school on time."

"I get help when I need it. Colby, my office manager, goes above and beyond when I ask her. Berty's a godsend year-round but especially in December. She loves it as much as the rest of us, so that helps." He scrubbed the last pan. "I suspect Skyler will get so caught up in all the holiday stuff, she won't have time to think about Kizzy's house or the way things used to be."

"I hope you're right."

As Ben handed off another pan and I took it, he bumped his hip into mine. "We'll get you into it too if you just give it a chance, Ems."

"That sounds like a threat," I said, but I couldn't help smiling. Maybe it was the nickname. I'd been called Em plenty but never Ems.

"It is. You're going to have fun or else."

That made me laugh. "I didn't know how scary you are when I agreed to stay here. You should come with some kind of Christmas-obsessed warning."

"Now you know."

As I dried the last pan, he wiped the sink down. When the kitchen was sparkling, Ben took out the dwindling cookie supply and offered me one.

"You're sharing the llama's stash?" I greedily accepted the cookie, llama be damned.

"Sugar's closed tomorrow, but I'll have Friday and Saturday to buy more."

I leaned against the cabinets and ate the cookie,

thinking about the guaranteed insanity of the next few days. The next few weeks.

In theory, I agreed with Ben that an overdose of holiday events could be just what my kiddos needed, especially Skyler. Xavier was already settling into the Holloway routine. He loved living with his buddy, Ruby, taking the bus to and from school, and helping with the animals. He'd taken to the changes like a duck to water.

"So...tomorrow's Turkey Day on steroids, then the tree-lighting ceremony in the evening?" I asked after devouring the last bite.

Ben opened the oven to check on the pie, then closed it with an approving nod. "I'll take the kids shopping downtown on Friday. They love the scavenger hunt the shops on the square put together."

"Friday's Black Friday. We have a product sale at the salon. There's no way I can get away."

"I'll take Xavier and Sky with us. The clinic is closed until Monday, barring any emergencies. They can pick out gifts for you."

I'd planned to take them to work with me. Shopping and scavenger hunting with Ben and his kids would be so much better. "You're sure you're up for double the children?"

"I can't wait." He was grinning like a kid in a candy store, his eyes lighting up, leaving me no doubt that he was into this and he wouldn't mind my kids tagging along.

Damn, did that get to me deep in my chest. I was overcome with a mix of relief and gratitude. Add that on top of the fatigue and stress of the day, and I found it hard to get words out. With my stupid eyes tearing up yet again, I merely nodded, pressing my lips together to hold it all in.

"Hey." Ben stepped in front of me and peered down at me. "Emerson?"

I wiped at my eyes before they could spill over, then met his gaze. "I'm okay. Just...overwhelmed. Your idea to keep the kids busy is probably exactly what they need. I need to figure out how to fit it all in."

In spite of my efforts, one traitorous tear plummeted down my cheek.

Ben caught it with his finger and wiped it away. He took a gentle hold of my upper arms and leaned down to force eye contact. "We're in this together this year. You don't have to do it alone. Partners in Christmas mayhem."

I couldn't help a laugh. "Mayhem might be an understatement."

"We've got Grandma Berty on our side too. The three of us will tag team. If there's something you can't make because of work, we can cover and vice versa."

"I have Mondays off," I said, thinking that might be a day when I could pull my weight.

"It's all going to work out," he said. His eyes held kindness and determination. "We'll get Skyler through this tough time together. Partners. I already love your kids, Ems. I want what's best for them too."

I studied him closely, those compassionate, handsome blue eyes. What I saw was straightforward honesty. He meant what he said.

"You're a good man, Ben Holloway," I whispered.

"We go way back. We dissected frogs together. Come here."

He pulled me in for a hug, and I surrendered to it. I wound my arms around his middle and held on, breathed in. I couldn't help noticing his scent, masculine and clean with a hint of pie. It made me feel comfortable, secure.

We held on for several seconds, a silent shared moment where we seemed to come down from a traumatic day as well as gird our loins for the coming chaos.

With my head nestled against his shoulder, I could feel his heart beating. Gradually I became more aware of him as a man, his strong arms, solid chest, and that alluring man scent that awakened something different in me.

Without pulling away, I looked up at his face again, and he gazed down at me. The air changed, became charged, and my pulse picked up speed.

I saw him lowering his head, coming closer. On some level I recognized he was going to kiss me, and I wanted that too. I didn't stop to think about it, just went with it as his lips touched mine.

My eyes fluttered closed as everything female in me responded to him, his lips soft but demanding. I wanted to give him everything he needed.

He pulled me even closer, flush against his body, as we explored each other's mouth. His hands trailed down to my hips, and my sluggish brain registered his erection pressing into me. I moaned, loving that I could still have that effect on a man.

Ben put a little space between us and moved one hand to my face as he lightened the kiss, then kissed my forehead.

My senses were reeling, still trying to catch up when he spoke, his voice gravelly.

"It's been a hard day. We both need to get to bed." He hugged me again, his chin resting on the top of my head as I burrowed into his chest.

I nodded, still going with sensation more than thoughts, loving how it felt to be in his arms. Warm, safe, not alone.

Only later, when I was tucked into my bed by myself, would I wonder what the hell I'd been doing kissing Ben.

Chapter Nine

Ben

Happy fucking Turkey Day, I thought to myself as I put out kibble for the barn cats then headed toward the house, the three dogs playing tag with each other and getting their morning stretch.

Thanksgiving had dawned cold but sunny while I was tending to the horses and llamas. Arguably a gorgeous morning for late November, but I wasn't feeling it.

I was feeling more like the proverbial turkey and in a foul mood, no pun intended. Sleep-deprived, worried, and pissed at myself. For once, the dogs' antics weren't pulling me out of it.

I never, ever should've kissed Emerson.

After a fitful night, I still didn't know what the fuck I'd been thinking. Obviously my brain had shut down, and my body had done whatever the hell it wanted to, consequences be damned.

I wasn't sure what those consequences would be, but I'd soon find out.

"Daddy we're done!" Ruby called out.

She and Xavier had decided to help Evelyn with the chickens today, probably because they'd sensed I wasn't in a fun-loving mood the second I'd woken them up.

"Everything go okay?" I asked as the three kids made their high-energy way toward me, the dogs racing to greet them.

"We got seven eggs!" Xavier hollered.

"That's a decent haul," I said halfheartedly, making a point of smiling when they caught up to me.

I wasn't in the mood for company, too mired in regret and self-disgust, but alone time was a luxury for a single dad and not happening anytime soon. Barn time was usually it, and that hadn't lasted nearly long enough today to put a dent in my mood.

I didn't need to worry about making more chicken conversation though because the three of them ran the rest of the way to the house, the dogs at their heels, leaving me in the dust.

I slowed my steps, trying to make the walk from barn to kitchen last a little longer, nervous about facing Emerson.

Upon entering the house, I found a fully cooked breakfast on the dining table, three kids pouring themselves juice and digging into bacon, eggs, and toast, the dogs at their water bowls, and no sign of Emerson.

She'd obviously cooked, as she'd been doing daily while the three oldest kids and I handled chores. Skyler was still adapting, most days sleeping until breakfast was ready.

"Where's your mom?" I asked Xavier as I walked into the dining room.

He shrugged. "Must be upstairs getting ready or helping Sky," he said, unbothered. He was the most easy-going kid I'd ever known.

Back in the kitchen, I poured myself a second travel mug of coffee and wondered if Emerson was avoiding me or if she was doing what her son had suggested.

When Skyler came down alone a couple of minutes later, fully dressed and looking more animated than the past few days, I had my answer.

Emerson might very well be avoiding me.

"Morning, Sky," I said. I suspected she'd dressed herself as she wore a pink leopard-print shirt, blue leggings with rainbow unicorns, and a red-and-white-striped skirt. "How are you today?"

"Hungry!" she said, her eyes lighting up as she took in the spread on the table. Nugget pranced up to her, tail wagging.

The other kids greeted her and passed the food her way as soon as she climbed up on her chair.

"Is your mom coming?" I asked.

She looked at me with wide eyes and shrugged with her arms spread. I cracked a grin in spite of myself because she was such a cutie. I was relieved to see her excited about food and not fixated on where her mom was. It seemed like progress.

I eyed my place setting and the food, knowing I should sit down with the kids and act like everything was fine. I couldn't pull it off though. I needed to resolve things with Emerson. I set my coffee on the table.

"Everybody have what they want?" I asked.

I got four positive answers as Skyler stacked bacon on her plate next to a large heap of eggs.

"Help Skyler if she needs it," I said to Evelyn. "I'll be right back."

"I will, Daddy," she said.

I jogged up the stairs, my head down in concentration,

trying to figure out what to say to Emerson. As I reached the top, she rushed out of the bathroom at the same moment, and we collided hard in the narrow hall.

I caught her upper arms to steady her and realized she wore nothing but a towel. Her long hair was wet, cheeks slightly pink, and drops of water beaded on her chest above the towel, drawing my gaze downward. I popped it right back up and swallowed.

"You okay?" I asked.

With a nod, she said, "Forgot my clothes in my room," and crossed an arm over her chest to hold the towel in place.

I took a step back, but there wasn't far to go before hitting the wall. "I was afraid you were avoiding me."

She darted her gaze down the hall. "Where's Skyler?"

"All four kids are stuffing their faces in the dining room." Their chatter was audible.

Emerson nodded once, then said in a low voice, "This is awkward."

"Doesn't have to be," I said, unsure whether she meant because she was nearly naked or because of what had happened last night.

I was about to ask if she wanted to get dressed and then talk when she barreled right in.

"Last night... Ben, that can't happen again. I'm sorry if I led you on—"

"You don't owe me an apology. *I'm* sorry."

She frowned. "Yesterday was nuts. We were exhausted and wrung out emotionally."

I nodded. "I only meant to offer comfort, companionship, a partner through Skyler's struggles. I didn't mean for that kiss to happen."

She surprised me with a slight smile as she met my gaze directly. "No premeditation?"

85

I chuckled, thankful as hell we were able to joke about it. "None. Temporary insanity."

"Same."

"I won't do it again," I said with conviction. Blake might be gone from this earth, but it still felt wrong to kiss the woman who'd been married to him.

For the dozenth time, I shut down the thought that the kiss had also, in other ways, felt very right. That was me being all kinds of wrong.

"We're okay then?" I asked.

She nodded. "We're okay."

I breathed a little easier, still making a point of keeping my gaze on her face, not letting it drop to where cotton met cleavage. Hoping to lighten the moment, I said without thinking, "But you at least liked it a little bit, right?"

She laughed. "Oh, my God, really?"

"Save a guy's ego. I'm fragile." I was full-on teasing, trying to bring us back from the awkwardness even as I flirted with making it worse.

Emerson shook her head and scoffed, but there was still a smile on her face. In a quiet voice, so there was no way the kids could overhear from downstairs, she said, "You're good at kissing. Just don't let it happen again."

I laughed, relieved. "Deal."

Inside, I was a little too pleased with the compliment.

"Get dressed and join us," I said. "An amazing breakfast fairy cooked us a hell of a meal to start the day."

"Breakfast fairies are the best," she said. "I'll be down in a few."

As she walked toward her room, I lost the battle to keep my gaze in check and drank in the sight of her long, bare legs from behind, noting the towel hung just barely low enough to hide her ass from my prying eyes.

Proof positive that I was a fucking idiot and a glutton for punishment.

———

Emerson

I'm fine. This is fine. Everything is fine.

As soon as I closed my bedroom door, I leaned my back against it, still holding my towel in place.

If you were to measure my heart rate, you'd find out I wasn't quite fine.

After a deep breath to try to level myself out, I stepped away from the door and hurriedly dressed.

Ben had so totally called it right. I *had* been avoiding him. Normally I showered first thing and got ready, then cooked. Today I'd cooked first then retreated upstairs before he could finish chores.

My head was a messy place after last night.

When Ben had kissed me, it had just...happened. It'd felt almost like an extension of our friendship. Almost. But then it'd awakened something inside me that'd been dead for years: desire. I hadn't felt a twinge of it since Blake died. As a grieving single mom, I didn't have energy for more than getting through the day. It was like my hormones had died with my husband.

Except now I knew they hadn't.

Something about being in Ben's arms had made me feel my femininity again. His kiss had affirmed that I was still desirable and still had working woman parts that might eventually want some attention. Though I hadn't missed any of that, hadn't let myself miss it, I couldn't deny it was reassuring to know it might be a possibility.

Maybe someday I'd want sex again. Maybe there'd be room in my life for a casual fling. Eventually.

It wouldn't be with Ben, because we were too good of friends. It wouldn't be a serious thing, because I'd promised myself I'd never go there again. But maybe someday, when my life was more stable and my kids were more secure and everything lined up, I'd let myself cut loose and get my "lady needs" met.

For the time being, my life was anything but stable. At least one of my kids was struggling big-time, and I needed to focus on getting us all through the next couple of months unscathed.

Chapter Ten

Emerson

By the time our last client left Friday, my stylists and I were exhausted but in good spirits. We hadn't had a single no-show all day, all of us with our chairs filled with a nonstop stream of customers, most of them regulars, getting prepped for the holiday season, sharing Thanksgiving stories, and tipping generously.

"That was a heck of a day," Gustie said as she switched the sign from open to closed. She was seventy-six years old, a dear woman who'd been doing hair for longer than I'd been alive. She swore she'd work till the day she keeled over, not for the money but for the socializing.

Edith, a lifesaver who did everything *except* hair for us, proclaimed, "We've never sold so much product in one day. I've already started an order to restock."

"The snacks were a hit," Claire, our newest stylist, said.

"I know they saved my life," Raelynn said in her deep drawl. "I didn't have an extra second for lunch. Couple bites of cheese and a slice of summer sausage between clients was perfect."

"You all did fantastic today," I said, ducking into the back room to grab a bottle of champagne. "Thank you, ladies."

"Black Friday tips always make it a worthwhile day," Willow said, and everyone agreed. "I could sleep until Monday though."

"I know you all want to get home as soon as possible, but we deserve a quick toast."

"Mmm, it's bubbly time," Raelynn said.

I poured a flute for each of the seven of us. "To the best team anywhere," I said, meaning it. We clinked and sipped and hashed out the day and the best stories we'd heard.

I'd brought champagne last year too as an insufficient but well-received thank-you. No question we'd all rather shop till we dropped or stay at home out of the crowds on Black Friday, but these girls pulled together to make it a festive, high-energy, lucrative day.

I guess maybe I did have my own little holiday tradition, Black Friday champagne for the girls, I realized, my mind slipping to Ben not for the first time today.

I'd fielded questions about him and me throughout the day and taken the opportunity to set the record straight that we were just good friends who went way back. Of course, that elicited more than a couple responses insisting that's what the best marriages were made of. I'd laughed it off heartily every time, hiding the way the m-word made me shudder.

Thanksgiving with Ben, his kids, and Berty was everything he'd promised, the kind of holiday depicted in Norman Rockwell paintings. Every last one of us had helped prepare the feast. We were blessed with way more delicious food than we'd eat in a week.

Before eating, we'd gone around the table and shared what we were most thankful for. When Ben had mentioned it a few days earlier, it had sounded simple and cliché, but the reality was a touching few minutes that reminded my too-busy self of the purpose of the holiday. I'd needed that reminder more than I'd realized.

We'd ended Turkey Day downtown on the square for the annual tree-lighting ceremony, with hot cocoa for everyone. Ben and I had kept the kids between us, like a silent promise to not touch each other again.

We'd focused on the children, making sure they had a magical time, ensuring Skyler was caught up in it every minute. My daughter had chattered nonstop on the way home in Ben's oversized truck that shocked me by seating six. It was as if it was made for our group.

Thanksgiving had been an alternate reality in a good way, and I had no complaints.

I was packing up what was left of the charcuterie and cookie trays when the bells on the front door of the old-house-turned-salon jingled.

"Mommy!" Skyler hollered before I could turn to see who'd entered. She ran over to me, all the ladies greeting her, Xavier, Ben, and his kids.

As I reached down to catch Skyler, I met Ben's warm gaze across the room and felt a spark down to my toes. He smiled, and it felt like it was just for me.

Then I did a reality check and reminded myself, *Of course he's happy to see me. He's been in charge of four kids under ten for hours on end.*

"Hey, guys," I said, picking up Skyler and pulling

Xavier into my side with my other hand. "How are my favorite humans?"

I listened as my son told me all about the scavenger hunt, with the other three kiddos excitedly adding details about the grab bags they'd received at the end. My stylists got into the conversation as we sipped our champagne. Ben came closer and said how well behaved the kids had been.

"We've had a fun day, haven't we, kids?"

All four of them enthusiastically agreed. I set Skyler on the floor and watched dutifully as they displayed the trinkets from their prize bags.

"With all that loot, Santa won't have to worry about you guys this year," I teased.

"Noo!" Ruby said. "We have to write our Santa letters, Daddy."

With a laugh, Ben said, "Of course we will. You can use your new glitter pen."

"I got a purple one, and Evelyn got green," Ruby said.

"I didn't get a glitter pen," Xavier said. "I got a silver marker."

"I got a pink one!" Sky hollered.

"You must be exhausted," I said quietly to Ben.

"I'm doing okay. You're the one who worked all day. I bet you're ready to relax."

"That wouldn't suck," I said. "I'm also starving, so let me lock up, and we can go home for dinner. I'll cook." It was the least I could do.

"Nope."

"Nope?" I stopped in the middle of packing the last of the cookies. "You don't like my cooking?"

"I fucking love your cooking," he said so only I could hear, in part because the stylists were fully engaged with the kids and weren't paying attention. "But tonight we're all going to Henry's."

"I love Henry's, but you realize there's probably a two-hour wait?"

"There might well be, but not for us. We've got reservations."

I snapped my gaze to him to gauge whether he was serious, because...a meal cooked by professionals? An adult beverage or two? A chance to sit on my tired butt without lifting a finger? It sounded like pure heaven. "Are you serious?"

"Yes, ma'am. We've got about fifteen minutes to walk there and claim it." He looked startled for a moment. "If you're not done here, the kids and I can go save it, and you can join us when you're able."

"We're nearly done." I glanced around. Most of the flutes were empty and stations were tidy.

"I can lock up tonight, Emerson," Gustie said as she approached, as if she sensed my dilemma.

"Ben made reservations at Henry's for us," I explained.

As Ben leaned down to address something Skyler was saying to him, Gustie said next to my ear, "Honey, if you don't get out of here with that handsome fella, then I will. Go have fun."

"The kids are going too," I clarified, because the growly tone in her voice said her thoughts had gone somewhere else entirely.

"Mm-hmm. He's a catch. Enjoy yourself, kids or not. We girls'll be outta here in a few."

"It's not like that," I said in a quiet singsong, then switched to a normal volume. "But thank you for locking up."

Soon we were making our way down the crowded

downtown sidewalks toward Henry's, Evelyn and Skyler leading the way, holding hands, Xavier and Ruby following them, and Ben and me bringing up the end, side by side.

With my guard down after a really good day, I wove my arm through his and grasped his biceps, noticing how solid they were. This man... He was something else. His superpower was sensing exactly what I needed at any given moment. That might just be my kryptonite. And honestly, as the champagne started to buzz through my veins and make my brain fuzzy and warm, I wasn't entirely sure weakening temporarily where he was concerned was off the table. As long as it was understood that it was in fact temporary.

———

"Do you feel it?" Ben asked in a low voice.

We were at Henry's at one of the high-top tables. The kids had fought for the four swiveling stools with backs as if they offered as many thrills as an amusement park ride, leaving Ben and me sitting side by side on the elevated booth that ran the length of the wall.

"Feel what?" I asked. I was for sure feeling a lot of things at the moment, from the heat of his leg just inches from my thigh to the rum in my Santa's hat martini.

"Holiday spirit?"

I raised a brow at him, trying to keep a straight face.

"Even a little?" he persisted.

Giving in to a smile, I said, "You must think I'm a big Scrooge. This *is* festive."

My cocktail itself was enough to make a girl love Christmas. It was bright red with a sweetened coconut rim to look like the white fluff of Santa's hat. It tasted even better than it looked, of cranberry, grenadine, and coconut.

Henry's was decked out to the hilt in a tasteful, classic way. The full wall of windows that looked out on the lake during the day was rimmed with evergreen garlands and white fairy lights. The deck was closed to diners for the season, but it held a dozen lighted Christmas trees that were visible from every table inside. The walkway to the water, and even the dock, was lined with thousands of white fairy lights and also visible from inside.

"Confession?" I said even more quietly, leaning closer. "I was overdosed on holiday music before noon today."

Ben laughed. "That's fair. I've always wondered how retailers can stand the same songs over and over for a month."

"It makes me crave a little Nirvana or Pearl Jam."

"The grunge bands of our childhood will never get old," he said.

The kids were engrossed in coloring pictures of Santa standing in front of the restaurant, chattering back and forth about their day, generally ignoring Ben and me. It was a blessing how well these four got along.

"I'm done," Xavier said, holding up his artwork.

"I love the colors you chose," I said. Coloring wasn't really his thing. He was the opposite of a precise, stay-within-the-lines kid. He'd chosen a deep purple for Santa's suit.

"Santa should be red," Ruby told him. She wasn't even halfway done with hers yet because she was taking her time and going for perfection.

"My Santa's red suit is in the laundry," Xavier said, making all of us laugh. "What's this?" He reached for the triangular table tent. "'Your entry in the Dragonfly Lake

Holiday Parade could win a prize,'" he read out loud. His brows shot up his forehead as he continued reading to himself. "Oh, we could win a hundred-dollar gift certificate to Earthly Charm! Or A Novel Place! Mom, can we make a float?"

There was nothing that sounded worse to me at that moment. Not even a school science project. "I don't think so, Xav," I said with zero hesitation. "That would take weeks of working every day on it. I have to work at the salon."

He frowned. "I could do it by myself."

I laughed softly. "Make a float? Let's leave that to grown-ups, kiddo. We can go to the parade and pick our favorites, okay?"

"Dr. Ben could help me," my son said, his tone hopeful.

With another laugh, I shut that down immediately. Ben was just crazy—and unselfish—enough he might consider it. "Dr. Ben has to work too, plus take care of all the animals. I'm sorry, sweetie. That's a big project, and there just isn't time for it."

"What about our new gramma?" Skyler asked.

I was still puzzling through the new gramma bit when Ruby blurted out, "Grandma Berty could help us!"

My mouth gaped open, and I met Ben's gaze for a moment. His eyes sparkled with amusement. I was more worried about setting the record straight.

"Even though we call her Grandma Berty, she's not really our grandma," I said carefully. "But we can still love her like a grandma, can't we?"

"I love her already," Skyler said.

"Grandma Berty's the best," Evelyn said authoritatively.

"We like Nana Kizzy too," Xavier said, "but she lives far away now."

The discussion switched to Kizzy's upcoming visit, the big hotels in Vegas, the desert, the jungle, and a dozen other topics. Our appetizers of fried mozzarella and chips and artichoke dip arrived, and we dove into them, the kids' conversation not missing a beat.

My festive cocktail was two-thirds gone. I made a point of stretching it out until the main dishes arrived, in part to prevent me from ordering another. With the champagne pre-drink, I was definitely feeling the effects of the alcohol in my vision and my level of relaxation. Ben had told me when I considered ordering a cocktail that we could leave my car parked behind the salon for the night so I wouldn't have to drive home.

Once again, he'd sensed I'd had a hard day and could use a drink, even though I was sure his day had worn him out just as much.

"Do you have any flaws?" I asked him quietly enough that the kids paid no attention. Maybe that was too personal, but I was relaxed and didn't care. I was legitimately trying to find anything wrong with the man sitting next to me.

He laughed. "That's a joke, right?"

"Not a joke. You put your kids first—and mine now—you take care of a jillion animals, you're good to your grandma and include her in your daily lives. You're thoughtful and seem to care about, like, everyone you meet. You always have a smile for people, even in the morning."

"I like mornings."

"That could be counted as a flaw in some circles," I said, thinking hard about it and deciding it was not, in fact, a flaw because who wanted to deal with a grumpy grouch in the morning?

"You cook pretty good," I continued, "run a successful

business, and offer to take in homeless friends and their kids, over the holidays no less."

"Plus I'm a good kisser," he said into my ear.

Without thinking, I went for his thigh that was so close to mine with a half smack, half grab. "You're awful," I said as I turned my head and met his gaze, unable to hide my grin.

"Am I awful or perfect?" he asked, peering down at me and looking so damn handsome. He nudged his upper arm into mine as he said it, leaning against me for an extra moment.

Our gazes locked as I tried to think of how to answer, my brain just addled enough by alcohol that I found it a perplexing question. I stopped trying to answer, caught up in the depths of his cornflower-blue eyes with the crinkles just starting at the outer corners that spoke of years of kindness and laughter.

"Are you guys gonna get married?" Ruby asked in a voice that wasn't at all quiet or private.

I whipped my head toward the kids, my heart skipping a beat. Too late, I realized my hand was still clinging to Ben's thigh under the table. I slid it away and put it in my lap, scanning the surrounding tables to check if anyone besides the four urchins at ours had noticed. No one appeared to have heard, not surprising since the acoustics of the room kept it difficult to hear specifics over the ongoing din of the crowded restaurant.

"Miss Emerson and me?" Ben said with a chuckle. "No. Remember, we're friends from way back? We sometimes tease each other."

"Do you sometimes kiss?" Ruby asked.

"Eww," Evelyn said.

A lie was on the tip of my tongue just as Sarai, our

server, popped up to the table with a large, dinner-laden tray.

"Who had the chicken tenders?" Sarai asked, drawing all four kids' attention away from us.

"Saved by the server," Ben muttered with a sheepish grin.

I tried to smile too, then turned my attention to the food.

It had become crystal clear in a heartbeat that, alcohol or no alcohol, I needed to be a lot more cautious about my growing attraction to Ben. There were four little humans who'd be deeply affected if they ever thought something was between him and me.

Chapter Eleven

Ben

I should've been in a holly-jolly mood Saturday evening for the single dads' night, Christmas edition, but I wasn't. I was tense and not myself.

Living with Emerson was becoming a daily dose of torture. Kissing her was the dumbest thing I ever could've done, because now I could barely talk to her without remembering what she tasted like, how her lips felt. I loved being with her, and I fucking hated it at the same time.

It was getting harder to keep my guard up and keep my hands to myself. Last night at Henry's, sitting next to her, nearly touching, had felt natural and right...until Ruby had blurted out the marriage question. It'd had the effect of a bucket of ice-cold water being poured over our heads.

Unfortunately, the chilling effect had worn off. There were only so many cold showers a guy could get away with taking. And getting myself off to thoughts of Emerson didn't quench my need. Only she would.

I had no fucking idea how I was going to get through the next few weeks without losing my damn mind.

"You okay tonight?" Knox asked as he joined me at his kitchen counter, where a slow cooker of chili was simmering.

The five of us—including Chance, Max, and West, who were parked in the living room in front of a college football game—had already devoured a good portion of it.

"Sure," I said, summoning a smile. "Chili's damn good. Did you make it or did Quincy?"

"I did, thank you very much. I've been trying to cook more."

"Well, you nailed it."

"Anyone can follow a recipe," Knox said humbly. "The cornbread's a mix. I know my limits."

Knox was hosting tonight, a rare occurrence since he was one of the two who'd fallen prey to a happily-ever-after and technically no longer met the "single" part of the single dad qualification. He and Max were still dads, single or not. We had an unspoken agreement that once you were in, you stayed in. The ties we built with our weekly get-togethers were strong.

"Where'd you say the girls are tonight?" I asked.

"Quincy's out with the sisters-in-law. Girls' night at the Barn Bar. I'm sure I'll get a call for a ride in the wee hours." His goofy grin told me he didn't mind. "Juniper's with Faye and my father for a sleepover."

"Nothing like a sleepover with the grandparents," I said. "For the parents, I mean."

"You aren't lying." Knox set his empty bowl in the sink.

A knock sounded at the door. Then it opened, and Luke walked in.

"Hey, gents," he said to the group. "Sorry I'm late. The

Amy Knupp

farm was record-setting busy today. We didn't get the last family taken care of till almost seven thirty."

"Tis the season," Chance said in his friendly way. "Get your ass in here and take a load off."

"Mighta left you a little chow," West said.

Luke came over to Knox and me and peered into the pot of chili. "I could eat."

I suspected that was an understatement. The guy worked his ass off on a normal day. The Saturday after Thanksgiving running a Christmas tree farm likely wasn't a normal day.

"Help yourself." I moved away from the food so he could dig in.

"We're glad you joined us," Knox said.

"Thanks," Luke said as he set a wrapped box on the island, grabbed a bowl, and filled it. "Didn't want to miss the presents." He shot us a shit-eating grin that told me he might've gone the gag gift route like I had.

An hour later, the game on the TV was a blowout, the chili pot was empty, beverages were replenished, and we sat around the living room.

Chance checked his phone, undoubtedly ensuring his teenage daughter was still where she was supposed to be. "I'm ready for presents," he said, telling me Samantha was behaving herself tonight, at least so far.

"You're worse than a little kid," West said.

"Who's staying with your three tonight?" Luke asked the ex-military guy.

"I got a high school gal off the Tattler," West replied. "Good references, loves kids."

West was a burly badass I wouldn't want to piss off, but he had a soft spot a mile wide for his three little girls. When his live-in girlfriend had dumped him and moved out a couple of months ago, he'd been more upset for his daughters than himself.

"Is that the Tatum girl?" Luke asked.

"Allison Tatum," West confirmed.

"I saw her post," Luke said. "Let me know how she does."

"You're not stealing my babysitter," West said. "You got your built-in childcare, man." His tone was good-natured but also adamant.

"My built-in childcare's sixty-four years old with health issues," Luke reminded him.

"How's your dad doing?" I asked.

"Stubborn," Luke said. "Hates not helping with the farm stuff, especially this time of year. He loves the holidays."

"Grandma Berty always says getting old's not for the fainthearted," I said.

"I'm only in my forties, but I can tell that's going to be true," Knox said.

Chance grinned at him. "Good thing you've got a pretty, *much* younger wife to keep you young."

"Jealous?" Knox shot back.

"Oh, hell no. Have you tried raising a teenager? Full-time contact sport that takes all my focus." With that, Chance checked his phone again like a habit. "So far she's still at the friend's house she's supposed to be at."

Chance stood and went to the pile of wrapped gifts on the table between the kitchen and living room. He plucked one off, walked over to Knox, and tossed it on his lap. "Merry Christmas, old guy."

Knox laughed. "I'm forty-three, asshole."

"That box doesn't look like it has a cane inside," Max joked.

"I'm first?" Knox asked.

"Must be something good since Chance can't sit still," West said.

"Open it." Chance sat back down, grinning.

Knox ripped open the box and took out a placard of some kind.

"What's it say?" Max asked from one of the chairs.

"'Please do not annoy the writer. He may put you in a book and kill you,'" Knox read, laughing. "Hell yes. This goes on my office wall. I should get Ava one too," he said of his writing partner and sister-in-law.

"There's more," Chance said.

Knox set the plaque aside and pulled out a T-shirt. Laughing, he shook his head and said, "Asshole," again, then held it up.

The T-shirt said, *Who's your daddy?* in big, bold letters.

A collective explosion of laughter broke out.

"That's perfect," West said, then howled.

"Double duty," Max said.

There wasn't a more appropriate saying for Knox, as he'd not only showed up in town last year as Simon Henry's secret love child but also had baby Juniper left in his SUV with a note claiming he was her father. The claim turned out to be true, and he'd been smitten with that little girl ever since.

"Maybe triple," Chance said. "We'll have to ask Quincy."

"I'll wear it with pride," Knox said like a good sport.

"Who'd you draw?" Chance asked. "You're next as Santa."

Knox set aside his gifts, stood, and went to the table. He picked up a gift bag and delivered it to Luke.

"You got me, huh?" Luke said, taking the bag. He dug

into it and pulled out another T-shirt. He chuckled as he read it.

"What's it say?" I asked.

"'Things I do in my spare time,'" Luke read. "'Drive tractors, look at tractors, research tractors, talk about tractors, think about tractors, dream about tractors.' I don't talk about 'em that much, do I?"

"You do love your tractors," Chance said.

"Heck yeah, I love my tractors." Luke's expression said, *Duh*.

"Okay then," Knox said as if that settled it. "There's more."

Luke dug back in, pulled out a coffee mug, and howled. As he held it up, he said, "'Get plowed by a pro. Sleep with a farmer.' That's what I'm sayin'. Thanks, man."

"Knox pretty much nailed you," West said.

"Knox is the last person I want nailing me," Luke quipped.

"You're missing out," Knox shot back. "Who'd you buy for?"

Luke set his gifts on the floor by his chair. He headed to the island, where he'd left his present, picked it up with both hands as if it was heavy, and handed it to Chance.

"Damn. Some barbells?" Chance asked.

"You could use some," West said. "Mr. Soft Job."

"You just wish you could get paid to market beer too," Chance said. He ripped the gift wrap off and tossed it aside. He leaned forward and put the box on the floor, then lifted out a growler. "Beer?"

"Hard cider," Luke said. "Because apples are better than hops any day."

In addition to Christmas trees, Luke grew apples and strawberries on his land. Chance was the marketing manager for Rusty Anchor Brewing and lived and breathed beer.

"Did you start brewing the hard stuff?" Chance asked.

"It's not mine. I got it from a cidery on the west side of the state. I'm looking into the possibility. We might be in competition soon, my man," Luke said.

"Eh, not direct though. Bring it on. We might even be willing to carry a local cider at the Anchor for the nonbeer folks." He twisted the lid off and sniffed. "That's nice...for apples."

Luke told him the four different varieties in the box.

"Hey, this is actually cool," Chance said. "My mind is open to multiple kinds of alcohol. Thanks, Luke."

"You might have to share," Knox said, reading the label on one of the growlers.

"After gifts, we'll do a taste test," Chance said. "Who's next?"

"I'll go," Max said, then delivered a bag to West.

West sat forward and pulled out a large water tumbler perfect for his construction job. "Jesus. I love it," he said. He turned it so we could read it.

It had a hard hat on it and said, *Always use protection*, eliciting more laughs all around.

"Use protection for sure," West said, shaking his head. "Unfortunately not much opportunity for that these days."

"I feel you," Luke said.

"There's something else in there," Max said to West.

Like a kid, West's eyes lit up, his lonely bachelor state forgotten. He pulled out something bright yellow. "Socks?" He unfolded them and read, "'Want to hear a joke about construction?'" He flipped them so he could read the rest. "'I'm still working on it.' Ha. Funny guy. Sadly one hundred percent true." He laughed. "Thanks, Max. I'll wear them to work and flash them at appropriate moments when we're behind schedule."

"What does it say that we all went the gag route?" Knox asked.

"That we're funny fuckers," West said. As he stood to get the present he'd brought, he chuckled to himself in a way that made me nervous. Max and I were the only ones who hadn't gotten anything yet.

West carried a box past Max and held it out to me. I met his eyes, and the spark in them did nothing to put me at ease.

As he sat back down, I unwrapped the box and opened it. Nestled in straw was a bottle of white wine. I puzzled over that as I dug deeper. Next up I pulled out two taper candles. I shot a look at West.

"You fixin' to wine and dine me?" I asked in a fake deep drawl.

"Keep digging," he said.

Next I pulled out two small silver items. "Candle holders?"

"You got it, Romeo," West said. "One more thing in there."

I lowered my brows at him as I dug. I hit cardboard and pulled it out to discover a box of condoms, thirty-six count.

Before I could put two thoughts together, West said, "Since you got a live-in lady now, I thought you could use some help with the romance—and the protection."

"Always use protection," Chance bellowed, laughing.

"Fuck." I closed my eyes, trying to smile, but I was already in such a state over Emerson that this was hitting flat for me.

"Come on," Luke said beside me, punching my arm. "You've gotta admit that's funny."

I forced a laugh, but it sounded as fake as it was. The room went serious in an instant.

"It's just a joke," West said.

"Yeah. Thanks." Again, I tried to laugh, but the fact was, I'd had the thought last night about what if... What if I snuck up to Emerson's room and seduced her? What if she let me? What if...

And then it'd hit me: I didn't have any condoms anyway, so that couldn't happen. In fact, I'd sworn to myself I wouldn't buy any for as long as she was in my house. Maybe that would help me keep my hands off her. Now I had a damn box full.

"Something happen between you and Emerson?" Max asked sincerely, all teasing gone.

"I told you she was my best friend's wife," I snapped, then caught how shitty my tone was. "Sorry." I exhaled and said a dozen more swear words in my head. "Sensitive subject."

"Emerson's husband was your best friend?" Chance asked. He and Knox were the only ones who hadn't grown up in Dragonfly Lake.

"From the time we were three years old," I told him. "When he and Emerson moved away and I went to college, we lost touch a little. We were different from each other in a lot of ways, but we were tight even in high school."

"He thinks Emerson is off-limits," Max said to the group.

A few seconds of silence passed. Then Luke spoke up. "Blake's gone. As awful as that is, it means Emerson is single."

"I know she is," I said.

"You have feelings for her?" Knox asked.

Denying it would be pointless. I nodded and said, "Sure

fucking do. For some time now." No sense in admitting *some time* equaled almost twenty years.

"I mean, she's hot," West said.

Hot didn't begin to encompass my attraction to Emerson, though hell yes, she was hot.

"Is she dating anyone?" Chance asked.

I ground my teeth together. "No." Thank fuck.

"But she could," Max said. "Because she's single."

I narrowed my eyes at him across the living room.

"Just laying it out there," he continued. "If you don't pursue her, how's it going to feel to see her out with another guy?"

Like son-of-a-bitching shit.

"If something happened to me, I'd want Quincy to have a happy life," Knox said. "I'd hate for her to be lonely for the rest of her years."

"From what I knew of Blake, he'd feel the same way," Max said.

"You really think it'd be okay to move in on my buddy's wife?" I asked bluntly.

"I do," Luke said without hesitation.

"The bigger question is whether Emerson's interested," Knox said.

"Say she is," I said. "This town that talks about everything... It's not going to see a thing wrong with me being with Blake's woman?"

"First off, screw the town," West said, "but yeah. Emerson's got plenty of good years ahead of her. The chances of her not remarrying? I don't know her, but I wouldn't blink an eye if she did. Whether it's to a friend of Blake's or not. It's a small town. Everybody knew him."

"If you care about her, you should let her know," Max said. "See where it goes."

"I care about her." I couldn't see telling her the truth about that though.

"It's either you or someone else," Luke said. "Maybe West here."

Luke chuckled, but I eyed West to see if there was reason for me to hit him.

West raised both hands as if surrendering. "Hey, dude, I'm not touching her. Not with that death-threat look in your eyes."

I was starting to see their way of thinking. When I imagined Emerson moving on with someone else, it was like a blow to the gut. But they were right. She likely would eventually. Who knew how soon?

"It's not a thing," Chance said.

I raised my brows to see if there were any differing opinions around the group.

"Not a thing," Knox agreed. "Blake is gone. If you're the one who can make Emerson happy, he'd probably give you thumbs-up from beyond."

The others nodded as if they wouldn't think twice about it.

"Max's turn," I said, done with being the center of a serious moment. I gave Max a large gift bag and sat back down.

"The biggest one's for me," Max said. "With this group, that makes me nervous."

"Justified," Chance said.

Max shoved the layers of tissue paper aside and hooted. "You're fucking kidding me." He pulled out a twenty-inch plush white llama that looked a lot like Esmerelda.

"You're halfway to llama expert by now," I told him.

"I know how to catch a llama on the lam, anyway," he said, laughing again as he stared at the animal.

"When I was down with the flu, Max and Harper captured Esmerelda like pros," I told the others.

"That's what friends are for, I guess," Luke said.

Esmerelda had a history of getting out of the corral. Every damn time, she headed straight for Sugar Bakery, which had inspired the next part of his gift.

Max riffled through the tissue paper some more and pulled out a box with the Sugar logo on the side. "I hope this is full of cookies." He opened it. "Yes. Thank you." He stuck one in his mouth, then passed the box around, saying, "Enough for everybody and then some" around the cookie.

"One more thing in there," I said.

He drew the bottle of top-shelf whiskey from the bag and said, "If we don't like the cider, we'll have whiskey. Thanks, Ben. Whiskey and cookies are a heck of a combo."

There were several cracks about llamas and protection and God knows what else. I acted like I was listening, but my thoughts veered back to Emerson and the guys' opinion that my friendship with Blake didn't mean she was off-limits.

I'd received the message loud and clear, not just through my ears but maybe in my brain as well. But I couldn't let myself think too hard about it, because Blake was only one of several reasons I wouldn't be going home and taking Emerson to my bed.

Chapter Twelve

Emerson

By Sunday evening I'd like to say the kids and I were settling into our temporary new normal. Xavier was completely comfortable, and Skyler was a lot more content and seemed to be getting used to living with the Holloways. The problem was me. I didn't know if I'd ever be able to fully relax around Ben. I was too drawn to him.

I suspected it was because I'd been alone for so many years. I longed for a man, a partner, in general. Ben was a wonderful person, but I kept reminding myself this was because of our proximity more than anything.

I'd caught myself more than once today nearly reaching out to touch him as we laughed at something the kids said or almost leaning into his side as we walked next to each other. In other words, if I dropped my guard, I might cross a line or three.

As the six of us walked with Luke Durham toward the section of his tree farm that had the type of tree Ben wanted, the tiny snowflakes falling from the sky became bigger at once, as if a switch had been flipped.

"Nice effects, my friend," Ben said to Luke, laughing. "It's like you powered up a snow machine."

"Wish I had that kind of control," Luke said. "We'd crank out just enough to drive business."

"I bet so." Ben had a daughter on each side, holding their hands like the loving father he was. I wasn't sure which of the three of them was most excited.

"Douglas firs are through here," Luke said, his words coming out with puffs of frost in the air. "As far as you can go that way." He pointed. "Text me if you need any help cutting it—"

"I won't," Ben said. "You've got plenty of other customers tonight who might."

"Okay, then happy tree hunting, guys," Luke said to all of us with a friendly smile that looked tired around the edges.

"Thanks, Luke," I said as he headed back to the open-air shelter that served as tree HQ.

"Have fun, kids," he called as he walked away.

"Come on, Sky," Xavier said, bursting with enthusiasm as he took his sister's hand. "Let's find a perfect Christmas tree!"

"We're gonna find a perfect one too," Ruby said with more glee than competition. "Let's go, Evelyn."

"Here's the deal," Ben said, stopping all four of them in their tracks. "Xavier and Sky, you go down this row." He pointed. "Ruby and Evelyn, you come over here and check out this row." He indicated one row over. "Let us know when you find a good one. Miss Emerson and I get final approval."

"Let's go!" Xavier said.

Skyler let out a happy giggle as she looked up at her brother, and they rushed down the row. It never failed to make my heart contract in my chest when Xavier took his little sister under his wing.

"You and I will keep an eye on everybody," Ben said to me as his kids skipped over to their assigned row.

"They'll be okay even when we can't see them?" I asked. Xavier and Sky were already a good forty feet away.

"We can hear them," Ben said.

I realized he was right as I heard Evelyn ask Ruby what she thought of a particular tree. When Ruby replied, "It's too little," Ben and I laughed.

"While they're busy," Ben said, taking a thermos out of an inside pocket in his thick coat, "I brought us a hot adult beverage." He handed the top, which served as a cup, to me, then unscrewed a second cup from the bottom.

"What is it?" I asked, catching a whiff of chocolate.

"Hot cocoa with Bailey's. It's cold tonight."

He poured some for each of us, and we clinked our stumpy metal cups together, laughing.

The warm, sweet liquid went down easily as we kept an eye on all four kids and embarked in a lighthearted debate about which trees were contenders and which weren't. His preference was for a fat tree that was nearly as wide at the bottom as it was tall. Knowing the living room corner we planned to put the tree in, I was worried about it fitting and pointed out thinner, more elegant-looking trees.

There wasn't a lot of spiked cocoa, just enough for the beginnings of a warm, buzzy contentedness. As the huge snowflakes came down heavier and accumulated on the ground, I felt like we were in a magical, insulated-from-reality snow globe where everything was peaceful and beautiful and in harmony.

Ben and I kept things between us light and full of laughter as we checked in on both sets of kids from time to time and tried to convince them there wasn't one perfect tree but rather many of them that could serve our purposes. They were having none of it and in no hurry.

For once, I embraced that. I let them go at their own speed, sipping my cocoa, enjoying Ben's company, laughing more than I had in ages.

I didn't want the evening to end.

When the cocoa was gone, I handed my cup to Ben. He returned them both to the thermos.

"Didn't even have to fight the kids off from the adult beverages," he said, grinning. "That was the objective all along."

I laughed. "Mission accomplished."

"Let's go see if they're close to deciding on a tree." He extended his arm, and I wove mine through his.

The kids had disappeared from our current row, so we slipped between two bushy trees to the next row over to find Skyler and Xavier running in our direction.

"Mommy, we found one!" Skyler called out.

"It's way down there where Ruby and Evelyn are standing," Xavier said.

Ben let go of me, leaned down, and picked up Skyler when she reached us. "Is it a fat tree or a skinny tree?" he asked.

"A big, fat one!" my daughter said joyfully.

Ben shot a private, handsome look of victory my way, making me laugh.

"Show me the way, Sky Blue."

"Hey, Xav," I said before my son could run off after them. He turned back to me, his eyes lit up and curious. I bent down and hugged him. "Thank you for being such a good big brother. I love you, kiddo. Your sister does too."

He hugged me back, wrapping his arms tightly around my shoulders. "This is the funnest night ever, Mom! It's like...Christmas magic!" He ended the hug and took off toward the others, his excitement too much for him to stand still for things like moms and mushy stuff.

My heart overflowed with gratitude and love—gratitude that Ben had included us in his family's special tradition and love for my kids and this experience I'd unknowingly deprived them of for all these years.

With our noisy group in my sights down the way, I took a few moments to myself to soak everything in. The smell of pine filled the brisk, snowy air. Laughter rang out frequently, warming me as much as the Bailey's had. I leaned my head back and looked up at the zillions of snowflakes fluttering down so peacefully, several of them landing on my face.

I sucked in a deep, cleansing breath of fresh, cold air, imagining it replacing the lingering stress from another jam-packed day at work and the season in general. This was what it should be all about. Families. Memories. Snowflakes and laughter.

By the time I finally rejoined our group by the chosen tree, Ben was lying on the ground, reaching under the branches, sawing the thick trunk, a lantern nearby. Ruby and Skyler stood behind him, out of the way, and Evelyn and Xavier were on the other side of the tree, pulling it slightly as Ben directed them.

"I can tell this isn't your first time," I said as I joined the two older kids to help.

"You're just in time," Ben said, pausing the saw. "You

kids move over here with Ruby and Sky. Let Miss Emerson hold the tree. I'm about through to the other side of the trunk."

We all did as he said, with me reaching into the branches to grab the trunk up high so it wouldn't fall on him.

Minutes later, the tools and supplies were stashed back in Ben's bag and the kids were practically jumping up and down with adoration for our "perfect tree" that was, indeed, an extra-wide one.

As I picked up the bag, Ben singlehandedly hoisted the tree up to his shoulder. Not gonna lie...the sight of him being all lumberjackish, lifting a heavy tree, his eyes lit with happiness, had me lighting up on the inside in forbidden ways. *Down, girl*, I thought.

The kids raced ahead of us, two by two again, toward the shelter and checkout, leaving Ben and me alone.

"I understand it now," I said, walking next to him on the opposite side of the tree.

"Understand what?" he said on an exhale, telling me the tree was heavier than he made it seem.

"Why you go to all the trouble to pick out a tree, cut it yourself, take it home. The kids will remember this forever."

"Yeah," he said, his lips stretching into a sexy grin. "It's always a special night."

While I wasn't committing to cutting our own tree next year, when I wouldn't have Ben's help, *I'd* remember the evening too...to say nothing of Ben carrying that tree as if it weighed ten pounds.

_____

Ben

I'd set out to show Emerson and her kids what the Christmas season could be like. Based on what she'd said as we headed to pay for the tree, I suspected I'd succeeded tonight. What I hadn't counted on was screwing up my own head even more in the process.

We'd just hung the last few ornaments from the branches, with Emerson-approved instrumental holiday music playing quietly in the background. The rotund tree overfilled the corner of the living room, as Emerson had feared, but I didn't regret our choice for a second. We couldn't go tall because of low ceilings in this old farmhouse, but we could go wide, and we had. It gave the room a cozy warmth.

There'd been a poignant moment early on when we'd unpacked the heart-shaped ornament with a verse about remembering loved ones we'd gotten in memory of the girls' mom. Our ritual was for Evelyn to read it out loud, then both girls kissed it and hung it together. Xavier and Skyler had respected the moment by listening solemnly and watching.

Emerson had sidled up to me and quietly asked if I was okay. I'd easily nodded. At moments like that, my heart ached for my girls and the loss of their mother, but the pain of my own loss had dimmed significantly over the years as I'd come to terms with the ups and downs that had been life with Leeann.

Now Emerson and I were packing up the empty ornament containers as the kids chattered about the prettiest decorations and whether white lights or multicolored ones were better.

"The aroma's pretty incredible; I have to admit,"

Emerson said to me. "Not sure we'll be able to go back to fake after this."

"You'll smell it every time you walk in the house from now till New Year's."

"Nice." She stacked some of the boxes. "I told your girls I'd take them shopping to buy gifts for you next weekend. I hope that's okay."

"Of course." I straightened and stretched my back before taking the load to the basement. "On a similar note, Xavier pulled me aside earlier. He has a special idea for you."

"Oh? Should I be worried?"

I laughed. "Not at all. But it'll take some time. We're planning to start on it Sunday, so that'll work out well."

"You don't have to do that, Ben."

"I know. I want to," I reassured her.

"Is Skyler helping?" she asked.

I shook my head. It'd be a surprise for Skyler and my girls as well as Emerson. "Would you mind taking her with you and the girls?"

"We'll make it a girls' day."

Xavier and I had come up with an idea for the parade after all. He had hopes of winning a prize for his mom, but we'd have a backup plan in place just in case, because there were a dozen variables of this thing even working.

Though it'd be a multiday project, I was all in. I liked to think Blake would approve of his son and me bonding over a project that would require power tools and manual labor.

"Mommy, come see," Skyler called out.

All four kids were lying on the floor on their backs, shoulder to shoulder, in a semicircle, their heads partially under the tree, gazing at the lights above them.

When I came back from taking boxes to the basement,

Emerson had joined the kids, lying next to her daughter on the end, her knees up, caramel hair draped across the floor.

"Come on, Daddy!" Ruby said.

"Is there room for me?"

"We'll scoot." Evelyn directed the group, and they made room for me next to Emerson.

I lowered my big frame onto the floor and wedged it in between Emerson and the hearth. I had to lie on my side to fit. I shared a smile with Emerson, which put our heads just inches away, so I quickly turned my head and averted my gaze to the lights above.

"Magical, right, Daddy?" Evelyn said.

"Absolutely," I confirmed.

We did this every year, usually just the three of us. Another tradition. An attempt to ensure we all took time to stop and take in the beauty of the tree. I knew from experience how easy it was to walk by it without seeing it. The girls had taken to it immediately and never let me skip it or forget it.

I breathed in the pine and noted the hint of Emerson's feminine scent mixed in. Letting the calm and peace of the rare quiet moment settle into my bones, I watched the sparkle of the colored lights reflect off our beloved ornaments.

As contentedness seeped through me, I rested my hand on Emerson's arm, which was draped over her middle. I propped my head up on my other arm just enough that I could see past her to the four smaller faces. All four kids gazed upward with expressions of enchantment and wonder. I couldn't help but feel the moment deep inside me, and with it came a kernel of a thought, an inkling of *What if this was forever? What if this was my family?*

I couldn't deny the warmth that shot through me.

Seconds later, the moment was interrupted by Emerson's ringtone. I shifted my hand away as she rolled partway over to get her phone out of her back pocket.

"What time is it?" she muttered.

"Ten till nine," I said.

Once her phone was out, I could see the name on the screen—Darius Weber. He was a real estate agent in town. I knew she'd been looking for a home, checking online listings, but his name in black-and-white made it more real.

Emerson sat up and answered.

Unlike me, the kids were unbothered and uninterested in Emerson's conversation. They pointed out the ornaments that sparkled the most, trying to one-up each other.

I tried to give Emerson privacy by tuning in to the kids' talk, but she sat right there in the middle of the living room floor. I couldn't miss that something had come on the market, and Darius thought she'd want to look at it as soon as possible.

Before ending the call, she stood, paced to the dining room as she asked questions.

I waited until it sounded like her call was over, then I joined her with a questioning look.

"That was Darius," she said, her face lit with hope. "A three-bedroom house came on the market outside of town, on the road to Runner. He hasn't seen it yet, just saw it pop up a few minutes ago, but we're going through it tomorrow morning."

That was all it took for the contentedness and the what-ifs from under the tree to float away.

"That's great," I said, reminding myself it was indeed a step toward her goal.

I needed to be happy for Emerson, not sad that my farfetched pipe dream moment under the tree had been crushed. She'd made it clear what her plans were and that they didn't include me.

Chapter Thirteen

Emerson

Tuesday evening all hell broke loose.

I was nearly finished with Everly Henry's cut and highlight, my last client of the day. We were running a little late because she'd required extra toning time, so the other stylists had gone home, and I'd told Edith she could go as well.

As I turned Everly to the mirror for the final reveal, she preened and oohed and aahed, and my phone rang. I allowed a few seconds to gauge her reaction and felt the pang of satisfaction when her eyes lit up and her smile widened genuinely.

"Emerson, I love it," Everly said.

"Excellent! Going one shade lighter really makes your eyes pop. You're gorgeous!" Finally I pulled my phone out and saw Ben's name. "I better take this. Give me two minutes, and I'll get you checked out." I gave her the hand mirror so she could see the back.

"Take your time," Everly said, admiring her new do from every angle.

"Hey, Ben," I said into the phone, pacing away from her.

"Hi, Emerson." His voice was all business. "I got an emergency house call for a horse. I just got off the phone with Berty, so she knows the change in plans. I'm not going to make it to the play tonight."

"Oh," I said. "That's fine. Berty and I can handle the kids. I'm sorry you can't make it, but go take care of that horse. We'll be okay."

"Thanks. I don't know how long this'll take, but I'm still twenty minutes out from the horse."

"I'm running late myself, but I'm betting Berty's already got the kids eating."

"She does."

"Is it snowing?" I asked him, glancing out the salon's back window.

"Tiny flakes. Just started."

"Word is they changed the forecast tonight from flurries to six inches." Everyone had been buzzing with their take on the weather all afternoon. "Keep an eye on that."

"Will do. Enjoy the play, okay? Sorry to miss."

"It can't be helped. The kids'll fill you in when they see you, I'm sure."

We disconnected, and I checked out Everly, hugged her, and said goodbye. I quickly cleaned my station, locked up, and rushed out to head home so I could grab a few bites before the kids, Grandma Berty, and I headed to the high school holiday production.

I'd no sooner turned onto Honeysuckle Road toward Ben's than my phone rang again. Darius's name appeared on the dash screen.

"Hi, Darius."

"Hey, Emerson. I wanted to let you know an offer came through this evening on that property we looked at yesterday. You still good with your decision?"

"I am," I said without hesitation.

As we'd gone through that house, I'd tried to keep an open mind, as he'd suggested. It needed a lot of work. *A lot.* There was enough room in my budget that I could've handled some of the more pressing projects right away, but that wasn't the reason I'd easily decided it wasn't the right property for my kids and me.

The twenty acres were partially wooded, but the section the house was on included a vast, heavily landscaped yard that was painstakingly cared for by the previous owners until they'd become no longer able to handle the work. Apparently they were a retired couple who loved gardening more than home maintenance and spent most of their days tending the gardens, weeding the flower beds and stone paths, and keeping more than twenty bird feeders full. Though everything but the evergreens was dead and brown right now, the photos from other seasons had shown a stunning landscape suited for a garden show and full-color magazines. I couldn't imagine keeping it up.

"You passed the litmus test," Darius said with a chuckle. "That's good news. I like to make sure there's no second-guessing. Personally I think you made the right decision."

"My only concern is how soon I'll have more options," I said. "But I know you'll keep me posted."

"You know I will," he repeated. "I'm watching every day, checking in with my colleagues. We'll find the right place for you and those kiddos."

"Thanks, Darius. I appreciate you letting me know."

"Hopefully I'll talk to you soon with more options," he said. "You have a good evening."

After ending the call, I turned into Ben's driveway, noting the clinic lights were out for the evening, and all the cars were gone, including Ben's truck with his supplies. As I pulled up to the house, I noticed the animals were still in the pasture. Ben had likely forgotten them when the emergency call had come in.

"Crap," I said as I turned off the engine and grabbed my purse. I knew enough to understand we needed to get them in before too much snow fell or the temperature dropped for the night. "Looks like we're going to figure out how to get horses and llamas inside."

I jogged inside and found Grandma Berty and the kids at the table, eating.

"I'm sorry we didn't wait," Berty said. "I wanted to have them ready in time for the play."

"I'm glad you got them started." I noted their plates were nearly empty. "We have a problem. The horses and llamas are still out, and Ben's—"

"Out on an emergency," she finished for me. The dear, seventy-something woman stood. "Did he close the barn doors today?"

"Daddy said he closed them because he wanted the animals to get some exercise," Ruby said. "Since it's supposed to be snowy for the next few days and they'll have to stay inside."

"We just need to open the doors and feed them," Evelyn said.

Perfect. Just feed the animals who were six times my size and could trample me in a heartbeat. "Okay," I said.

"The kids can go out with you and take care of it,"

Grandma Berty said, thankfully unaware of my feelings toward the llamas. "They're just about done eating."

Her lack of concern helped me relax slightly. "Okay." I picked up a dinner roll and ripped off a bite, my coat and boots still on.

"You want to eat first?" Berty asked.

I shook my head. "I want the animals in. The snow's picking up."

The older woman went to the window. "Goodness gracious. Evelyn, are you about finished, honey?"

"I'm done, Grandma."

Thank God.

"You should put on your snow boots," Evelyn said as she carried her plate past me to the sink.

"Good idea." I was so out of my element with barn stuff it wasn't funny. My outdoor boots were in the mudroom. I slid my brown cowboy boots off and replaced them with the weatherproof ones.

Five minutes later, the three older kids were bundled up and ready to help. While Skyler helped Berty take care of the kitchen, I led the older three outside, acting confident. I was mostly just confident Ben's girls knew what they were doing, and probably my son did too.

As we approached the pasture, I noted the three horses were gathered at the fence, watching us, as if to say, *Hurry up, humans. We're hungry!*

I spotted one of the llamas along the fence on the opposite side of the property and scanned for the other one. I frowned, not immediately seeing the white one, a knot forming in my gut.

Not losing hope, I kept searching the pasture, easily visible with the whiteness of the snow cover reflecting light.

I angled out to better see up against the barn, thinking maybe she'd huddled for protection from the weather.

Panic welled up in me, but I fought it down and said, "Where's the other llama?"

"Oh, no," Ruby drew out. "Esmerelda, not tonight."

Her dramatic tone would've been amusing, except I was so far into freaking out that I couldn't appreciate it. I looked to Evelyn, who'd moved ahead of me, her head going left, then right, then left again.

"I don't see her," Evelyn said. "I have a bad feeling she escaped again."

Shit, shit, shit. Worst nightmare, happening now. "What do we do?" I asked.

"She's probably going to the bakery," Ruby said matter-of-factly.

"Super."

"You'll have to take the van to get her," Evelyn said.

"I'm going to text your dad and see if he's almost home." I knew he wasn't. It hadn't been a half hour since I'd talked to him. He'd probably barely arrived at the sick horse's barn.

One of the horses—Bay, I thought—whickered in greeting as we reached the fence.

The four of us verified that we were down a llama. I stifled a whole stream of swear words and took out my phone as Evelyn led the other kids into the barn to feed the animals and opened the big doors. I typed a message to Ben.

> SOS. Very sorry to bother you, but one of the llamas got out. What do I do?

I paced helplessly, trusting the kids could feed the animals. I settled my gaze on Betty, the brown and white llama, as she hurried toward the barn along with the horses.

When my phone sounded, I exhaled in relief and realized Ben was calling me instead of texting.

"Hey," I answered before the first ring ended. "I'm so sorry to interrupt you, but I didn't know what to do."

"Do you know where Esmerelda is?"

"Not yet. We just realized she's missing."

"Fucking llama," he muttered quietly. "I'm sure she's headed to Sugar. Call Max. He and Harper know how to catch her and load her up. You'll need to take the llamamobile to pick her up. The keys are hanging by the door."

Just pick up the llama like she was a kid who'd gone to a party and was ready to come home. In the llamamobile. Sure thing.

"Can you send me Max's number?" I said, fully aware time was precious on his end.

"I will. Max will be able to help with everything. I have to go. Sorry, Ems."

Ems. The nickname soothed me ever so slightly in this otherwise panicked moment.

Almost as soon as the call ended, Ben sent Max's contact info. Without wasting time feeling bad for interrupting his night, I dialed Max and explained the problem to him and let out my breath when he said he'd help me.

———

The ridiculously named llamamobile was stupidly hard to drive, thanks to an old, temperamental manual transmission nightmare. The worsening snowstorm didn't help.

Grandma Berty had happily volunteered to take the kids to the play and had them pack a bag for a sleepover at her house afterward. She was incredible and maybe half-crazy to take on all four of them, but I trusted her completely and was grateful for one less thing to juggle.

By the time I made it the few miles to town, Harper had called to let me know Esmerelda had turned up on Main Street and actually tried to enter the bakery when Tansy Harrelson had gone in to pick up cookies for her daughter's preschool class. Harper was waiting in the car with Danny while Max, Cade McNamara, and his mom worked on catching the rogue llama.

"How is this my life?" I asked out loud after disconnecting from Harper so I could find a place to park the llama transporter.

When I turned onto Main, traffic was stopped for the would-be cookie thief. I wish I was joking about that. On the bright side, hopefully that meant no llama roadkill today.

I shuddered. I might not love that llama, but Ben and his kids did. Probably Xavier too. I had to get Esmerelda home safely.

I pulled the llama buggy up as close as I could, a few doors down from Sugar, turned on the hazards, grabbed the harness, and got out. As I crossed the street toward the commotion, I took in the scene. Cade and Mrs. McNamara were handling crowd control, keeping the onlookers well out of the way, while Sheriff Lopez began addressing the traffic bottleneck.

Esmerelda, in all her shaggy white glory, eyed Max disdainfully from the covered entryway of the bakery as he slowly approached her.

As I got closer, I spotted the cookie in Max's hand. So much drama for a four-inch disk of sugar.

I took the harness to Max, moving slowly to avoid

spooking her. Max grabbed it with an outstretched hand and whispered, "We'll meet you at the van."

Inside the bakery, a handful of people had gathered to watch the operation through the glass door.

When I reached Cade on the sidewalk, about twenty feet down from the llama, I stopped, looked at him, and said words I'd never in a million years thought would come out of my mouth.

"I'm here to give the llama a ride home."

Cade laughed. "Better you than me. Max seems close to capturing her."

"Hallelujah?" I joked. "Life is weird."

"Indeed. Ben's unavailable?"

"He's saving a horse."

"And you're saving his llama." Cade laughed again.

"I've got her," Max called, his voice gentled.

Sheriff Lopez had diverted traffic around the square, clearing the street in front of the bakery, so I jogged back to the llama limo and pulled it close to where Max had the fugitive. The snow was now coming down so hard I needed to turn on the windshield wipers to see.

I got out of the llama getter, determined to not look like a sixteen-year-old boy honking in the driveway to pick up a date, but the truth was, I stood by the driver's door and let Max and Cade load her.

As I watched them lead Esmerelda to the back doors of the van, using the cookie like a carrot, I made a point of not shrinking up against the vehicle. The llama didn't eat people. I knew this. As they passed, she gave me the side-eye, as if she knew I was the one who'd discovered her escape. I was the one raining on her sugar parade.

"You're getting a cookie," I pointed out to her. "Spoiled beast."

Mrs. McNamara approached me from the side, holding out a bakery box. "Just in case," she said. "Tansy came out the back way with an extra dozen."

"Either that llama's going to gain a hundred pounds or I am," I said, smiling, sincerely grateful because I still had to somehow get the llama into the barn.

The back van doors shut, and Max came around to my side. "One llama locked up for your transporting pleasure."

"Thank you so much, Max," I said. "I literally could not have done that without you."

"Ben knows my whiskey brand," he replied, laughing. "It was no problem. She's pretty docile, really."

I eyed the llama, whose funny-looking head was facing forward, close to the metal mesh that would keep her from taking a bite out of me on the way home. She met my gaze as she smugly chewed her cookie.

"Anything else we can help you with?" Cade asked kindly, obviously having no trepidation around llamas.

For a split second, I considered asking this llama-wrangling team to follow me home and get Esmerelda in the barn for me. But the snow wasn't letting up. Harper and Danny were waiting for Max, and for all I knew, the McNamaras had people waiting for them too. I could put on my big-girl panties and get this fucking llama in her pen by myself.

I shook my head and forced a warm smile. "I've got it from here. Thank you all. *So* much." I hugged each one of them in gratitude, watched them walk away with more than a little anxiety, then climbed into the driver's seat without a glance at my prisoner.

I started the engine and pulled the van over to the right lane, turning the wipers up a level against the relentless wet snowflakes. The most direct route to get her home would be to take a right and circle the square instead of winding through residential areas.

There were a lot of cars out tonight, in part due to the backup from Ms. Traffic Stopper herself, so it was slow going. As the car in front of me stopped, I hit the brakes, trying to figure out what the holdup was. Then I spotted a gloved hand popping out of the driver's window and motioning me around them.

Slowly I drove forward, waved at the courteous driver, then realized the next car was pulled to the curb as well... and the one in front of that. They were all letting me pass them, as if I was driving a parade car with the president of the United States in back.

"You're getting a pretty high opinion of yourself, aren't you?" I said as we took a right turn onto Honeysuckle Road by Henry's and headed home.

She huffed out a snort that startled me so badly I went airborne in the seat, my heart taking off in a sprint. In my defense, it was the first sound I'd heard her make tonight, and it was right behind my ear.

"That was rude," I chided once I caught my breath and avoided driving into the ditch. "And not safe at all."

That was apparently the wrong thing to say, because the llama began groaning, sounding like a long, drawn-out moo that kept on going.

"You don't have to be a drama queen," I said, noting that the snow had started sticking to the road, making it slick and slushy. "If you land me in the ditch, we're eating llama for Christmas dinner."

Ben's driveway was less than ten miles from town, but between the snow pelting the van and the llama groaning nonstop, the drive was the longest ten minutes of my life.

When I pulled up as close as I could get to the barn door, I realized the fun had only just begun.

Chapter Fourteen

Emerson

Two hours and a glass and a half of wine later, I'd finally calmed down from the llama business. Now I was worried about Ben driving in bad weather.

The storm had only gotten worse, with the wind picking up and the snow falling harder. By the time I'd walked from the barn to the house after locking Ms. Llama Pants in her pen, there was close to two inches on the ground.

I'd come into a house empty of humans, let the three dogs out to do their business, loved on the cats, who were nestled together in one of the chairs, then poured myself some merlot I found in the cabinet above the fridge. I'd turned on the fireplace and collapsed on the sofa to come down from the llama antics.

Less than three minutes later, I'd popped up off the sofa and funneled my restless energy into cooking chicken and rice soup.

I couldn't remember the last time I'd had a house—any house—to myself. It was an odd feeling.

Berty had texted when she and the kids made it to her home in town after the play. I'd talked to Xavier and Skyler both on her phone, letting them tell me all about the production and the cocoa and popcorn they got before bed.

Berty's idea for a sleepover had been fortuitous, preventing her from having to drive them out this far. We agreed there'd likely be a snow day tomorrow, so we'd touch base midmorning. Despite my misgivings, she seemed genuinely happy to have her four kiddos, as she called them, staying over.

Once I'd put the leftovers in the refrigerator, I changed into my most comfortable pj's, went back to the couch, pulled a blanket over my legs, and stalked the weather app on my phone, fretting over Ben's safety instead of diving into my cozy mystery.

When I heard his key in the lock, I threw off the blanket, startling the cats, then hurried to the kitchen, the dogs at my heels. I waited by the counter, the only light the dim one over the sink, while he greeted the tail waggers one by one in the mudroom, then let them out one last time for the night. Finally he came in from the entryway, having shed his boots and coat, looking exhausted but so damn handsome.

I was so relieved on multiple levels, I couldn't help it— I rushed over and wrapped my arms around him, burying my head in his chest and breathing in his masculine scent.

"Hello," he said with a low laugh.

It hit me we weren't on a hugging-hello basis, but then I felt his arms go around me and let myself soak in the feel of him.

"It's bad out there," I said. "I'm glad you made it okay."

His scent was alluring, no hint of soap or shampoo, just the unique smell of a man who'd been working hard all day. Leaning on him after an evening that had tested me made me feel safe. Protected. No longer so alone.

He let out a quiet groan and didn't move away. "You had quite an evening."

"Your llama's home safe and sound."

He loosened his hold enough to look at me and chuckled. "I got your *the llama has landed* text. Thank you, Ems. That had to be an ordeal for you."

Ordeal was one word for it. *Trial. Nightmare. Trauma.* Those were others, but I'd made it through. There was no reason to draw out the drama for Ben.

"She's relaxing in her pen," I told him.

"I checked on her before I came inside, filled up her hay trough," he said. "You did great. She looked no worse for wear."

"It took me three cookies to get her from the van to her stall." I made myself untangle from him and give him space. "How's the horse?"

"Holding his own. I got some meds in him. We'll see how he does over the next twenty-four hours, but I think he's going in the right direction."

"I'm glad. I'm having wine. Can I pour you some?" I went to the counter and held up the half-full bottle.

"Sure, I'll take some. It's been a day."

"I second that." I laughed at the understatement as I filled a second glass.

"Berty let me know the kids did great. I hope she's still saying that tomorrow morning," he said.

"Right? The woman is a saint."

I handed him his glass and picked up my own. Holding it up, I said, "To surviving."

"To saving horses and llamas," he said as he clinked.

We both took a sip, then our gazes caught, and the energy in the room changed. Ben set his glass on the counter and held out his hand, palm up. I put mine in his, my pulse picking up. Even though he'd just come in from outside, his hand was warm, strong, rough.

"I know you're not a fan of llamas, Ems, so I appreciate what you did all the more," he said in a low voice that resonated right through to my core.

"She gritched at me the whole way home," I said, stepping closer, "but we made it through."

"She groans sometimes in the van. I think she's voicing her displeasure at losing her freedom." He smiled. "She's a pain in the ass, but I love that fucking llama."

I laughed quietly, distracted by the way his blue eyes were so focused on me, so intent. For once there were no kids anywhere in the vicinity. The llamas and horses and chickens were taken care of for the night. The cats were sacked out again in the living room. With the dogs outside, it was just the two of us and a tangible tension arcing between us.

I set my wineglass on the counter, my eyes never leaving his, and stepped closer yet. Somehow our other hands became entwined, and I took it as a green light. Before I could second-guess myself, I went up on my toes and pressed my lips to his.

As our mouths connected, a spark of need shot through me, my insides going liquid and hot. I let go of his hands and grasped the back of his neck, pressing my breasts into his hard chest. I couldn't miss his hardness against my belly, telling me he was as into this as I was.

The kiss became urgent, fervent, as he pivoted us and trapped my body between him and the cabinets. As our tongues twisted and teeth collided, Ben's hands slipped beneath my pajama top and slid upward along my sides until they were just under my heavy breasts, so close to my needy flesh. He paused there for long enough I was silently urging, begging him to touch me with those work-roughened hands. When he finally lifted one thumb to my nipple, I gasped into his mouth, then intensified the kiss, my wordless way of telling him *more, please.*

He palmed my breast, kneaded it, fingered and pinched the tip, eliciting a moan from me. I lowered my hands to his ass, pulling him into me, needing to quell the pulsing ache between my legs.

A *thunk* sounded at the outside door, and we froze. Next came scratching, then a dog's whimper, then a bark.

"Shit." Ben put space between us. "I forgot they were out there."

I ran a finger over my lower lip, catching my breath as I registered that we'd left the three dogs out in the cold. "Sounds like they're done."

"I've got 'em."

As he walked toward the door, he adjusted his jeans, making my lips flicker up in a lust-struck smile.

The outer door opened, cold air swept in, and three dogs galloped inside, bringing their energy and the jingle of tags with them. Each one of them rushed up to me and sniffed. Milo and Sprocket apparently registered me as okay, trotted over to the water bowls, and started slurping. Nugget did a lap around me, rubbing up against my legs, campaigning for attention.

I reached down and rubbed the sides of her head. "Who's a pretty girl? Did you get cold out there, Nugs?"

Ben ducked into the bathroom and returned with a towel. "I wasn't prepared," he said as he bent down and dried Milo's, then Sprocket's paws. He called Nugget over and sweet-talked her as he lifted each of her paws and dried them as well.

In a flash, the three headed out of the kitchen, probably to curl up in their dog beds.

Ben tossed the towel into the mudroom for next time, then settled next to me, both of our butts leaning against the counter.

"That was probably good timing for an interruption," he said, his voice rough.

I pressed my lips together and considered what to say. "Stupid dogs" was what came out. I laughed, then sobered, doubt flashing through me. "I... Did you not enjoy that? The kissing, I mean."

"Are you kidding me? I was two seconds from lifting you to the counter, stripping your sexy flannels off, and having my way with you."

I laughed again, giddiness rushing in at his admission. "Flannels are not sexy." The shorts showed off my legs, but the top was literally buttoned up tight.

His response was a quiet, rumbly growl. "I'm sorry that was getting out of control. You said it couldn't happen again. As much as I want that to happen and more, I respect your needs."

Yeah, those needs...

With an ache still thrumming deep in my core, my thoughts went to Olivia's suggestion of letting Ben help me get back on the bike, so to speak. I was dying to ride that bike, or rather, Ben. The question was, did I have the nerve to ask for it?

"I did say that, didn't I?" I said.

His answer was an affirming grunt.

I nodded, searching for the right words. "What if I said I wanted that and more to happen too?"

He swung his head to look at me from the side.

"Sort of," I added.

"Sort of?"

I ran my tongue over the inside of my tender lower lip, then raised my hand, palm up, urging him to take it. He pressed his palm to mine but didn't grasp it, so I wove our fingers together and lowered our entwined hands, then turned toward him.

"I don't want a serious relationship with anyone," I said. "Ever."

"Never?"

I shook my head. "I can't do it again. I can't... I can't lose somebody else the way I've lost Blake, my mom, my grandma." Years-old grief bubbled up in my throat and threatened to take my breath. I fought it down, focused on the man in front of me. "It hurts too much."

"Losing someone's fucking hard." His voice was low but laced with conviction, leaving me no doubt that he'd suffered gravely when his wife died. Not that I'd had any question.

"I'm not up for it."

He raised our joined hands and brushed his lips over the back of mine. "You've lost the three people you loved most."

I swallowed and nodded, shutting down on the pain again before it could seep in because I didn't have the energy for it...and I didn't want it to ruin the evening. I had hopes it could go in a different direction.

Ben unlaced our fingers to slide his arm around my waist, pulled me into his side, and kissed the top of my head like a supportive, caring friend. I appreciated the hell out of that, but it wasn't what my body was thrumming with need for.

I inhaled a courage-steeling breath, then turned to face him.

"The thing is, I haven't been with a man in four years." I lifted my chin and tentatively sought eye contact. As soon as our gazes connected, my courage sparked, or maybe it was raw need driving everything. "I miss sex."

I stopped breathing. Ben swallowed as he peered down at me, his pupils enlarging.

Before he could answer, I rushed on. "I'm not to the point where I could go out for a one-night stand, but I trust you, Ben. And it seems like we're physically compatible."

He let out a low rumble of a chuckle. "And you miss sex."

"Maybe you have someone already," I said as soon as the possibility occurred to me. Oh, God. What if he had someone else on the side?

His laugh was heartier this time. "Surely you know me better than that, Emerson."

I let out my breath. "I don't know. Maybe you have a whole team of *special friends*, and you told them things were on hold while you had house guests." I couldn't help a wide grin.

"Like a different lady for each night of the week?" he teased back.

"Sure. For all I know, you meet them in the barn and roll around in the hay after the creatures are fed."

He laughed wholeheartedly and pulled me into him, then sobered. "No. I don't have any fuck buddies who meet me in the barn or anywhere else."

Thank God.

"So you want to be friends with benefits? Is that what you're proposing?" he asked.

"At the risk of sounding like a rom-com that could have a bad ending..." I tried to laugh at my own joke, but nerves were taking over. "Yes? I mean, maybe. Roommates with benefits. If you're interested."

"And what happens when you find a house and move out? We're done?"

I nodded. "If we're not living together, the temptation should be gone, right? Back to just friends?"

"Nobody gets hurt?"

"Right," I said. "We go into it with an approximate end date. The kids won't know, so none of them will get hurt either."

He continued to gaze into my eyes, all kidding gone, not a single sign on his face of what he was thinking. I waited, wondering if I'd misjudged and just screwed up our friendship for good, my heart hammering in my ears.

"I just have one more question," Ben said.

I pressed my lips together nervously. "Yeah?"

"What the hell are we still doing standing in my kitchen with our clothes on?"

Chapter Fifteen

Ben

When the woman who was your teenage crush nearly twenty years ago proposes getting naked, you don't take the time to think through the downside.

As I swept Emerson into my arms cradle-style and hightailed it to my bedroom, I wasn't sure there *was* a downside. There was only this beautiful woman with full, tantalizing tits I hadn't had the privilege of laying my eyes on yet, kissing me till my eyes crossed, suggesting we screw.

Sign me the hell up. Every day.

When I got her in my room, I lowered her feet to the floor, went to the nightstand, and flipped the lamp on low, bathing the room in a dim, warm light. I wasted no time returning to Emerson, who watched me, looking...hesitant? Hadn't she been the one to suggest this?

"Something wrong?" I said, cradling her cheek in my palm and guiding her chin up so she'd look at me. I was confused. She hadn't flinched when she'd stood in my kitchen and propositioned me.

Her gaze darted toward the lamp, and her chest rose with a deep breath in.

I held my breath, my gaze locked on her, afraid she was having second thoughts.

"I'm...still trying to lose weight from my pregnancies."

"Oh," I said on a relieved exhalation. In my opinion, she didn't need to lose a pound. "Beautiful, sexy Ems, I want you exactly the way you are. Every curve just as it is."

She still looked uncertain, so I pulled her body against my erection. "Does this tell you how sexy I think you are?"

Her eyes fluttered shut. "Mmm. I guess you can't fake that."

"If you'd feel better with the lights off, we can do that, but I assure you I will fucking love every inch of your body because it's yours."

She met my gaze, seemed to measure my words and turn them over in her mind. "The light's okay," she whispered as she lifted my thermal shirt up my chest, her fingers teasing me along the way. I took over from her and yanked it the rest of the way off, then tossed it on the floor.

As she ran her hands up my chest, seeming to like what she saw, I kissed her again, hoping to get her back to where we'd been a few minutes ago in the kitchen so she'd forget about her self-consciousness.

I tunneled my fingers through her gorgeous silky hair, angling her head, plunging my tongue between her lips so I could taste her, feel her heat.

I knew Emerson was right there with me, about to combust, when I felt her fingers at the button on my jeans. She had it undone in a heartbeat, then unzipped them. Pulsing with need, my dick was jutting out of my boxer briefs. When I thought she'd shove my pants down, instead she touched my tip, dipped her fingers into my underwear, and grasped me, pulling a groan from me.

"Fuck," I bit out, my head falling back at the heavenly feel of her touch. "Let me catch up."

I fumbled with the buttons on her flannel pajama top, my fingers feeling big and clumsy at first. My hands shook with need. I was thirty-five years old, and I felt like this was my first time with a woman. It'd been a while, a long while, but not so long I didn't know what I was doing. I guess that's what happened when you'd been hot for a girl so many years ago, then finally had her in your bedroom.

When the last button was unfastened, I left her top in place while I undid the drawstring of her pants. I kissed her again, forcing myself to slow down. I tended to her mouth, exploring it, relishing the connection I'd longed for for so long. She was turning me inside out just with her mouth on mine, with the sexy gasps and moans she made, the way her fingers clung to my nape, holding me close and insistently.

She arched into my chest, teasing me with her breasts mostly covered by flannel. With our mouths still connected, I filled my palm with one ample, luscious globe, eliciting a sexy, slow moan from her as she pushed into my hand.

I tugged the top off her shoulders. It fell to the floor, and I palmed both of her tits, desperate to touch every millimeter of her soft, supple flesh. Ending our kiss, I bent down to suck her nipple into my mouth, swirling my tongue around the tip, teasing it with my teeth.

"Oh, God," she breathed out.

I needed her stretched out on her back on my bed so I could take the next twelve hours to worship her body at my leisure. At the same time, I was aching to bury my dick deep inside of her till both of us exploded.

I reluctantly lifted my mouth from her, straightening and directing her backward to the edge of the mattress. As I dipped my hands into her shorts and sent them tumbling to her ankles, I distracted her with another hot, fervent kiss on the lips, my hands sliding to her tantalizing ass once it was bare.

"You still okay with this?" I asked, knowing once I laid her out on my bed, it would be damn hard to stop.

"More than," she said, shoving my jeans and boxer briefs down.

I stepped out of my pants and kicked them aside as she did the same. My hands were on her hips, our bodies flush from knee to chest. I was dying to feast my eyes on her but also conscious of her timidness. If only she could grasp how much she had me about to come out of my skin just with the feel of her body, she'd understand there was no possible way I wouldn't love how she looked.

We eased onto the bed, and she shifted up so her head was on my pillow, pulling me with her by one hand, our gazes locked intently. I pressed a kiss to her lips, then could no longer resist. I kneeled between her knees and feasted my eyes on her.

"Jesus," I growled out. "You're so fucking beautiful, Ems. Don't you ever, ever feel shy about your gorgeous body."

I lowered to her breasts and filled my hands and mouth with them, spending a good long time showing her how much I adored her. I couldn't remember ever being so turned on.

Eventually I trailed kisses lower, until I was nestled between her legs, loving her with my tongue, tasting her intimately, my blood pounding through me.

I set out to see how many times I could make her come,

with my tongue, with my fingers. Hearing my name on her lips as she shattered... I'd never, ever forget what that was like, would never tire of it.

Her body responded to me as if we'd been together for decades, not minutes. After her third orgasm, she went limp, breathing hard.

"Ben."

When I glanced up at her face from between her legs, her expression was lust-drunk, satisfied, and a little disbelieving.

"Mm-hmm?"

"What are you doing to me?" she asked on an exhale.

I feigned concern. "You don't like it?"

"I'm not sure I can survive it." She let out a lazy, satiated laugh as she tugged at me. "Come here."

I stretched over her body until we were face-to-face, then kissed her, letting her taste herself on my tongue and lips. Blood pounded through my cock as it nestled against her softness.

"It's your turn," she whispered as she kneaded my ass with one hand and ran her foot over the back of my calf, her body cradling me closer. "Do you have protection?"

A laugh slipped out of me as I remembered the gift from West. "As a matter of fact, I do."

"What's so funny?"

I kissed her a few more times, then rolled to the side of the bed to get my box of thirty-six. "West Aldridge got my name in the gift exchange for my single dads' group. Smart ass gave me supplies for romance since you're living here, including a big box of condoms."

"Oh, my God. For you and me?"

"Quit looking so mortified. Thanks to him, we have protection."

"How did he know?" she asked, cracking a grin as I stood, went to the top drawer in my dresser, and took out the box.

"He didn't, technically. What he knew is I have a hot woman living with me. He didn't want me to miss an opportunity."

I opened the box, took out a packet, and ripped it open, watching her as she thought that over.

"Well then, thank you, West," she said lightly, her eyes roving hungrily over my erection as I sheathed it. Then she went serious again. "We're not going public though, right? This is between us."

"It's between us." I crawled back over her, her legs falling away as I positioned myself at her opening. "People can think what they want. They already do."

Before she could ponder that too hard, I pushed into her slowly, biting down on the inside of my cheek to keep myself in check, remembering it'd been a while for her.

Emerson gasped, then bit her lip, her head falling back and eyes closing. I watched her face for any sign of discomfort or doubt, but what I saw was bliss that mirrored mine. Because her tight, wet channel felt like fucking heaven.

She looked like the goddess of my dreams, with her gorgeous hair spread over my pillow, her irresistible body stretched out under me, mine for the taking. I wouldn't forget the way she looked in that moment anytime soon.

I entered a little farther, felt her muscles contract around me, her body going tense.

"Are you okay?"

Her eyes popped open and met mine as she nodded with a slight smile. "You're not small."

"I don't want to hurt you."

Emerson took in a deep breath and let it out. I felt her relax around me.

"You're not," she said. Then she grasped both my ass cheeks and pulled me into her at once, until I was in so deep it truly felt like we were one.

Her eyes fluttered closed, and she moaned and moved her hips just enough that the friction had me fighting to hold on. I was already worked up from loving on her body so much and watching her come apart. I wasn't going to last long at all.

I slid out of her, pushed back in, slowly, savoring every incredible bit of sensation, my eyes on her as I repeated the movements again and again, because a part of me still couldn't fathom that I was finally inside Emerson.

As much as I was trying to hold on to these moments, stretch them out into more, my blood was on fire, my self-control on the verge of unleashing. My brain and thoughts shut down, and my body went rogue, hammering into her on instinct and hot, throbbing need, climbing, reaching...

I had just enough awareness left to realize she hadn't come yet. I reached between us and found her tight little nub of nerves. Her eyes rolled back as she arched up into me, sexy little gasps and whimpers spilling from her, telling me she was close.

I held on until I felt her muscles explode around me and she ground into me, clung to me, reaching, arching, then plunging over with a "Ben, omigod, Ben," and a keening as her body convulsed.

That was all she wrote for me too.

"Ohhh, fuck," I bit out as I stiffened and held on to her, unsure I'd come out conscious on the other side.

When I'd emptied myself, it took a good second for my breathing to restart and my heart to beat again.

"Holy fuck," I said on an exhale as soon as I could muster words. "What you do to me, Ems…"

She let out a low, lazy laugh. "Pretty sure you were the one *doing*." She slowly, distractedly ran her fingers through my hair in an affectionate caress. "You're good at that."

Even as my blood took its time trickling back into my brain, I was pretty fucking sure it was the combination of the two of us, because I'd never in my life had sex like *that*. That was next-level.

I eventually gathered the strength to roll sideways, bringing her with me, reluctant to break our connection. As our breathing leveled out, I ran my hand down her hip, over her perfect ass, and back up, loving the feel of her soft skin and curves. I nestled my chin on top of her head, inhaling the smell of her hair.

"You smell like lemons," I said, my voice not much more than a rumble in my throat.

She laughed. "That's better than fear and llama breath, right?"

"Llama breath isn't nearly as bad as cat breath with dental disease."

"Animal nerd."

"But I'm *your* animal nerd. For tonight," I clarified, though this was *not* going to be the last time we were together if I had my way. Not by any stretch of the imagination.

"For tonight," she repeated. "You don't happen to have a secret bathroom in here, do you?"

I laughed. "Afraid not."

"So I have to trek through half the frigid house buck naked to get to one?"

"You can throw on your pj top, but I'd like it a lot better

if you didn't. I'll just have to take it off you again when you get back."

"Presumptuous that you think I'll come back," she teased.

"I'll warm you up if you do."

She pulled back to look in my eyes. "Compelling offer."

"It's not every night we'll have the whole place to ourselves."

She frowned and sat up, glancing around at my modest bedroom. "I guess that's confirmation you've never had a secret lover in this place."

I sat up too, banding my arm around her middle and pressing a kiss to her lips. "I've never had any kind of lover in this place. It's not a decision I make lightly, not with the kids here."

"Have you been with anyone since Leeann?" she asked quietly, as if hesitant to bring up my late wife's name.

I shook my head. "It's funny how your priorities change when you have kids."

"That's for real," she said.

She climbed over me, her legs straddling me for a few seconds as she leaned in and kissed me. "I'll be back in two minutes for that getting-warm offer."

She slid off the bed. I expected her to throw her pajama shirt on, but she strode away without a stitch of clothing covering her irresistible body. I didn't see any sign of an extra sway as she walked out. She wasn't even trying to get to me, but even so, I started to get hard again from watching her.

I got rid of the condom and pulled the covers back as it hit me how chilled the nighttime air was, particularly with a sheen of sweat covering my skin.

As I waited for Emerson to come back, I felt on top of

the world. Maybe it would've been just as good between us without the backstory, the teenage crush, and all that, but I couldn't deny that was part of it.

Had I loved my wife? Yes, but in a very different way. It wasn't fair to compare the two. The fact was that when I'd been married to Leeann, Emerson had been off my radar, living across the country and married to my friend.

That didn't lessen the satisfaction or the thrill of finally, *finally* getting to be with Emerson.

I locked out thoughts of Blake, reminding myself I'd decided this was okay, that he'd want her to be happy. I might not be her forever happy place, but based on her sexy sounds and signs of enjoyment a few minutes ago, I believed I'd made her happy for tonight.

So far.

Chapter Sixteen

Emerson

After multiple rounds of sleep alternating with superlative sex, I stirred again to find Ben's strong arm around me.

I cracked an eye open to verify it was still dark in that snowy, brighter-than-usual way, telling me the world outside was covered in a white blanket. Filled with warmth and contentment that was practically foreign to me, I relaxed back into him and closed my eyes again.

Sleeping cuddled next to a man was a luxury I'd rarely gotten to enjoy in my life. During all the years I was with Blake, we went from high school, where we both lived at our respective parents' homes and woke up alone, to a couple of weeks of married bliss before he went into basic training. From then, he'd rarely been in my bed for more than a few nights at a time.

The last four years it'd been more normal to wake with a little girl or sometimes a boy in bed with me. It made cuddling with Ben that much more glorious.

I must've dozed off again when I realized with a start that he was sneaking out of bed on the other side.

"What are you doing?" I whispered. "Did we miss Gordon's wakeup call?"

"We must have. He's not as loud on this side of the house. It's time to feed the animals. Somebody kept me up too late."

"Mmm. Not sorry."

He leaned across the bed and kissed me. "Me neither. Go back to sleep if you want." He took clothes out of his dresser, then left the room.

I did want to go back to sleep, but he probably did too. He'd woken me up twice last night, and I'd returned the favor once.

I laughed quietly, like a satisfied cat. Had we really done it four times? The delicious tenderness between my legs said yes.

I had zero regrets.

I stretched my legs, appreciating the warm cocoon of blankets for a few seconds, then tossed the covers aside and sat on the edge of the bed. When I crept up the stairs to my room, Ben was still in the bathroom.

In my room, I threw on warm sweatpants, a long-sleeved tee, and a thick sweatshirt, plus wool socks. Twisting my hair up on my head in a scrunchie, I hurried down to the kitchen and found Ben starting a pot of coffee.

"What are you doing?" he asked as I walked into the room.

"Feeding the beasts with you. It's time for me to learn the ropes."

"You don't have to. Have you looked outside?"

I went to the kitchen window and peeked out. "Snow." It was tough to judge how much, but there were drifts a third of the way up the garage door. I shrugged. "Esmerelda and Betty still have to eat."

Ben laughed. "They do. You're welcome to come out with me if you want."

We put our boots, coats, gloves, and hats on. Ben picked up a shovel from the entryway on our way out. I immediately saw why. Pristine white snow covered everything in every direction, drifting over the steps and giving no hint of the usual route to the barn.

He scooped a path down to the driveway. "I'll have to get the plow going to do the rest. Animals first though."

Taking my gloved hand, he waded through snow that was probably seven or eight inches deep, with me following in his footsteps, literally. When we entered the barn, one of the horses nickered and another made a snuffing sound.

"Morning, everybody," Ben called, making me smile.

This was Ben's version of walking into the office and greeting everyone for the day.

He made his rounds to all three horses, rubbing their necks, saying good morning, and giving them compliments. I stuck next to him, telling each horse hello but not going close enough to pet them. I wasn't really afraid of the horses, just a little intimidated, but this was me taking a first step toward getting used to them.

"I'll need to go up to the hayloft and get more hay, but first we'll refill their water and get them their grains."

"Will you show me what to do?"

His brows shot up. "Really? You want to feed the horses?"

"I didn't like having to depend on the kids to do it last night."

Ben nodded, then showed me how to fill the water

buckets, where the corn was stored, how much to give each horse, and how to secure everything in the stalls.

Ben's horse, Smoky, nuzzled me as I gave him his grains. I caught my breath and then laughed because it tickled.

"He likes you," Ben said.

"What do I do?"

"He likes to have his neck rubbed, although he's picky and doesn't usually ask for attention from anyone but me."

"Really?" I looked at the horse, who was studying me with those big, astute eyes. Even though his corn was there for the taking, all his attention was on me.

Ben came up to us. "Hey, Smoke. You know a pretty lady when you see one, huh? You trying to steal my woman?"

"Temporary woman," I said in a stage whisper, grinning and playing along.

"He doesn't need to know that," Ben said. He stroked Smoky's neck. "Try doing this."

I reached over and rubbed the other side of the horse's neck, tentatively at first. He nuzzled me again, startling me and making me laugh.

"Who knew he was such a flirt?"

"He just likes me because I gave him corn."

Once all three horses had corn and water, Ben went to a staircase at the end of the aisle and started up.

"Can I come?" I asked.

He paused. "Sure. It's just a lot of hay."

"I've never seen a hayloft."

Ben laughed and shook his head. "Got me a city girl, huh?"

"Small-town girl who's never been around barn animals." I caught up to him and followed him up the stairs.

They opened to an expansive loft filled with rectangular bales from one end to the other. "That's...a lot of hay."

"It should last us all winter. The llamas each go through about a bale a day."

"Each?"

"They don't have grains like the horses, so it's all hay in the winter."

"And cookies."

"And cookies."

There wasn't a lot of room for us to walk up here, just stacks and stacks of hay, with some of the stacks on this end shorter, making a kind of stair-step pattern. As I took it all in, he grasped my hand and pulled me flush against him. He'd taken his thick work gloves off.

"Wanna roll around in the hay?" he asked.

I eyed the hay, grinning at his reference to my teasing accusation last night.

"Missing your many ladies?"

He went serious and tugged me in for a hot, lingering kiss, which served to stop my smart-ass remarks. Instead he pulled a moan from me as heat shot through me from just a kiss. Let it be known that Ben Holloway could work magic with his mouth even with all my clothes on.

He gripped my butt and pulled me against his erection. "I didn't start anything in bed because I meant to let you go back to sleep, but here you are."

"Here I am. Feeding the horses. If anyone asks."

"No one's going to ask," he said in a sexy rumble, "because the kids are with Berty. Trapped by a snowstorm."

"Mmm. The whole town is stranded by a snowstorm." I'd likely need to close the salon for the day.

I kissed him, my arms going around his neck as I wished for fewer layers between our bodies.

Ben slipped both his hands under the waistband of my sweatpants and palmed my butt, his fingers dipping lower between my legs. As if he'd hit a switch, a persistent ache ramped up deep in my hollow core, throbbing to be filled by him.

With our mouths still locked in a frantic kiss, I unzipped his coat and ran my hands under his thermal shirt, over his ridged chest, as he teased the apex of my thighs. I'd never ached so bad for someone. If I didn't fill myself with him in the next sixty seconds, I was going to lose my mind.

"Ben," I gasped.

"I know."

I went after his jeans next, unbuttoning them, trying to be careful as I worked the zipper down over his erection.

He'd undone my coat and shoved it off, then unfastened my bra so he could get his hands on my breasts. He lifted my sweatshirt and leaned down to take my nipple in his mouth, making me moan and gasp and throb deep inside.

I guided him backward to a bale of hay stacked about three feet off the ground, and he sat on it, in perfect alignment with my intentions. I toed my boots off, shoved my sweats and underwear down my legs, and stepped out of them.

"God, Ems," he said, shoving his jeans down a few inches, enough to free his big, beautiful penis. As I straddled him, my core rubbing against his hardness, he said, "I didn't bring a condom."

"I'm on birth control and clean."

"I'm clean too."

He barely got the words out before I lowered myself onto him, biting my lip at the heaven of having him inside me again.

The sensation of his heat filling me and the cold air on

my butt drove my need even higher as I ground into him, pumped my hips, and rode him like the crazed woman he'd turned me into in about two heartbeats. I lost myself, driven by sensation and need, everything else falling out of my consciousness.

My eyes locked with Ben's intense ones, the connection between us like nothing I'd ever experienced. As exposed as I felt, I couldn't look away as he bucked and thrust into me, over and over again, meeting every motion of my hips, our rhythm, our need in unison like a masterpiece of a song.

"Come for me, Ems."

As if the words in that growly, demanding voice were the final push I needed, I shattered, every muscle in my body contracting and reacting to this man, heat exploding through me and my brain blacking out.

"Look at me, Emerson," he said in the roughest, need-filled voice.

I forced my eyes back to his and felt a swoon in my chest. He was so familiar, so much a part of me, so dear. At this moment, he was everything to me, the very reason I took in air and gasped for breath.

Ben gripped my butt tighter into him, bucked up hard, and held on tight as he emptied himself into me.

I wrapped my arms around him, clung to him, and closed my eyes. Memorized what it felt like to have this strong, virile man come apart because of me. Even as my own body still trembled and contracted, it was a rush to know I could wield that kind of power over him.

Eventually he seemed to regain some control over his body and sat up straighter, his arms banding around me like he'd never let me go.

"If that was an audition to be my Wednesday roll-in-the-hay lady, you got the gig."

I laughed. "But only Wednesdays when the kids are trapped at Berty's by a snowstorm?"

"For now."

As my body came down from Ben Holloway, the temperature of the barn air registered, and I shivered.

"How is it I'm half-naked, and you're still wearing your coat and jeans?" I asked.

"Hey, you did that yourself."

I smiled, a little embarrassed at how aggressive I'd been. That wasn't typical for me.

"I fucking loved it," he added, as if sensing my thoughts.

"I'm glad, but now I'm freezing." I kissed him, then disconnected our bodies and scrambled to get my sweatpants back on.

Ben stood and put himself back together too. When we were both dressed, if not desperately in need of a hot shower, he advanced on me, put his arms around me, then pressed my back into the support pillar that went to the roof as he kissed me soundly.

"You turn me inside out, Emerson."

"You make me rip my clothes off and mount you," I said back, laughing.

"Feel free to do that every day."

We kissed some more, slower now, more affection than urgency.

A human-like humming sounded, startling me.

Ben broke contact and laughed. "Esmerelda's hungry."

"That's her?"

He nodded. "She communicates a lot. She wants her breakfast."

"Last night in the van she was louder, more distressed."

"She groans in the van. Hums when she thinks it's past time for a meal."

Amy Knupp

"What about Betty?"

"She's hardly ever in the van since she doesn't run away like Esmerelda. She doesn't vocalize much at all."

The humming sounded from below us again.

"Demanding llama," I said.

"She's special." He laughed. He heaved a bale of hay and tossed it over the railing to the large center aisle below, then sent a second one behind it.

We headed down the steps, and Ben showed me how to fill the llamas' troughs with hay. Esmerelda was first. I felt bad for Betty, the better-behaved llama, because Esmerelda made sure she was served first.

As Ben spread Esmerelda's hay out in her trough, I watched and gathered my courage. I knew llamas didn't normally bite people, and I had made it through getting Esmerelda in her stall last night. Ben had reassured me they only spit when they felt threatened.

Betty stretched her neck out over the half wall of the stall, watching as her sister-in-llamahood dug in to the hay.

"You're hungry too, aren't you?" I said to her. She looked at me with those big, pretty eyes as if to confirm that she was starving and just as worthy as the loud, demanding creature in the next stall.

"I got you," I told her, then grabbed a mound of hay and spread it in her trough.

Following Ben's lead, I gave her several armfuls until we'd split the bale between the two.

"There you go, pretty girl," I said as Betty chomped her hay and eyed me, not in an unfriendly way, more just curious. "Yes, I called you pretty. I love your spots."

Ben sweet-talked Esmerelda, the high-drama llama, while I muttered praise to mellow Betty as she ate. Betty stuffed her mouth with hay for a few seconds at a time, then

162

lifted her head, stalks of hay sticking out every which way as she chewed and studied me.

Now that I was this close and receiving no threatening vibes from this gentle creature, I was intrigued. Maybe even fascinated. Llamas were so funny-looking, but the longer I watched Betty, the cuter I thought she was, with her understated enthusiasm for hay, her unabashed interest in me, and maybe even some gratitude around the edges.

"The horses need hay too," Ben said, heading toward the second bale he'd thrown over.

"Okay," I said without moving. "I'll hang out with you," I told Betty in a softer voice.

Before taking another mouthful, she paused, stepped closer to me, tilted her head slightly, then ducked her head for more hay directly in front of me, telling me she was comfortable. I wasn't sure why, but she seemed friendly and approving of me in spite of my nervousness.

On the other end of the barn, I could hear Ben talking to the horses as he delivered their second course. His affection for all these animals was obvious and oddly endearing. So was what he could do to me in a hayloft, to be honest.

I kept up a one-sided conversation with Betty as she ate, admiring her brown spots and her thick coat. A few minutes later, when she finished her mouthful, she paused and looked at me, poking her snout over the trough and half wall so she was inches from my face. I froze and waited to see what she would do; not gonna lie, I felt a little intimidated.

"Hey, sweet girl," I said, working hard not to flinch or jolt away. I was starting to trust her.

Before I could register what was happening, she pressed her snout against my cheek then straightened. It tickled and drew a giggle from me.

"What is happening here?" Ben asked from behind me

as he approached. "Betty, you big sweetheart. First Smoky goes for you, and Betty just kissed you, Ems."

"Yeah?" I looked at Betty, then turned to gauge Ben's face to see if he was serious.

"Without a doubt. That was her way of saying she likes you."

I'd never given thought to a llama's approval or friendship, but as I looked into the gentle beast's eyes again, I felt a gratification and affection that stunned me.

"Can I pet her?"

"Try rubbing her neck," he said.

I stepped up to the half wall and tentatively reached for her. Betty leaned into my hand as I rubbed her soft, furry neck and laughed quietly. She moved forward and nuzzled me in return.

"You are a lovey," I said, hugging her with a hand on the back of her neck. The hug ended quickly, and I wondered if I'd interpreted it right. I looked to Ben as he came up to my side.

"I've never seen her do anything like that," Ben said, his tone awed. "I believe Ms. Betty has a new favorite human."

I laughed and petted her neck again, thoroughly charmed by the big, furry girl with the gorgeous eyes.

———

Ben

"I'm going to feed the chickens. You're welcome to stay here with your new bestie if you want," I told Emerson. "I'll come back in fifteen or twenty minutes so we can trek back to the house together."

"You don't mind if I don't help with the chickens?"

"Not at all."

As a matter of fact, I needed a minute.

I pressed a kiss to the side of her head only to have Betty stick her nose between us possessively, making Emerson laugh.

"Back in a few," I said.

I hurried off, absently telling the horses goodbye. When I stepped out into the cold morning, where a cloudy day had dawned, I inhaled deeply, trying to get my mind right.

I'd realized in the barn, as Emerson looked awestruck at her newfound friendship with my llama, something not good at all had happened without me realizing it.

I was in love with her.

Emerson, not the llama.

The woman who'd made no bones about swearing off forevers and happily-ever-afters for good.

I took my time getting to the chicken house, hoping again that the biting wind would straighten out my head.

It didn't.

There was something to be said for a quickie in the hayloft in the middle of a snowstorm. Emerson, who I never would've expected to get naked in a barn, had stunned me with her brazenness and sent me to the stars with her gorgeous body.

Then, to watch her, so uneasy around the llamas just a week ago, laugh with pure joy at Betty's friendly advances?

Be still my traitorous heart. I was a goner.

And that, of course, was a big fucking problem.

Chapter Seventeen

Emerson

The only thing more blissful than an unexpected day off from work was a twenty-four-hour break from the kids.

We loved them to pieces. Of course we did.

"But they come with a nonstop, underlying frenetic energy," Ben had said a few hours ago.

The entire town of Dragonfly Lake had shut down. No school, businesses were closed, nothing was happening until our one city plow could make the rounds. Ben had had Colby reschedule all his patients for the day, and between Edith and me, we'd contacted everyone with a hair appointment to do the same.

After breakfast, Ben had plowed the long driveway and the clinic's parking lot so it was ready in case of a pet emergency, but so far our day had been uneventful and, frankly, indulgent in a neither-one-of-us-had-had-sex-in-years way.

Point in case, we'd just taken a midafternoon shower

together, pleasuring each other until the water ran cold, then moving to Ben's bed to warm up. It wasn't just the blankets that had done the warming either.

I'd lost track of how many orgasms this man had given me in the past twenty-four hours. I was sore, my inner thighs tender, yet I was practically humming with an over-flowing contentment as we lit a fire and curled up together under a large, super-soft blanket on the sofa. Pixie and Jett were lying under the tree as if it was their God-given right. Sprocket and Milo had settled close to the fire. Nugget was MIA, most likely napping in Skyler's bed upstairs, still pushed up against Evelyn's. The girls' joined beds had become our dog's favorite sleeping spot in the Holloway house, both during the day and at night.

The Christmas tree was lit, all the other lights off, curtains drawn to shut out the gloomy day as we settled in with a lineup of holiday movies. *The Polar Express* was first, one of Ben's favorites.

We were stretched out on the couch, and he was spooning me, warming my back as the fire brought up the temperature of the room. My hair was still wet from the shower, mainly because I'd spent the half hour afterward in Ben's bed instead of wielding a hair dryer, so the blanket, fire, and warm-blooded male were appreciated.

We were no more than ten minutes into the movie when Ben's body stiffened behind me, and I don't mean in the good way. His head went up, and he muted the television.

"What's wrong?"

Before he could answer, I heard the back door open, a cacophony of kid voices blowing inside with a cold draft.

I jumped off the sofa as if it were a sinking ship, yanking

the blanket with me, my heart racing as Ben bolted upright. We shared a panicked look.

He stood. "Curl up with the blanket. I'll meet them in the kitchen." Without waiting, he turned the sound back on and headed that way. "Who's that sneaking in the door?" he called out.

I laughed quietly to myself in a half-hysterical way as I planted my ass in the corner of the sofa and tucked the blanket around me. With my heart still racing, I fought to look nonchalant as it hit me how close that had been. How lucky we were the front door was rarely used and they'd come in the mudroom. For that matter, it was a damn good thing the living room wasn't visible from the mudroom.

All of that paled in comparison to how fortunate it was we'd pulled clothes on after our latest round. If I hadn't been so cold...

"Mommy!" Skyler ran into the living room, so overjoyed to see me that I felt momentarily guilty for celebrating our day-long break.

"Hey, sweetie," I said, shoving the blanket aside and leaning forward to catch her in a hug. "What are you doing home already? How did you get here?"

"Gramma Berty drived us," she said, holding on to me a few extra seconds. I breathed in her little-girl smell, noting Berty had managed to clean the kids in addition to everything else.

I hoisted my daughter into my arms as I stood, then walked through the dining room toward the others in the kitchen.

"Did you hire a sleigh to get you here?" I asked Berty.

"The plow's been through most places," she said with a wave of her hand.

I suspected the drive wasn't quite as easy as she made it

seem. I also couldn't help but wonder if she'd reached her admittedly generous limit with four children under ten. "Did they do okay?" I asked.

"They did real good. Little troopers."

Ruby had discovered the movie still playing in the living room and called out, *"The Polar Express* is on!" The other three kids rushed in to join her.

"Sky was starting to get a little antsy without her mama," Berty said quietly. "I didn't want to push her too long. She did so well last night."

"I'm relieved to hear that," I said.

At the mention of last night, I met Ben's gaze for the quickest instant before I glanced back at his grandmother.

"What did you bring there?" Ben asked, pointing at the grocery bags in her hands.

"The perfect activity for a snow day," she said. "Gingerbread houses."

He took the bags from her.

"You baked with the kids?" I asked.

Berty squawked a laugh. "Not gingerbread. I know my limits. That stuff never works out right, but the Country Market sells kits. I stocked up a few days ago."

"You're too good to us," Ben said, setting the bags on the counter and unpacking them.

"Benny, you know gingerbread decorating's my favorite," Berty said. "I got a house for each of us and enough candy that we can rot our teeth and still have plenty to deck our halls."

A few minutes later, all seven of us sat around the dining table with frosting tubes, bowls of every type of colorful candy ever invented, and prebaked, precut gingerbread walls.

I'd helped Skyler construct her house with the frosting

along the seams, then gathered the M&M's and kisses as she requested, knowing full well she'd eat at least as many as she used for the house. I couldn't fault her for that.

Xavier chose red and green gumdrops to start and was building a fence around a white-frosting snow-covered yard. One of Ruby's walls collapsed, so Ben was rescuing it, while Evelyn used a squeeze tube of blue icing on her roof. All three dogs were at our feet, keeping a vigil for any bits that hit the floor.

"Shoo, you guys," I said to the canines, snapping my fingers, urging them out of the room. I didn't want any of them to get chocolate.

"Bed," Ben said in his stern, dog-master voice. Sprocket and Milo headed to the living room. Nugget circled my chair, then headed into Ben's room behind me. It wasn't quite what she was supposed to do, but as long as Ben didn't mind, I was just glad she'd left the room.

I sat down to start my own construction, eyeing the candy canes and peppermint hard candies for my design. There was no sense in wasting good chocolate on a house.

"Oh, Nugget," Ruby said, laughing. "What did you find, silly dog?"

I was so focused on getting my walls to stick together that I didn't immediately register what was going on behind me—not until Xavier said, "That's Mom's pajama pants, Nugget! How did you find those?"

I whipped my head around. Sure as shinola, that cretin dog had my flannel pajama shorts in her mouth, as if she'd found a pirate's booty.

"Nugget!" I called out. "Get those out of your mouth!"

"Which one of you three carried those in there?" Ben scolded. I realized the other two dogs had trotted out to see what their coconspirator had discovered. Then it hit me that he was a genius to come up with that white lie, because I knew just as well as I knew my own name, I'd left those shorts on Ben's bedroom floor last night after he'd peeled them off me.

The kids thought the theft was hilarious as Nugget took off up the stairs with her treasure. Ruby and Xavier sprinted after her, along with the other two dogs. With my head spinning, I glanced at Ben, then darted my gaze away, afraid I'd reveal our secret if we made eye contact.

I was fully aware of Berty's attention going from me to Ben and back, but I made a point of avoiding her gaze too. "I guess I'll go rescue my shorts and make sure I didn't leave anything else out for the canine thieves," I said as I stood.

"Dr. Ben, can you help me get these unwrapped?" Skyler asked.

Knowing Ben was on it, I didn't bother to see what she needed help with. I rushed to the stairs, mainly to get out of Berty's line of sight and breathe.

One day in and we'd nearly been busted? By the dogs?

The good news was that the kids seemed to believe Ben's story. They had no reason to wonder why my shorts would be in his bedroom.

Berty, on the other hand...

Nugget had taken her treasure to Skyler and Evelyn's room and was hiding under the bed with it. When I walked in, three kids were on their bellies on the floor, peering under the bed, trying to reach the dog. I laughed in spite of myself because they were so darn cute with their three little bums in a row.

"You kids go back down and work on your houses. I'll get the little thief out."

That was all it took for them to sprint away for more candy.

By the time I made it back to the dining room, the kids and Berty were singing carols as they decorated their houses, laughing when they messed up the words. The moment had been forgotten.

"This calls for cocoa," I said at the end of "Jolly Old Saint Nicholas." "Who wants some?"

A chorus of *me*'s and *I do*'s rang out, so I headed to the kitchen to make hot chocolate for everyone.

The kids were belting out the chorus of "Up on the Housetop" as I poured the milk into the mixture on the stove. I sensed someone behind me and turned to find Berty.

"Almost done," I said, stirring the pan constantly with one hand as I took seven mugs out with the other.

"I'll get the marshmallows," she said. She stood next to me, facing the cabinets. "It's none of my business what goes on between you and my grandson, but Emerson, please be careful with him."

I frowned, stunned she'd brought the subject up so bluntly, though I shouldn't have been. The kids' silliness and singing had me letting my guard down, I guess.

"There's not anything—"

"Honey, don't insult me with a denial. I'm not blind, nor am I stupid just yet, though I might be slower than I used to be. I'm in this house with you two nearly every day of the week. I can sense things." She took the first mug from me after I filled it and poured a heap of marshmallows in. "And I know that dog of yours did *not* drag your pajamas from your room to Ben's."

"I'm sorry," I said contritely. "I didn't mean any offense. It's embarrassing to be outed."

"I've been on this earth for darn close to eight decades, my dear. I've seen some things."

I laughed. "I'm sure you have."

I filled the next two mugs, and she added marshmallows, the two of us working together amiably, as if she wasn't in the process of busting my chops.

"Emerson, I mean it. Do not hurt that man. If you do—"

"It's not like that," I said, keeping my voice down as the revelry continued in the next room. "It's not serious, Grandma Berty."

She turned her head toward me and gave me a weighted look, one I was sure had functioned as her *don't mess with me* expression while she was raising her children.

I raised a hand as if surrendering. "Really. We're having fun. That's all. Nothing long-term."

"Does he know this?"

"Of course. We've agreed."

She went quiet as she filled the last mugs with marshmallows, and I sensed she was going to say more, but then she didn't.

"The kids won't know," I said in case she was worried about them getting hurt. I was worried enough myself. It was already going to be difficult for Skyler and Xavier to transition to yet another living situation when I found a house.

"Kids are resilient, but I think that's wise. Just remember you're dealing with a man who feels things deeply and prioritizes the whole world's needs before his own."

"He does," I agreed. That was part of what made him so easy to like. "He's a wonderful man, and he's also smart. He and I are on the exact same page."

"I hope you're right," she said.

Ben understood my needs as well as my limits. He'd been through similar losses.

We were being smart, communicating. Acting like adults, albeit sex-starved ones.

I had to believe everything would work out fine. I could explore this little treat for myself, and no one would get hurt.

Chapter Eighteen

Emerson

I walked into the holiday party at Max Dawson's house at Ben's side, keeping space between us like friends would. Because we *were* friends. The sleeping together part was literally just a benefit of that friendship and our temporary circumstances.

"Come on in," Max called out as he walked toward us.

"Hello, llama savior," I said, handing over my coat.

Ben handed him a bottle of whiskey. "Yeah, thanks. Yet again."

"The things we do for a little libation." Max laughed and took it from him. "Happy I could help. Grab a drink and some food."

"Thanks for having me," I said as I made a point of separating from Ben.

I smiled warmly at everyone in the vicinity, greeted Harper and her business partners and friends, Cambria and Dakota, who stood nearby welcoming guests, then scanned the room for drinks. I was going to need at least one, stat.

My nerves were on edge from the challenge of being with Ben in public, acting like the best of friends but not slipping too close.

My body wanted to be too close.

The crowd was bigger than I'd expected, with the open-area living room, kitchen, and dining area all filled with people, most of whom I knew. It appeared there were more guests out on the deck despite temperatures that hovered around thirty-five degrees.

Anna and Ava, Cash and Seth and his singer wife, Everly, were in my immediate view, with another three or four dozen scattered throughout.

"Emerson!" Olivia called out from a corner between the dining area and kitchen.

I waved and headed that way, taking in the details of the former NFL player's home as I went, finding it down-to-earth and homey. I wasn't too surprised since I knew Max to be humble and unpretentious. Harper was one of the easiest people to like as well.

My pace quickened as I got closer to part of my girl tribe—Olivia, Chloe, and Maeve—particularly when I caught sight of three partially full wine bottles on the counter next to them.

"Hey, ladies," I said when I reached them.

Chloe gave me a side hug, and Maeve squeezed my hand in greeting. Olivia plucked an unused wineglass from the kitchen counter and held it out to me.

"Red, white, or bubbly?" Maeve asked.

"Yes," I said and laughed.

"If you don't care, then you're getting champagne. We're celebrating how gorgeous you look with your sparkles," Maeve said.

"Seriously hot," Olivia said.

"You all look fantastic too," I said as I held my glass up and Maeve filled it.

The girls raised their glasses for a toast, so I clinked with them and relaxed. These girlfriends made me feel better even without the alcohol.

The invitation had specified holiday casual, and the house was filled with cute dresses and sparkly, blinged-out black, gold, silver, and green. I'd decided on leather-like black pants and a glittery, golden tunic-style sweater. Festive but comfortable.

"There's a table over there overflowing with finger foods," Chloe said, pointing.

When I glanced in that direction, what caught my eye instead of the food was Ben. Just seeing him made my heart speed up.

"And more importantly, another one over there with sweets," Olivia said, gesturing to a different side of the room.

I coached myself to turn my gaze from my hot roommate and keep up with the conversation.

"Half of them baked by Olivia herself," Maeve said. "So you know they're killer."

"Aww, thanks. I've had a little practice." Olivia had worked at the bakery since before I'd moved back to town.

"This was my priority," I said, holding up my glass of champagne. "But sweets? A close second, especially if you brought chocolate cherry bombs."

"Of course I did," Olivia said.

"So tell us what's up with Ben," Chloe said, closing our circle even more tightly.

My brows popped upward, and I lifted my glass for another drink, this one less sip, more gulp.

"You could let her arrive for a minute first," Olivia scolded, laughing. "But yes, we're dying to know."

"Why beat around the bush?" Chloe said, grinning. "We won't have this corner to ourselves all night."

"He and I are *friends*," I said, inspecting my short, gold-glittered nails as if they were the most interesting things ever. When I lifted my gaze, all three women were leaning forward as if I were about to impart the secret of life. I laughed and shook my head. "Surely there are more interesting topics?"

"Nope," Olivia said.

"Uh-uh," Maeve agreed.

"You two looked cute together when you came in the door," Chloe added.

"Friends," I said again, because that was the truth. Just maybe not the whole truth.

Maeve, who was on my left, leaned into my side and said, softly, thank God, "With bennies?"

I looked around the circle, meeting their eager, curious gazes one by one, unable to get the hint of a smile off my face. "Maaaybe," I said simply, which elicited laughter and a "Yessss!" with a victory fist from Olivia.

My smile faded. "Please," I emphasized quietly. "Keep it between us?"

"Absolutely," Olivia said.

"Your secret's safe," Chloe added.

"Of course, Em." Maeve's eyes were lit with joy. "I was hoping for that news."

I laughed again. "Why?"

She shrugged. "You deserve some sexy times."

"We all do," Olivia said. "Even those of us who are getting it on the regular." She gave Chloe a lighthearted, accusatory look.

"A ten-month-old makes it trickier," Chloe said, "but"—she shrugged—"guilty."

Olivia threw a wadded-up napkin at her, then lifted her glass. "Here's to all of us having Chloe's luck."

There were clinks and laughter all around, but the party was so loud and crowded no one took any notice, which was how I liked it, particularly considering the topic.

"So..." Olivia's grin widened as she zeroed in on me again. "How did it happen?"

"Olivia London, you should be ashamed of yourself for being so nosy," Chloe scolded.

"Don't lie," Maeve said to Chloe. "You're dying to know too."

"I am," Chloe admitted.

All eyes turned to me. My closest friends waited expectantly. I wasn't one who'd ever give them graphic details, but I said, "Five words for you." I glanced around to make sure we hadn't captured anyone's attention. "Snowed in without the kids." I counted the words on my fingers as I said them.

All three of them laughed, and Olivia held up a hand for a high five.

"That'll do it," Maeve said. "Or so I've heard."

"It just proves your attraction was off the scales," Chloe said.

That was the truth.

I took another swallow, glancing around, worried about being overheard again. Kemp Essex, Chloe's husband, Holden, and Max's brother, Levi, were engrossed in a conversation nearby but paying us no mind.

"So are there feelings involved here?" Olivia asked in a hushed voice.

"No," I answered quickly. "It's just the bicycle thing. Getting back on with someone I trust."

An uneasiness rooted in my gut, but I shut it down.

"The bicycle thing is legit," Maeve said. "I might need to find a guy to help me back on the bike one of these days." She laughed.

"What's going to happen when you move out?" Olivia asked me.

"Nothing." My answer came automatically, but I couldn't help but imagine a flash of living in a different house with my kids but without Ben and his girls. It would be...different. Quiet. Another adjustment.

Lonely.

Especially at night.

"You don't think you'd keep seeing him on the sly?" Olivia asked.

"For booty calls?" Maeve added.

I laughed. "It's hard enough to rendezvous in the same house with four kids involved. Two separate addresses?" I shook my head. "I don't think that's what either of us has in mind."

"I guess you better get it all out of your system now then," Maeve said. "How much sex can you have in, what, a month?"

"Any luck on houses?" Chloe asked as she refilled her glass with white.

"Zero luck." I told them about the one place Darius had taken me to. "That's exactly the full list right there. It's depressing."

"Well..." Chloe, who was starting to show signs of tipsiness, put her arm around my neck and leaned in. "I'm sorry to hear that. Something will eventually turn up and be perfect. In the meantime, here's to riding bikes!"

We laughed and toasted yet again and drank.

"I need a trip to the dessert table," I said. "And I should probably say hi to more than just you three. I'll be back in a few."

I walked off, registering a kernel of unease blossoming in my gut. Then the reason for it hit me. It was the thought of moving away from Ben. I would miss him way more than I'd ever imagined. I'd miss the naked gymnastics, of course, but even more, I'd miss his company. Not because of feelings that had gotten too deep. Just because he was a good friend and a partner with the kids.

That was all I could let it be.

———

Ben

Emerson proved to be fucking impossible to keep my eyes off at Max and Harper's party.

No matter who I was talking to, my Emerson radar was tuned in to her, knew where she was at all times. At first I didn't even realize I was keeping an eye on her, but then Max came up to me, handed me a Rusty Anchor IPA, and said, "If you don't want people to know your secret, you might want to stop staring at her."

I snapped my gaze to his amused one as his meaning sank in. I hadn't told him how things with Emerson had evolved, hadn't talked to him since the single dads' party nearly a week ago. I realized I'd just given up my secret to him without saying a word.

"Fuck." I made a point of looking at everyone *but* her.

He chuckled. "I don't think anyone else noticed. Yet."

"Yeah. Thanks, I think."

There was a part of me that wanted the world to know I was with Emerson. She'd picked me to play naked games with. I suspected that was the seventeen-year-old boy inside me though and not the responsible father or town veterinarian.

Ty Bishop, the high-school basketball coach, joined us, as did Finn and Cade McNamara. I forced myself to get lost in the conversation about last night's college basketball game, the Anchor's holiday beer flavors, and Max's kittens, who were closed in a room for the duration of the party.

I fought hard to stop scanning for Emerson. There were solid reasons we were keeping our new closeness private. Reasons number one through four were our kids.

I filled up on finger foods and bite-sized desserts as I mingled with the half of the town that was here tonight. Many of them were clients, so I spent a chunk of time catching up on my furry patients. Cash Henry cornered me to get my input on surprising his pregnant wife, Ava, with a puppy for Christmas.

"Are you sure she's up for caring for one more being?" I asked him.

"I'll take care of the pup," Cash assured me. "I just want someone to keep her company when I'm working late. Need a dog that'll be good with a baby."

"Goldens or Labs are great with kids," I told him.

"Kemp's are Labs, right?"

"That's right. Talk to him. He doesn't have babies around, but he can give you an idea of how much work they are."

"You trying to talk me out of it?"

"Never," I said, laughing. "I fully support informed pet adoptions. It's just a lot to take on a few months before a first child."

He nodded. "I hear you. It's terrifying, but I can't wait for this baby. Ava and I'll make it work. You know of anyone with puppies available?"

"I've got a couple of reputable people I can check in with. I'll call you this week after I've asked around."

"Thanks, Ben. Hopefully you'll have a new patient soon." He moved on, searching for Ava, I suspected.

We'd been at the party for close to two hours, and it had only gotten more crowded. The football coach and his artist/business owner fiancée knew how to throw a good party.

I went out to the deck, where there were two heaters running, to get some fresh air. When I saw I had it to myself, I breathed a little more deeply and took in the view.

Max's home was lakefront. The water was frozen around the edges, the docks all removed, boats put away for the season, giving it a lonesome but beautiful look.

I stood at the railing of the deck, soaking in the relative quiet, although I could still hear the din of the party, and wondered briefly how Berty was doing with the kids. Likely just fine, but the further into December we got, the more revved up they became. Emerson's kids could hardly wait for Kizzy and her wife's visit a few days before Christmas. Though the newlyweds were staying at the Marks Hotel, our household would definitely level up in chaos. I couldn't wait.

Needing to lay my eyes on Emerson, I turned away from the lake, took a swallow of beer, and scanned the party through the windows. It didn't take me long to spot her, talking to Anna, Ava, and Cash just off the kitchen. She laughed, and even though I couldn't actually hear it, I could hear the sound of her in my head.

The door opened, and Chance and West ambled out to the deck.

"What are you doing out here by yourself?" Chance asked when he saw me.

West turned and followed where my gaze had been. "Creepin' on his lady friend's my guess."

I laughed. "I'm not creeping on anyone, just getting some air. It's louder than a full kennel of barking dogs in there."

Chance turned to see Emerson as well and raised a brow as they came up to the railing next to me. "It is loud. A lot of people came out."

"I'll show up to any party Max throws if he does the food like tonight," West said.

Max and Harper had it catered, probably by Henry's Restaurant. I agreed with West's assessment. "Did you try those sausage and cream cheese croissant things?"

"Try?" West scoffed. "I had a half dozen. And the maple caramel bacon things?" He made a noise of appreciation.

"I liked the little egg roll ones best," Chance said.

We spent another few minutes discussing the top-notch food before Chance said, "So why are you out here staring in the window at Emerson instead of by her side?"

I'd been taking a drink and nearly spit it out at his bluntness. I covered my reaction with a laugh. "Why would I do that? We're not a couple."

"But you want to be," Chance said.

I'd already told the guys as much, so I didn't bother to deny it.

"You out of condoms yet?" West asked.

"You gave them to me a week ago. There were thirty-six.

I'm no math teacher, but that's something like five a day. I do work for ten hours a day."

We all chuckled.

"You said *were*," Chance said. "So how many are you down to?"

West cackled at that. "Good point, buddy." He fist-bumped Chance. "Somebody's having a *good* week."

I drank another gulp of beer, neither confirming nor denying.

"Sounds like you two are a couple after all," Chance said.

I shook my head, expelling a breath that came out as a white burst in the cool air. The heater in the middle of the deck didn't reach this far. I turned toward the lake, and the other two followed suit, not getting the message that I didn't want to discuss this.

"You going to let her get away?" West asked.

I scoffed. "You're assuming it's my choice. You know what they say about assuming."

Chance hummed a sound of comprehension. "If it were up to you, you'd be all in," he guessed.

My silence must have given them their answer.

"Have you told her how you feel?" West asked.

I shook my head. "She's not interested in a long-term thing."

"Maybe she would be if she knew where you stand," Chance said.

"She wouldn't." I gulped down more beer. "She's pretty cautious. She's had a lot of losses in her life." I didn't figure I was giving away anything private since everyone knew her husband had been killed in combat, and her mom's and grandma's deaths years ago had been common knowledge.

"You have too," Chance said.

"Which means I understand where she's coming from," I said. "You of all people should get it." He'd lost his wife as well, though it'd been even longer ago than Leeann's death.

"I saw you two together a couple of days ago when I was heading to pick up cookies for my girls at the bakery," West said. "You have a connection, man. It was tangible."

I hadn't noticed West when Emerson and I made a bakery run. We'd had all four kids with us, but thinking back, I'd likely been more focused on Emerson. I'd have to be a lot more careful.

"Connection or not, she's expressed her fears, and I respect them," I said.

Both of them shut up for a while. I was happy to no longer be the topic of conversation and considering heading back inside when West spoke again.

"I still think you need to tell her how you feel. You love her?"

I grunted. Fuck this conversation.

"Tell her," Chance drew out.

"That's not what she needs," I said.

"What about *your* needs?" Chance asked.

"Yeah. You're the giving type," West said. "You nurture the hell out of your kids and animals and, it sounds like, Emerson. But your needs count too."

"He's right." Chance leaned forward to look at West on my other side and nodded emphatically. "You've got a soft heart under all that badass, don't you?" he asked West.

It was West's turn to grunt.

"But back to you," Chance said. "Your needs are just as important as hers. Especially on this. Tell her."

"Not going to do that," I said, then finished off my beer.

"You sure?" West asked.

"I'm sure."

"Okay," Chance said. "Your call. If you're sure, you're sure."

"I'm going back inside. It's cold as balls out here, and I'm out of beer." I turned and left those two asses outside.

I *was* sure I was doing the right thing by not pressuring Emerson. It wouldn't work and would likely ruin the short-term thing we *did* have, to say nothing of our friendship.

Chapter Nineteen

Ben

This thing between Emerson and me was unofficial, difficult to label, and no obligation.

Frankly, I hated it.

Not the thing itself, not Emerson, but the lack of definition.

It was supposed to be that we'd hook up when opportunity arose or when the mood struck, but I was aching for more.

Literally aching tonight.

Two hours had passed since we'd left the party together. Casually, hands-off, just friends.

What I'd wanted to do was put my arm around her, hold her hand, whisk her away, park along the side of a dark road, and ravish her in my truck like a desperate high school kid.

I still felt the desperate part in my blood. In my dick.

In the week and a half since the snowstorm, since our first time together, she'd sneaked down to my room each night after all the kids were asleep, blown my mind with that body of hers, then crept back up to her room. With the kids home, she didn't allow herself to fall asleep in my bed, and I understood her reasons.

That didn't mean I had to like it.

So far tonight, when I was half expecting her and fully needed her, she hadn't appeared.

About an hour ago, I'd heard a floorboard creak above me, probably one of the kids going to the bathroom or maybe even Emerson. I'd held my breath to see if she made her way down to me, but she hadn't.

I'd rolled over and told myself to go to sleep. If she showed up, I'd wake up to bliss. If she didn't, I'd catch up on sleep.

But here I still was, wide awake, hard as hell after watching her from afar all night at the party and not being able to touch her or get my fill of her.

I'd considered texting her something sexy to lure her down, but I'd held off in case she had a kid with her.

I'd thought about going upstairs to check on the kids myself, maybe slipping into her room if everyone was asleep, but that felt like changing the unspoken rules and invading her space.

I already knew she wasn't as into me as I was her. I didn't want to pressure her, push her, or crowd her. Didn't want to do anything to scare her away or endanger what we did have before she moved out.

In other words, I was doing my best to take what she'd give me and not ask for more, but tonight, my body was throbbing for more.

I turned over to my opposite side for the hundredth time and fluffed my pillow, as if that would do a damn bit of good for the heat raging through my blood. As I settled back into the pillow, a faint tapping came from my door. I froze and listened.

Tap, tap, tap, tap.

It was deliberate, and it was human.

I popped out of bed, went to the door, and opened it a crack, preparing myself for a kid with a middle-of-the-night crisis, afraid to hope...

Emerson jumped backward, gasping, pressing a hand to her chest.

Opening the door farther, I tugged her into my room, against me, my arm banded around her while I closed the door with the other one. She wore a robe that hit her midthigh over short pajamas.

"I thought you were asleep," she whispered. "It's late, and I didn't want to wake you."

I moaned, pressed a kiss to her forehead, and said, "You can always wake me." I lined our bodies up so she wouldn't miss my erection.

"Yeah?"

"Always."

Our lips met in a kiss—a slow, tender one, full of gratitude on my side. Everything felt better when I was touching her. When she was in my arms.

"I didn't think you were going to come tonight," I eventually said between kisses.

"Xavier had a nightmare. I let him crawl into bed with me and got him calmed down."

"Poor kid. Did he say what it was about?"

She chuckled quietly. "He's worried he's not going to finish whatever you and he are working on."

"We'll finish it," I reassured her.

"What *are* you working on?"

"Top secret."

It wasn't the first time she'd asked. I'd given the same answer each time. This was Xavier's surprise first and foremost, and I wouldn't be the one to spoil it.

"You're no fun," she said.

"If I ruined your boy's surprise and broke his heart, you'd be as upset for him as I would."

"I guess that's true." She ran a finger along my jaw. "I'm so curious though."

"Your curiosity will be assuaged at the parade next weekend. That's all I'm saying."

She sighed as if I was the cruelest, meanest guy in town.

"Did you come down here to learn your son's secrets, or did you come down here so I could make you scream my name?" I asked, trailing kisses along her jaw, toward her ear.

Emerson laughed quietly. "You're mighty cocky."

I pressed my cock against her again. "Yes, I am."

With another laugh, she kissed me. "No screaming allowed," she whispered. "You know that."

"Watching you try to keep quiet as you shatter is my new favorite thing."

"Then by all means"—she ran her talented tongue along my lip—"you should do that."

I locked the door, shed my pajama pants, and got her naked in less than a dozen heartbeats. She crawled under the blankets, and I followed her in, covering her body with mine.

As I rubbed my shaft over her soft core, she moaned. "Make me shatter, Ben."

"I will," I promised. "Eventually."

I'd waited so long for her tonight, I wasn't going to let this be over in a few minutes. I set out to make her as desperate for me as I was for her.

Before this, we'd had plenty of urgent, hot, hard sex.

We'd gotten our respective years-long dry spells out of our systems. All of it had been stellar, and I'd be up for that again any time.

That wasn't how tonight was going to go though. I kissed her thoroughly, then trailed my lips to her neck, tasting her, nipping her, suckling as I moved lower. I spent a luxurious amount of time on each of her breasts, then slowly, torturously according to her, worshipped every inch of her body with my tongue, my fingers, my own body.

By the time I spent myself inside her, Emerson had come apart four times. Every last orgasm of hers had turned me inside out and made my blood pound that much harder.

Now I lay over her, coming down from a life-altering climax of my own, my first coherent thoughts once blood began trickling back into my brain: wishing she was mine forever and that nights like this weren't limited.

There wasn't a doubt in my mind I'd never feel for someone else what I felt for Emerson.

"I might be dead," Emerson said quietly, sounding spent and satiated.

At least I wasn't the only one.

Her arms were wrapped tightly around me, leaving no question whether she wanted me to move off her. That was handy since I wasn't sure I could move yet.

"Heck of a way to go," I managed, then summoned the strength to raise off her enough to find her lips again. When I rolled to the side, I took her with me, unwilling to lose the glorious feel of her heated skin against mine from head to toe.

We lay there quietly, my mind circling over what Chase and West had said tonight about leveling with Emerson about how deep I was in. At the time, I'd been sure that was a bad idea. I didn't want her to feel like there was any pressure. Absolutely didn't want anything to ruin what we had going. But my emotions were in the stratosphere, my chest light with the high of loving this woman. Love was more powerful if it was shared instead of nestled away as a secret. I could let her know how much I treasured her and still ensure I wasn't pressuring her for anything. Keeping my feelings to myself seemed nearly impossible at this moment.

I traced my finger over her jawline and looked into her eyes, just able to see them gazing back at me affectionately.

"It's been a while since I told you how incredible you are. Beautiful..." I kissed her. "Sexy." Another kiss. "Irresistible." And another.

She let out a drowsy, satisfied laugh. "You already had your way with me. I thought sweet talk was supposed to come before?"

"It's not sweet talk. Just the truth." I propped myself up on my elbow, becoming more serious as I weighed the right way to say this. "Ems..." I found her hand and wove our fingers together. "I know you're moving out in a few weeks. I know this is casual. No strings. No commitments. I just need to level with you about something."

"Okay." She drew the word out as if scared of what I was about to say.

I took a slow, silent inhalation, hoping this wouldn't be the wrong move. Giving myself every chance to come to my senses and let it be.

I couldn't let *this* be. I needed to speak my truth.

"My feelings... They're deeper."

"Oh..."

"I love you, Emerson. I'm in love with you. I know that wasn't our agreement," I rushed to say. "I'm not asking you to change anything, not trying to pressure you. I'm not asking you to stay forever, although if you said you wanted to, I'd be the happiest man in the world."

"I can't—"

"Please," I whispered. "You don't have to say it. I know where you stand. I respect that completely."

Had I hoped maybe she'd laugh in relief and say she loved me too? Maybe a little part of me, but I knew. She'd been honest. This was me being honest.

"I'm not asking you for anything at all, except...I hope this doesn't scare you away from our nighttime trysts."

"Trysts," she repeated, and I could hear the smile in her tone. Thank God. "That's such an evocative word."

"Mm-hmm."

"I like it." She let go of my hand and burrowed her fingers into my hair. "The word and our trysts. Our no-obligation trysts," she said meaningfully. "That's all I can manage, Ben."

"I know." I took her hand and pulled it to my lips, kissed it, then held on to it. "I understand your fear of getting in too deep. You know I do. I'm not asking you to change. It just felt... wrong not to tell you how I feel about you. Full disclosure."

I pressed my forehead to hers, relieved she didn't pull away.

"There's zero pressure," I repeated. "Just know that if you ever change your mind, if you ever want more..." I pulled my head back to look her in the eyes again. "I'm here. I'm so fucking here."

Her eyes fluttered closed, and her lips tipped up at the corners in a smile. I exhaled, relieved she didn't seem too spooked.

"Thank you," she said. "For being honest. And even more, for understanding."

"You're not going to be scared off?"

"I'm not scared of you," she said lightly. "And I'm not dumb enough to deprive myself of another few weeks of mind-blowing *trysts* either. As long as we're open with each other, as long as you really have no expectations beyond that..."

"I don't."

Maybe it was wrong of me to hope for more, to wonder how I could get her to let go of her fears and give herself over to loving me. Maybe I was the dumbest man alive. But I was pretty sure I was having better sex than ninety-eight percent of the population, and for now that would have to be good enough.

"Thanks for not running away," I said.

She kissed me, which reassured me we were okay.

"I *am* running away," she said. "Bathroom. I'm sorry."

I nodded, knowing this was it for tonight. She always went to her room after making what she called the long trek to the bathroom from my bedroom.

I sat up and awakened my phone to give her enough light to find her pajamas. She stood and pulled on her boxers and long-sleeved sleep tee, then slipped into her robe. I crawled out of our warm love nest and walked the short distance to the door with her.

Before she opened it to sneak away, I pressed her back into it and kissed her one last time for the night, hard, intently, like an exclamation point. With my forearms bracketed on each side of her head, I looked into her eyes in the dimness. "Sleep well, Ems. Dream of me."

I winked, then let her sneak out, biting down on the urge to make her promise to come back again tomorrow night.

───────

Emerson

I closed Ben's door silently behind me and crept through the dining room and kitchen. The floor was ice-cold under my bare feet, but I barely noticed. I was too absorbed with Ben's confession.

Did it scare me? Oh, hell yes.

It turned our fun, fast fling into something more serious, even though we agreed it wouldn't change the outcome. I couldn't help but be aware the chances of one of us getting hurt had just skyrocketed. One or both.

I shoved all that aside for now. Instead I closed my eyes and soaked in the warmth and elation of knowing Ben Holloway loved me. Was that self-indulgent? Maybe. I'd worry about the cons later.

I couldn't deny how good it felt to be loved. I hadn't thought I needed or wanted that, but between it and the things that man had done to my body, I was warm and buzzy inside, like when you drink just enough alcohol for inhibitions to slip a notch and you veer toward feeling quietly ecstatic.

He'd taken a risk by confiding, but I intended to keep our nighttime trysts going until the kids and I moved out. They were too good not to. As long as Ben knew where we stood, it wouldn't hurt anything. I felt sure of that because I took him at his word and trusted him.

When I finished in the bathroom, I headed toward the stairs as had become my routine, but at the foot of them, I paused.

I'd be sleeping alone soon enough. It would hurt

nothing if I went back into Ben's room for an extra few hours.

I went to his door, let myself in, and climbed under the blankets next to Ben.

"Hello," he said, his voice a low purr. "What's going on?"

"It's freezing out there."

"It's warm under here." He rolled toward me and wrapped me in his arms. I reveled in the heat and his scent and the feel of his solid body against mine.

"I haven't changed my stance," I said. "About long-term anything. I just...didn't want to go up to my cold, lonely bed."

"I didn't want you to go up to your cold, lonely bed."

I relaxed into him and inhaled deeply, content and tired and incredibly comfortable. "I just want to sleep."

"Do you want to go back to your room just in case?"

I shook my head. "Not tonight. Can you set an alarm for, like, four?"

"You got it." He rolled away and set the alarm on his phone, then came back and put his arms around me again.

I shoved away any worries about the future. I was going to relish the next couple of hours sleeping in this man's arms.

Chapter Twenty

Emerson

There were several events the people of Dragonfly Lake went all out for. The annual holiday parade was one of them.

I was embarrassed to say today was my first as an adult. Up until this year, the parade had been held on a Saturday morning, which conflicted with my job, so Kizzy had taken the kids. This year the organizers had voted to move it to Sunday after much debate over whether it would hurt or help downtown businesses.

"It's starting! It's starting!" Skyler jumped up from her kid-sized camp chair as soon as we could hear sleigh bells.

Evelyn and Ruby popped out of their chairs and squealed with my daughter.

The air was electric with anticipation as the square overflowed with people. Ben had told me they came from all around for this parade, and now I believed him. It looked like there were more parade goers than residents.

It'd been less than forty-eight hours since Ben's declaration of love. I'd slept in his room for most of last night again. There was something so comforting about sleeping beside someone you trusted.

I kept waiting to freak out about his confession. I was nervous around the edges, but he was insistent that he didn't expect more from me, wasn't asking for more, so mostly I'd savored the warm feelings and not let myself worry about the day I moved out.

"What do you imagine my grandson and your boy cooked up for this?" Berty asked. She was bundled up for the day like the rest of us, plus had two blankets tucked around her, saying her old blood wasn't as thick as it used to be.

"I'm thinking costumes are involved somehow," I said.

"Maybe Daddy's dressed up as the Grinch!" Ruby suggested, her eyes afire with excitement.

"Daddy's not Grinchy though," Evelyn pointed out. "Maybe reindeer?"

"Xavier might be Rudolph!" Skyler guessed.

At that moment, the red convertible carrying the mayor and this year's honorary grand marshal, Leo Montague, an eighty-five-year-old veteran, eased around the corner to our block, causing an uproar. Our three girls held hands and jumped up and down in front of Berty and me. Their joy was infectious.

Berty reached her mittened hand over and squeezed mine, her lined face reflecting the same ageless joy the girls emanated.

Finally I got it. I felt it completely. Holiday magic. Christmas spirit. Call it what you want, but it was tangible and real on the square today. And maybe even in my heart, thanks to Ben.

The kids were so revved up about Kizzy and her wife's

upcoming visit, never mind Santa and presents and Christmas morning. I found it impossible not to feel it with them, as Ben had predicted.

We watched the lead car go by, decked out in strings of flashing lights and holiday ornaments hanging from them. The grand marshal waved as the mayor played Christmas carols on a harmonica, pausing periodically to call out "Happy Holidays!" or "Merry Christmas!"

Elves of all sizes danced and frolicked behind the car and around the floats behind it, tossing candy to the crowd. The girls had brought grocery sacks to carry their treasures and were wasting no time filling them up.

The next vehicle was a Jeep decked out with light strings and a full-sized, decorated Christmas tree set up on the roof.

After that came the Earthly Charm float, a flatbed truck with literally hundreds of candles set up on dozens of platforms. Harper, Cambria, and Dakota were dressed in sexy, sparkly dresses, one red, one green, one silver, with Santa hats to match, waving and blowing kisses to the crowd. I was sure the candles were lit with LEDs, but the effect was magical, even in the daylight.

Behind them was the high school marching band, which had Skyler plugging her ears, making Berty and me laugh.

More floats followed, some more intricate than others, with most of them keeping the girls enthralled and helping them fill up their bags.

There were all kinds of characters, costumes, more elves, a group of reindeer made of pairs of people in each costume, which was hilarious to watch.

The organizers had picked winners in numerous categories—student, spiritual, nonprofit, musical, mounted, vehicle. I remembered Xavier's excitement about the prize list and wondered if there was any way he could've won something. Even something small. He'd be thrilled to get a prize, whatever his entry was.

The Rusty Anchor had a beer trolley powered by eight people on each side—Holden and his brothers included—pedaling as they imbibed. Above the pedalers was a banner that read, Green Award, Most Earth-Friendly Entry.

Berty leaned over to me eventually and said, "I think if Ben and Xavier were just doing costumes, they wouldn't've required so much time in the workshop. I think they built something."

"They did spend hours out there," I said.

Ben had devoted countless hours to my son's idea, whatever it was, in one of the outbuildings that had been deemed off-limits to the rest of us. They'd worked all day last Sunday and until Xavier's bedtime every night last week. I'd worked at the salon yesterday, but Berty had stayed with the girls so the guys could finish up whatever it was they were concocting.

There was a bagpipe group, several horses and riders, more floats than I ever would've believed possible from this small town, and candy. So much candy.

Loretta Lawson's Fat Cat Yarn Shop float featured two gigantic balls of yarn, one in red, one in green, with oversized needles sticking out. Loretta herself sat in an armchair in front of a decorated tree, knitting away. The impressive part was the display of hand-knitted mittens. Twine hung from one end of the float to the other, dipping in U-shapes, laden with pairs of mittens clothes-pinned side to side. There must've been several hundred pairs in every color of the rainbow, big ones, small ones. They were made by her knitting group, I knew, and she donated some to charity and sold the others, then gave the proceeds to charity.

I promised the girls we'd track down the mittens after the parade, and I'd buy them each a pair. They were entranced by the choices, animatedly discussing which ones they liked best until they'd see yet a different pair they preferred.

The crowd's excitement grew louder as the next float rounded the corner. Monty Baynes, owner of the Dragonfly Diner, drove the truck that pulled the float. In the back of his pickup, a large two-sided banner was proudly displayed: Overall Winner, Commercial Category. As the float got closer, I saw why.

The first thing I noticed was the dozens of strings of multicolored dragonfly-shaped lights. In the center was a Christmas tree and next to it, two kids pretending to sleep in a bed that was in the shape of a giant waffle. Above them, more giant waffles speckled with blue and purple sprinkles, cooked eggs, and strips of bacon were strung. On the side was a sign that read, Visions of Dragonfly Dust Waffles Danced in Their Heads.

"Isn't that the cleverest thing," Berty said with a hoot of amusement.

"Effective. I'm craving waffles now," I said, laughing. And we'd just had Humble's slices for lunch.

"They won, Miss Emerson," Evelyn told me with glee.

"I saw that. They deserved to, didn't they?"

"I want waffles!" my daughter said, clapping her hands.

"Big, giant ones," I said.

Several more entries went by with no sign of Ben and my son. My curiosity grew, which I hadn't thought was possible.

"Oh, my word," Berty said.

There was so much expression in her voice I glanced at her then followed her gaze to the float coming around the corner.

My mouth gaped open. Then I covered it with my hands and laughed.

"Mommy, they brought the llamas!" Skyler yelled, pointing.

"Look! Look! Look, Ev!" Ruby jumped up and down, and her sister gasped and jumped with her.

"I can't believe it," Berty said, dropping her blanket cocoon to stand up for a better look.

I stood too, speechless.

Knox Breckenridge's SUV pulled the float holding Esmerelda and Betty, standing side by side, wearing reindeer antlers as they chomped hay to their hearts' content and peered out at the crowd. Ben stood nearby, dressed as an elf, with a pointy green hat, a red elf shirt that stretched across his chest, dark green pants, and pointed red shoes.

"Oh, my God." I'd never seen a hot elf until now. An elf costume should make a guy look goofy, but this one fit in such a way that it showed off his muscular chest. Ben wore it well.

"Look at Xavier!" Ruby yelled.

At the back end of the float, behind the reindeer-llamas, was Santa's sleigh, and in it was my dear boy, dressed in a Santa costume, holding the llamas' reins with one hand and waving with the other. His grin was a mile wide, and then he spotted us in the crowd and jumped up from his sleigh driver's seat.

We all waved frantically at him and the girls called out.

"Unbelievable," Berty said, laughing.

I still couldn't find appropriate words as I took in the details.

There was a large green bag in the sleigh behind Xav overflowing with wrapped presents, and more presents lined the entire bed of the float. In front of my son was a ledge that held a mountain of rainbow-sprinkled cookies. Just as I noticed them, Ben walked back and grabbed two, then returned to the llamas and held out a cookie to each of them. The crowd went wild, pointing and laughing at the hilarious-looking reindeer wannabes as they greedily chomped their sweets.

"Look at Esmerelda up there!" Ruby shouted.

"And Betty!" Evelyn said. "Hi, Betty! Hi, Esmerelda!"

"I want cookies!" Skyler shouted.

"Looks like they have extras," Berty said, her tone filled with wonder. "I never expected anything like this."

As the float made its slow way past us, I was so focused on my adorable, amazing son that I almost missed the banner below him that said, Overall Winner, Individual Category.

"They won!" I yelled. "Xavier, you won!"

The yelling and cheering in our area tripled in volume as everyone else noticed the banner.

I didn't know if Xavier heard me, but he looked down at us, yelled, "We did it!" and swung his head in a joyful victory dance.

I raised my hands and clapped as I cheered for him and Ben. Incredible, generous Ben.

I dragged my gaze from my son, sought out Ben, and found him watching me with the happiest, sexiest expression on his handsome face. As our gazes met, I felt it down to my toes.

"Thank you," I mouthed to him. He winked, and that little gesture melted me.

"Mommy, does Xavier get a prize?" Skyler asked.

"I imagine he gets something," I answered, remembering when he'd first seen the parade info at Henry's, "but I don't know what." I hadn't paid attention because it'd been so far out of the realm of possibility in my mind.

"That float is unbelievable," Berty said, still staring after it with awe.

I was staring after it too, but my attention was locked on the big, sexy elf who'd taken my boy under his wing as if he were his own child. That was even hotter than the fit of the costume or the handsome crinkle at the outer corners of his eyes.

There were only a few more floats and entries after Ben and Xavier's. A police car pulled up the rear. After it drove past, the crowd spilled into the streets, meeting up with friends and making their way to shops or restaurants or heading home.

Berty sat back in her chair and bent over to collect her blankets. Her grandson's float had gotten her so excited she'd stood for the rest of the parade, and so had I.

"Best parade ever!" Evelyn declared as the girls showed off how full their bags were. There was enough candy to keep Joella Livingston, the town dentist, in business for the next fifty years.

As we mixed with the masses, I texted Ben to find out if we could meet up with him and Xavier and Betty and Esmerelda. I couldn't wait to hug my boy and congratulate him. I was dying to know how much of it had been his idea and how much Ben's.

And Ben... He was getting a special, private thank-you tonight.

"They're back at the staging area at the high school," I told Berty and the girls.

"Let's go see them!" Skyler said.

"I want to go on the float," Ruby said.

"I'll walk with you as far as my house," Berty said. She lived two blocks this side of the high school. We'd parked in her driveway, knowing public parking would be at a premium throughout town.

On the other side of the square, we found the mitten float doing a brisk business. The girls chose their mittens, and Skyler picked out a pair for her brother as well. Then we continued to the residential area that led to the high school. At Berty's house, we hugged her goodbye and promised to pick up our vehicle later.

The school parking lot was a madhouse, overflowing with people, floats, animals, and vehicles. We easily found Xavier, Ben, and the llamas, the animals still on the float, still chomping. The float, Knox's SUV, and the llamamobile were parked on the street about a half block down, out of the fray, probably for the sake of Betty and Esmerelda.

"Daddy!" Ruby yelled when we were a few hundred feet away.

"Xavier!" Skyler hollered.

"Esmerelda! Betty!" Evelyn called out.

"Girls, we need calm down and not run up to them. We don't want to startle the llamas any more than they're already startled," I told them.

I was bursting with as much energy and enthusiasm as they were, itching to run into Ben's arms to show him my gratitude, but I did my best to act like an adult, held Skyler's and Ruby's hands, and Evelyn held her sister's as we approached.

"Mom!" Xavier ran toward us, his face lit with pure joy and pride. "Did you see we won? We won! The biggest prize ever!"

He landed in my arms in a giant hug, and I soaked up

all his seven-year-old excitement, so absolutely happy for him.

Ben's girls ran to him for hugs, and Skyler hopped from foot to foot next to us until we pulled her into our hug.

Xavier was too revved up to be hugged for long.

"I'm so proud of you, Xavier! This float is incredible! You absolutely deserved to win," I told him as Ben and his daughters walked toward us.

"Did you tell them our prize?" Ben asked my son.

"We won a family boating afternoon on a pontoon from McNamara Marina and a two-person kayak and a gift certificate to Henry's and one for Lake Girl. That's for you, Mom." He looked to Ben. "And...what was the other thing?"

"A picnic lunch from Country Market," Ben said. "We got the grand prize basket, didn't we, buddy?"

"A boat ride, Mom!" Xavier said. "Can you believe it? We get to take our whole family!"

"Can we go too, Dad?" Evelyn asked.

"You're our family, silly," Xavier said.

"Close enough to go on the boat ride, anyway," I said, laughing, not letting myself think about how much our group of six could easily feel like a family.

The girls asked to sit in the sleigh, so Ben lifted each of them, plus Xavier, up on the float, telling them to stay at the back, away from the llamas. Soon all four kids were settled into Santa's sleigh, showing off candy and sharing it with Xavier. Skyler presented him with the mittens she'd chosen.

My attention went to Ben. Our gazes met.

"Can you believe it?" he asked as I went toward him.

There were people around, tons of them, but that wasn't going to stop me from hugging him. It *would* prevent me from kissing him till he forgot his name. I stretched to my toes and put my arms around him.

"I can't believe any of it," I said. "Never in a thousand years did I think you'd come up with *that*." I gestured with one hand to the float behind him but couldn't quite pull myself away from him yet.

"It was mostly your son," he said, pulling me in tight. "He had the idea for the sleigh and the llamas."

"And you made it happen." My eyes teared up. "Thank you."

We managed to come out of the hug, conscious of the kids a few feet away and the rest of the world in view.

"We had so much fun, Ems. He has an incredible imagination. Plus I got to teach him to use power tools."

"He's on top of the world. And that prize... A kayak, really?"

"A big, nice one from Lake Life Outfitters."

"I guess I'm going kayaking next summer," I said.

"And boating."

"And boating," I repeated.

The kids had found a fourth plastic bag, and the girls were absorbed in giving Xavier candy, piece by piece. I couldn't help myself. I hugged Ben again.

"You get a special thank-you later tonight," I whispered in his ear.

He growled low in his throat, which made me want to race home and thank him appropriately and privately right now. Unfortunately we had llamas and kids to see to.

I ended the hug long before I wanted to, still conscious of where we were.

"Working with Xav was sincerely my pleasure," he said. "A complete joy. And today was a blast. Happy early Christmas to all of us."

"Happy early Christmas," I returned, unable to get the smile off my face.

"Now...we need to get these ladies home before they make an escape." He gestured to the llamas.

I laughed and looped my arm with his in a friendly way as we went to coordinate llama transport with Knox.

This Christmas was looking like it could be the best ever.

Chapter Twenty-One

Emerson

Christmas was a week away.

The salon was having its best month yet, and in spite of all the hard work that entailed, my stylists were upbeat and festive, not to mention thrilled with their higher-than-usual holiday tips.

Today was the last day of school until after the new year, so I was certain Berty had her hands full with hyper kids. On top of winter vacation, mine could hardly wait to see their nana.

Kizzy and Shannon were arriving in two days and would be staying at the Marks Resort for a full week. Xavier and Skyler were extra excited because Kizzy had invited them to swim at the hotel's indoor pool as much as they wanted.

Having my mother-in-law and her wife take my kids off my hands for a few hours at a time would allow me to finish shopping and wrap their gifts in private—and maybe breathe for a minute.

The thing about extra holiday spirit, I was finding, was that it made me even more apt to spend on my kiddos. I'd never had this much fun with Christmas shopping before, and I wouldn't apologize for it or feel bad about how much money I sank into it. My business was thriving. I was grateful, as a single mom, to have enough to spoil them.

Willow and I were the last two at Posh. We locked up and left together, laughing about a story one of her clients had told her. It was dark, cold, and snowing again, but in a light, fluffy, happy way instead of a closing-down-the-town way.

We said goodbye, and once I had my SUV running, I turned up the country music to cleanse my ears from holiday songs. I might be feeling festive, but if I never heard another carol, I'd be ever so ecstatic.

As I turned onto Honeysuckle Road, my phone rang. Kizzy's name popped up on the dash screen.

"Hello, Mother-in-Law," I said cheerily.

"Hi, Emerson. Is this a bad time?"

"Not at all. It's good timing, actually. I'm driving home. Captive audience. The kids are so excited to see you they're like those yappy little dogs who run in circles when they're overstimulated." I laughed at the image in my head because it was so appropriate.

"Yeah." She didn't laugh right away, her tone setting off my concern. "About that... Our plans have changed rather suddenly, I'm afraid."

"What? Is everything okay?" Concern pulsed through me. The last I knew, Kizzy had been counting the days along with the kids. Every time they FaceTimed, they went on and on about her and Shannon's visit and all the things they'd do together.

"Everything's fine." She laughed self-consciously. "It's a crazy story and a rare opportunity."

I stiffened, unable to find it in me to laugh with her or even smile. "Okaaaay."

"We have these close friends out here, Marla and Lew. They booked a big, elaborate trip to Machu Picchu to celebrate their fortieth anniversary. All the bells and whistles, apparently. Well, they're supposed to leave Saturday morning, but Lew's been having some health problems lately, and he finally got a diagnosis yesterday. It's a rare type of cancer, and they've got to start treating it right away."

"I'm sorry, Kizzy. That's awful."

"It is. Prognosis is a little grim, but they think it's early enough he's got a decent chance, as long as he starts treatment right away."

"That makes sense," I said, my mind flitting ahead to how this was going to devastate my kids. "So you're going to help them out?"

"Ohh, nothing that noble, I'm afraid. They can't get their money back for this trip, but obviously they can't go. What they *can* do is transfer it to someone, and they've gifted it to Shannon and me. Since we didn't get a honeymoon, we thought it was a wonderful opportunity. We'll come to Dragonfly Lake in January and have a late second Christmas."

I drove with my mouth gaping open as I tried to figure out what to say. "Okay" was what came out, even though it wasn't. *I* wasn't okay. "The kids are going to be really disappointed," I managed.

"I know," she said. "I hate to postpone, but we'll make it up to them when we're there in January."

She made it sound like all would be fine in the end, and

it probably would be. It was the near future that was going to be hard—for me, Skyler, and Xavier, not Kizzy.

"Well, thanks for letting me know," I said, not even trying to insert pleasantness into my voice.

"Emerson, I'm sorry. I can tell you're upset." Her tone was empathetic and gentle, which made me feel unreasonable. "If there was a way for me to make everyone happy, I'd do it in a heartbeat. I was hoping you'd understand and welcome us a couple of weeks late."

I realized my jaw was clenched, so I took in a slow breath, trying to rein in so many emotions I couldn't even label them.

"I do understand, Kizzy. I'm all for your amazing trip and you and Shannon getting a belated honeymoon because you deserve it. It's just that my kids' hearts are going to be broken. They were already having a hard time with you moving away, selling the house...Skyler especially." She knew this. We'd talked about it multiple times.

"Bless her precious little heart," Kizzy said, her voice teeming with love and empathy, and that was exactly what made it impossible for me to lash out at this woman.

She did love my kids unquestionably. For four years, she'd sacrificed her privacy and her peace and let us live with her. I'd shared some of the expenses, and she'd shared nearly all the parenting responsibilities.

We'd moved in when Skyler was a baby and Xavier was only three. Kizzy had jumped in wholeheartedly to help with whatever I needed. Then when the only local salon had closed and I'd debated renting out the space and opening Posh, she'd volunteered to take on daily childcare.

Without her, my life wouldn't be what I'd built it into, with two kiddos who didn't question how much they were loved, a successful business, and soon, God and the real estate market willing, a home of our own.

So I found it tricky to begrudge her any of her happiness now—her late-in-life true love, her cross-country move to be with her wife, and a honeymoon. I would come across as spoiled and petty to rail at her for any of it.

But railing was exactly what I felt like doing.

"I'm pulling into the driveway," I said, deciding hanging up was the best way to avoid voicing the toxic comments in my head. "I need to go find a way to break it to the kids."

"Let me know if I can help in any way."

The way to help would be to show up as planned, but that obviously wasn't going to happen.

"I'll talk to you after your trip," I said and ended the call, unable to summon any genuine good wishes or even a pleasant goodbye.

I parked the car in the garage as usual, but I needed time to cool down before I went in that house. I was sure Berty had the kids handled, and maybe Ben was home from work too.

I got out and slammed the door hard. It felt good but didn't put a dent in the storm inside of me.

By the time I'd walked past the house, beyond the barn, and toward the east property line, my tears nearly blinded me.

"Dammit!" I yelled to the night.

I paced back and forth through the remnants of the previous snow, my anger growing with every step, drowning out the rest of the emotions with its intensity.

Who was going to have to tell my kids and break their hearts? Me.

Who would have to comfort them, get them to sleep,

wake up with them in the middle of the night when they were still upset? I would.

Who would have to be mom, dad, grandma, and grandpa to Xavier and Skyler? Yep. "Motherfucking me."

"Hey." Ben's voice came from several feet behind me.

I whipped around, on the edge, semihysterical, and now startled out of my skin. "Shit!" I put my hand to my chest, my heart galloping.

"Sorry, Ems. What's going on? What are you doing out here?"

"What are *you* doing?" I snapped back. I wanted to be alone.

"I heard you yell as I was walking home. What happened?"

"I let my guard down. That's what happened." I resumed pacing. "Stupid, stupid, stupid!"

"Hey," he said in a calm, reasonable voice. He took my hand, but I whipped it away. "Emerson, tell me what's going on. Maybe I can help."

"You can't help. I don't want help. That's where I went wrong in the first place."

He let me pace and rant in my head for a minute.

"Could you please tell me what happened? Something with one of the kids?" he asked.

I let out a scoff. "The kids didn't do anything wrong, but they're the ones who are going to be devastated. Kizzy canceled."

"*What?*"

"Kizzy and Shannon aren't coming for Christmas. They got a better offer."

"Why the hell aren't they coming for Christmas? Sky and Xav have been counting down the days."

"I know that!" I yelled, then realized I was being awful

and tried to rein myself in. A sob escaped me. "I know that," I said more reasonably.

"Come here," he said in his calm, caring voice.

I didn't want to be calmed.

I shook my head and stomped away again, clutching the ends of my hair that hung out of my stocking cap. I wanted to rant, rave, scream, and cry.

"This is why," I said, despair ringing through my voice. "This is why I don't ever want to depend on someone else again. I never should've moved in with Kizzy after Blake was killed. I should've known better than to rely on someone else."

"You were widowed with a newborn and a three-year-old," he reasoned. "You needed help. Anyone would."

"I should've made it work by myself. I could've come back to town without moving into Kizzy's. Without depending on her for so much. I know better!" My voice broke. "I fucking know better than to get too close. I know better than to care too much. It hurts too much when they go away or let me down."

I'd broken my own number one rule—twice now. With Kizzy *and* with Ben. My breath left me as that realization smacked into me.

I squatted down, hugging my knees, head buried in my arms. I was full-out hysterical, probably looked insane. Didn't care. My heart hurt so overwhelmingly with loss. With loneliness. With bone-deep disappointment, not in Kizzy but in myself. Because I knew better. I'd messed up, and now my kids—and I—would hurt because of it.

When I felt Ben's hand on my shoulder, I popped up, still unable to take comfort from him. I didn't want comfort. I needed to be self-sufficient even in this moment.

Putting space between us, I said, "This is why I can't

give you what you want." My voice was hoarse, quiet. I crossed my arms and hugged myself with my hands on my shoulders. "*This* is why I can't agree to anything long-term. Because it never lasts. Everybody leaves. They either die, or they go away and choose somebody else. My mom died. My grandma died. Blake died. Kizzy left, and here I am again, all alone." I threw my head back, pointing my face to the sky, then closed my eyes. More tears poured out.

"Dammit, Emerson," Ben said, his voice full of fire. "You don't get it, do you?"

"Get what?"

"I'm here. I'm right fucking here."

"Maybe for now," I said, "but it won't last." If my mother-in-law couldn't hang on, why would anyone else? I knew this in my soul. I'd just temporarily let myself forget because of a few orgasms and stolen moments.

"I'll be here, Emerson, if you'll just let me. For fuck's sake, I've cared about you since sophomore year in high school, before Blake ever asked you out. All these years and I still have these feelings for you."

"Stop." I shook my head, unable to fathom what he'd just admitted to. He'd married someone else. Made a life, had kids with her. It didn't make sense. I sucked in a deep gulp of frigid air.

"That's just it, Emerson. I apparently *can't* stop caring about you."

His voice had gone quieter but even more intense. It slowed my rant marginally.

"You're such a good, giving man, Ben, but life has taught me over and over not to get comfortable. Not to rely on anyone else. It's just me. It's better that way."

"Do you really believe that bullshit?" he said, looking angrier than I'd ever seen him.

All that did was reignite my own ire.

"Yes, I really do!"

How could I not? So many losses. So much pain, and it affected my children too. The hurt in my heart from Kizzy's moving away had been simmering for all these weeks. I'd tried to be understanding and accepting even as I'd felt like the kids and I weren't important enough for her to stay. Had she ever asked Shannon to move to Tennessee?

Now, with her skipping out on us for Christmas, the biggest thing the kids were looking forward to about the holiday, the cut went deeper. Whether it made sense or not, it took me back to all those other losses because, once again, in the end, I was left to fend alone and wrap my head around another big void in our lives.

I squeezed my eyes shut as tears gushed out. My chest physically hurt. My throat pulsed with pain, making it hard to breathe.

"It was supposed to be a long weekend she took to Vegas, a visit to a friend," I said, thinking back to just a couple of months ago when Kizzy had yanked the rug out from under us. "I was all for it. She deserved to get away for a few days. When she came back, she was married. No warning. Just, 'I'm moving a billion miles away.' And I was so understanding. Genuinely happy for her. I really was. I knew it would mean changes for us. We couldn't stay in that house forever. But then she sold it so fast..."

"I've always thought it was insensitive of her," Ben said. "She left you in the lurch, and you've been so damn understanding."

"How could I not?" I shrieked. "How could I ask her not to take that preemptive deal on her house?"

I cried harder, because that was the same predicament I was in now. Kizzy's actions weren't unreasonable. She was just living her life. But my kids and I were the ones being hurt by it. Again.

"The person I trusted most in the world to be there for my kids has hurt them three times now," I said, my voice quieter, calmer on the surface, mainly because I was suddenly drained. "Shame on me for letting that happen. This is on me, not Kizzy."

"There were better ways for her to handle it," he said. "And she sure as hell didn't have to blow off the kids' Christmas."

"It's up to me to make it okay for them." As the words poured out of me, I felt the truth of them in my bones. No more relying on others for that. No more relying on others for anything.

"You're not going to let me help?"

"No. We never should've moved in here. I appreciate your generosity, but I'm going to find an alternative solution. Maybe we'll rent after all, or we'll work out a long stay at the inn—"

"That's the dumbest thing you've said yet."

"It's what I should've done all along."

"So you're going to ruin my kids' Christmas because Kizzy hurt you?"

Dammit. *Dammit, dammit, dammit.* Of course I couldn't hurt Evelyn and Ruby. I didn't want to hurt Ben either. "We'll be here for Christmas just like we planned. But in the meantime, I'm going to see about a room at the Marks. My kids were promised a pool and fun times. If we can get a room, Ruby and Evelyn can come swim with us."

"You're running away."

I let out a laugh that had no humor in it. "I'm keeping myself safe, Ben. Protecting my kids. I can't take one more loss. Not ever. So call it whatever you need to, but I can't stay." I breathed, the panic starting to subside with my decision. "And now I need to go break my kids' hearts with Kizzy's news."

I stalked off before he could say more, feeling wrung out and heartbroken. I needed another couple of hours to level out, process everything, and work up my soothing-mom face, but I didn't have the luxury. I was a single mom. I'd tend to my own wounds later.

When I was almost to the house, I heard Ben yell, "Fuck!" at the top of his voice. I guessed he was letting out his own frustration.

I wished I wasn't the cause of it, but I had to do what was best for my kids and myself. I'd lost sight of that since moving in here.

Thank you, Kizzy, for the unpleasant reminder.

Chapter Twenty-Two

Ben

"You miss her too, don't you, Nugget?"

Emerson's black-and-white dog met me enthusiastically as I came out of Betty's stall Friday night, just as she had when I exited Esmerelda's and Smoky's and Bay's and Freckles's, pulling a shallow smile from me each time.

Emerson and her kids had been gone for forty-eight hours. My anger had mostly dissipated, but my heart was heavy, and my mood was in the shitter. I didn't foresee it improving anytime soon.

She'd booked a suite at the Marks Hotel and had herself and Skyler and Xavier packed up within the hour after getting Kizzy's news. Her kids had shed tears over their grandmother's postponement, but Emerson had presented their hotel adventure in just the right way.

When she'd seen the melancholy expressions on my girls' faces, Emerson had brought them in for a tight hug, loving words, and an invitation for a sleepover at the hotel the next night. That had raised Ruby's and Evelyn's spirits considerably, but they'd still begged me to let Ruby sleep in Evelyn's room, in the bed that was still pushed up next to Evelyn's, for that first night. I'd agreed, hoping they could comfort each other, because I wasn't at my best.

Last night had been the sleepover. Dropping them off at the Marks, leaving them in Emerson's care for a night felt like a divorced dad trading off with his ex. It'd been awkward, spring-loaded with a shit ton of emotions just under the surface, and polite exchanges like, *How's the pool? Really nice. The kids love it.*

Then I'd come home alone, drunk half a bottle of whiskey, and passed out watching Animal Planet.

Nugget circled me, her manic mood revolving largely around me. Emerson had asked me to keep her while they were at the hotel, and naturally I'd said yes. But the dog missed her family and seemed to have adopted me as her stand-in person. I was more than okay with that. I needed a stand-in person too, but maybe I was better off relying on dogs.

Yesterday morning, when I'd left the house to do the morning chores, the three dogs had gone out to do their duty as usual, but while my two played and chased around the yard, Nugget had trotted next to me and peered up with sad canine eyes at the barn door. I'd cautiously let her accompany me, unsure how she'd react to the barn cats, horses, and llamas.

The cats hadn't come out, and Nugget showed a healthy respect for the large animals, content to wait outside each stall for me. That reunion after each one was becoming the highlight of my days. I squatted down and scratched her ears and sweet-talked her.

"Who's my best barn helper, huh? Yes, who's a good

girl?" She licked my face, beside herself from the attention. "She'll come back for you soon." I let out a hollow laugh and muttered to myself, "I might be fucking jealous of that."

After a few more ear scratches and nuzzles, I stood. "Let's go feed the barn cats."

This was only the dog's fourth time "helping" me in the barn, but she already knew to sprint ahead to the container where I kept the cats' food.

"You're a natural, Nugs."

As I scooped out the right amount of dry cat kibbles, the barn door closed. I turned to see Berty bundled up and bearing toward me with purpose.

"What are you doing out here? Am I in trouble?" I asked.

"Not at all," she said as she reached me and gave Nugget a pat. "Just wanted to check on you and talk a bit without little ears around."

"Are the kids done with the chickens?"

"They're back inside. I've got them up in Evelyn's room wrapping their presents for you. I told them I was going to come divert you," she said with a conspiratorial grin.

"That sounds a little daunting for me," I tried to joke. She'd given me space so far, but I'd caught a couple of concerned looks when she thought I wasn't paying attention.

Once I'd set down the cat bowls, I walked over to Smoky's stall and rubbed his neck the way he liked. Berty came over to Smoky's other side and did the same. Nugget was sniffing something near the hay bales I'd brought down.

"How are you doing, Ben?" she asked in a tone that said this wasn't small talk.

My answer was a quiet scoff and an "I'm fine."

"That's a bunch of hooey, and you know it."

"I'm a grown man. I can handle a disappointment." As if sensing I needed support, Nugget trotted over and sat on her haunches at my side. I reached down and patted her head.

"I know you can," she said, relocating to my other side and putting a caring hand on my arm that rested on the stall wall. "I just wish you didn't have to."

"Me too, Berty. Me too."

"She's been through a lot, I know, but running away's never the answer."

I grunted in agreement. I didn't want to talk about the woman who'd broken my heart—again.

"Are you going to tell her you love her?" she asked.

"What makes you think I love her?"

"You do. I can tell. Are you going to deny that?"

Could a man *not* have secrets from his seventy-four-year-old grandmother? Apparently not when she was in his house every day helping him care for his children.

Nugget nosed my denim-covered leg as if urging me to level with Berty.

"I already told her how I feel," I finally admitted. "It didn't do any good. Maybe only served to push her away."

Berty nodded slowly. "She's a skittish one."

I laughed at the word I most often used to describe a horse. "She's been through a lot of loss in her life. It leaves scars."

"It sure does."

Smoky poked his head over to Berty, nuzzling her hand in search of a treat.

"I got nothing for you, boy," she said.

I narrowed my eyes. "Why would he think you might have a treat for him?"

"I surely don't know."

"Have you been sneaking apples out here? Carrots?"

A grin stretched across Berty's face. "You give those llamas cookies. A carrot here and there for these beauties won't hurt."

"You softie."

"Just an advocate for equal treatment."

I laughed.

"Quit diverting the conversation away from yourself," she said.

"I thought we were done. I told Emerson how I feel. She left. I'm sad, but I'll get over it. End of story," I grumped.

"People have to work through their wounds on their own schedule. Maybe she'll be motivated to work on healing."

"I used to hope," I admitted. Like, last week or so.

I'd gone into our fling with my eyes wide open. She'd been transparent about her limits. I'd genuinely understood. Hell, I'd lost my wife too. I was no stranger to tragic loss. A single one could derail a person for a good long time, never mind the number of losses Emerson had suffered.

I'd hoped though. I'd hoped like hell, in the next few weeks before she moved out, she'd fall in love with me and find the courage to take a chance on a future. But she'd cut our time short, put an end to that chance, and extinguished my hope.

"What are you going to do about Christmas?" Berty asked.

"She said she'll be back Christmas Eve. That way the kids will all be together to get up at the crack of dawn to see what Santa brought."

"That makes the most sense." She went silent for a beat, then asked, "Will that be difficult for you?"

"It sure as hell won't be a picnic." Closer to torture. "I'll get through it just fine. I'll focus on the kids."

And wasn't it fucking ironic that I was back to faking it till I made it as far as Christmas spirit was concerned? I wasn't at all optimistic I'd feel it in time for Christmas Day.

"I strongly believe if something's meant to be, it'll be," she said with conviction.

Before this, I would've said I did too, but I hated the position I was in now. Do nothing. Wait. See.

"I guess the big question is whether Emerson and I are meant to be."

Chapter Twenty-Three

Emerson

As I drove away from Ben's after leaving the kids with Berty on Monday afternoon, uneasiness unraveled in my gut.

Not that I'd had any easy feelings for the past four days since taking refuge at the Marks.

I missed Ben and his kids and Nugget and the other animals and Berty. Even that stupid screaming rooster.

That just showed how attached I'd gotten in such a short time. Kizzy had done me a favor by forcing me to see the mistake I'd been making.

My nervousness now was more immediate though and had everything to do with the real-estate showing I was on my way to.

Darius had called an hour ago about a house that was going on the market tomorrow. He could take me through it today if I could make it. As this was the first new listing that met my requirements in nearly three weeks, I would've rearranged whatever I had to in order to get there. Since the salon was closed today, I was more flexible than usual.

I'd debated taking the kids with me, but I'd decided to go alone to avoid getting their hopes up or, at the opposite end of the spectrum, worrying them about another change. Skyler was back to crawling into my bed every night at the hotel, so I didn't want to fill her head with possibilities that might not pan out. My kids needed solid plans. We needed to settle. I'd vaguely told them I had an appointment and asked Berty not to mention where I was going.

I followed the map app's directions to the house in the older neighborhood west of downtown to a house that didn't yet have a real estate sign in the yard.

As I pulled up along the curb, my brows rose. The house was adorable, with a cute little front porch, a postage-stamp front yard with a tree that looked climbable, and a long driveway to a detached, single-car garage.

Darius climbed out of his car and greeted me. "Just look at that curb appeal," he said excitedly.

"It's super cute from the front," I agreed. As we went to the door and Darius repeated the features he'd told me over the phone—three bedrooms, a partially finished basement, two bathrooms, a newly updated kitchen—I coached myself not to get my hopes up. I'd been let down every time so far.

Twenty minutes later, my mind was spinning. The house met every need on my list and looked cute doing it. The master was on the main floor. The two bedrooms upstairs were connected by a secret crawl space the kids would lose their minds over. The backyard was fenced in for Nugget. The basement would make a roomy play area. The kitchen was small but functional and remodeled in whites that brightened it up.

"What's going through your mind?" Darius asked me back in the living room.

"It checks all the boxes."

He scrutinized me more closely. "Sounds like a but."

I frowned, because I felt like there was a *but,* but I couldn't figure out what it was. "I'm not sure..."

"If you like it, we have to move on it."

I knew that was a fact and not some kind of manufactured pressure to get a sale. Darius wasn't like that. The market was.

"I'm going to walk through one more time by myself, if you don't mind," I said.

"Of course. Take your time. The owners gave us an hour."

"Thanks."

I went through the entire house again, logging all the positives, noting any negatives, though there weren't many. The linen closet was minuscule. The wallpaper in the upstairs bathroom was ugly but removable. The carpet in the upstairs bedrooms would need to be replaced. The garage was small but would protect the SUV just fine. All of these were minor.

Yet I was struggling to see the kids and me living here.

I squinted, trying to see past the current owners' belongings to the bare bones. The rooms weren't overlarge, but we didn't need that much space. The layout was practical. I liked that the master was on the main level with the kids' rooms above. The neighborhood was wonderful, with Posh just three blocks away and the grade school two or three in the other direction.

"Well?" Darius asked when I rejoined him.

"Do you know if anyone else is going through it tonight?"

"We're the only ones they're letting in early. They're longtime family friends granting me a favor."

"Wow. Nice of them. Okay." I blew out a breath.

Logic said I needed to jump on this and make an offer tonight. But something felt off in my gut, and I couldn't ignore it. I just needed to figure out what it was so I could determine whether it was valid.

"I need to think," I told him.

"Emerson—"

"I know. I know, I know, I know we need to act right away. I need a little time to think. How late can I call you tonight?"

"Nine o'clock," he said tensely. "I just don't want you to miss out on this."

"Me neither." My stress level climbed higher. "I understand the risk I'm taking if I push it until tomorrow. I'll do everything I can to call you before nine tonight, okay?"

He nodded tersely. "You might not have the luxury of being entirely comfortable with it."

"Right." I nodded again, distractedly, trying to put my finger on what was bothering me. "Thank you. So much. I appreciate you giving me this opportunity."

"Of course. As soon as I saw it, I thought of you."

We walked out and said goodbye, with a dozen puzzled glances from Darius. I got it. It didn't make sense. Feelings didn't make sense, but there was a feeling deep inside that I couldn't ignore, at least until I figured out what it meant.

Once he drove away, I sat there looking at the cute little house, taking in the well-manicured evergreen shrubs in the beds and the stone-lined walkway to the porch and the ideal spot for a porch swing.

I drove around the block, taking stock of the nearby houses, noting signs of lots of families with kids. I drove to the grade school and back, then pulled into the driveway of the house to turnaround and go back to Ben's to get the kids. Before backing out, I paused for one more long look. The most prevalent feeling in my gut was that I *should* fall in love with this. That was different than *falling* in love with it.

Was I being stupid to wait for some fleeting feeling? I suspected so, but I couldn't discount it until I had an idea of where it was coming from.

I had a lot to think about.

I backed out and drove on autopilot to Ben's, my mind churning, compelling my heart to speak up and tell it what the hell was holding it back from jumping on this.

Was it nerves over buying my first house? Fear about the financial commitment? The house was in my budget. I'd gone over the monthly payments multiple times. I could handle the mortgage.

I turned into the driveway on Ben's property and noticed the clinic was already dark. They must've closed early since tomorrow was Christmas Eve. Continuing down the lane toward the house and barn, I checked for the horses and llamas in the pasture, but they appeared to be inside for the night.

I turned left into the drive next to the house, and a strong wave of something rolled through me. I braked, closed my eyes, deciphered it.

Comfort. Peace. Familiarity.

Home.

I'd stopped the car a long way from the garage. I wasn't staying here anymore. This was where visitors parked.

And still the feeling undeniably washed over me, filled me with warmth.

Warmth that I hadn't felt in the driveway of the perfect little house.

I whipped my head toward Ben's home and peered at the kitchen window. There was Ben, as if an invisible force had drawn me to look at him.

The sensation deepened as I took in his handsome face, attention focused on the sink in front of the window. He was talking to someone I couldn't see. Laughing. I could hear that laugh in my head. I could feel the way he'd made me feel when we were cooking a meal together or getting the kids organized for school or playing a family board game. Everyday moments that were secure, companionable, safe, comfortable because we were side by side.

Watching him from out here filled me with contentedness but also longing. I wanted to be inside that warm, love-filled house with him, talking about nothing important, listening to the kids chatter or bicker, smelling whatever Berty had simmering on the stove.

"No," I whispered as tears filled my eyes.

I turned away and pressed my hands to my face, wiping the tears away as the truth settled in my head and my heart.

I'd fallen in love with Ben. And that scared me to the depths of my soul.

With my heart thundering, hands shaking, I had to get away. Needed to be alone.

I backed out of his line of sight and drove partway down the drive toward the clinic so he wouldn't look out and see me. Then I took my phone out and sent him a message, too shaky to call.

> I have a huge favor to ask. I looked at a house, and it was kind of perfect. I need to sort things out in my head. Could you possibly keep the kids for a couple more hours? I'll return the favor.

Three minutes passed before I saw signs he was typing —I knew because I watched the clock on the dash, feeling more desperate to run away with every minute that ticked by.

> They just started a game of Monopoly. Why don't they spend the night here? Would that help?

I cried harder because here he was again, being amazing even when I was anything but.

> Yes. Thank you, Ben.

> Good luck with your decision.

I could barely see through the tears as I reached the road. I stopped and tried to staunch the flow.

I'd gotten myself into a mess. I'd gone against my own rules. Now it was up to me to figure out how the hell to move forward.

Chapter Twenty-Four

Emerson

If I was going to make huge life decisions, I needed food first.

I drove back into town and parked as close to Humble's as I could get. Their pizza was something besides orgasms that Ben had gotten me addicted to.

Since I hadn't called in advance, I went to the counter and placed my order, then stepped back to wait.

"Emerson!"

I turned to find Chloe and Hayden huddled along an inner wall.

"Hey, ladies. Did you order to-go too?" I asked.

"We did," Hayden said. "Just got done with last-minute shopping and dropped in on a whim when we caught a whiff."

"The smell is killing me," I said, realizing how hungry I was. "Big family bash tonight?"

"*Au contraire*," Chloe said cheerfully. "Our guys took

the kids shopping in the city. They're staying at Faye and Simon's tonight."

"Which means Chloe and I have no kids to feed, clean, or put to bed," Hayden chimed in. "What about you?"

"My kids are at Ben's for the night."

"Oh, so you're taking dinner back to the hordes?" Hayden said.

"Nope. I'm..." I pressed my lips together, considering. I was as close to Chloe as anyone. I trusted her. And Hayden... I didn't know her quite as well, but I liked her and knew she was smart and trustworthy. While I didn't always rush to confide in others, I needed to tonight like never before. "I don't know what I'm doing." With a nervous laugh, I said, "I'm freaking out, to be honest."

"What's going on?" Chloe asked.

"It's a long story. Is there any chance you'd want to hole up in my hotel suite with me, eat pizza, and help me straighten out my head?" I directed the invitation to both of them. "Impromptu girls' night?"

Hayden and Chloe looked at each other, shrugged, and nodded.

"Absolutely," Hayden said. "Girl time is the best. We'll help you figure shit out."

"But what are you doing in a hotel?" Chloe asked. "I thought you were living at Ben's?"

"Yeah. That's part of the long story." I attempted to grin sheepishly.

"It sounds like we might need wine with our pizza," Hayden said.

"Yes," I said. "Please. We could get some from the hotel bar."

"I'm not sure by-the-glass is going to do it for this," Chloe said as Hayden's name was called out to pick up their order. "We'll stop by the Country Market and grab a couple of bottles and meet you. You're at the Marks?"

I nodded and told her my suite number. "I'll see you there. Thank you."

She brushed off my thanks. "This is perfect. Girls' night in the fancy hotel that brought me back to Dragonfly Lake in the first place. I can't wait to see your suite."

They headed out with their pizza, and I exhaled deeper than I had in the past fifteen minutes.

———

"Enough of the small talk," Hayden said forty-five minutes later as we drank rosé and devoured our pizza. They'd also brought a pound package of M&M's and a monster-sized bag of Twizzlers Chloe claimed would give us clarity. "What's going on between you and the handsome veterinarian?"

"At Max's, you were together but secret," Chloe said.

"And temporary," I reminded her.

I put my slice down and filled my half-empty wineglass to the brim.

The three of us were in the suite's living room, around the coffee table, with one lamp emanating warm, homey light. Leaning back into the surprisingly comfortable armchair, I caught Hayden up.

"It was good?" Hayden asked. "Between you two?"

My eyes fluttered shut, and I sighed. "The sex was incredible."

"Just the sex?" Chloe asked.

I swallowed a gulp of wine as I considered that. "Not just the sex. Everything. The partnership, the conversation, the coparenting..." Saying that out loud made me realize just how much I'd had my head in the sand the whole time to not see what was happening between us. "Even when Blake was alive, I didn't have that. I mean, we could discuss really big things on the phone sometimes, but the three thousand parenting things that come up in a day? It was all me because he was always gone."

"So it was like you were a single mom even when you were happily married," Hayden said.

"Right. I had mom friends on the base, and we traded babysitting and talked about potty training and nightmares and all the things, but they were just friends in the same position."

"So moving in with Kizzy must've been a godsend," Chloe said.

"Yep." I ate a bite of pizza, then said, "Until she defected."

"So you lost Blake, and then you lost Kizzy, just in a different way," Chloe said intuitively.

"And your mom, right?" Hayden asked.

I nodded. "My grandma too."

"Hell's bells, that's a lot. My mom died a few years back too," Hayden said somberly. "It sucks so bad."

Chloe, who sat next to Hayden on the sofa, pulled her in for a side hug.

"I'm sorry, Hayden," I said. "I didn't know her well, but I remember her always being so nice."

She nodded. "It's been a while, but you never get over it."

I shook my head, feeling that in my heart. "I have issues with letting people too close," I admitted. "Like, a deep fear in my bones."

"Heck yes," Hayden said. "Who could blame you? Zane

lost a good friend in the Navy, and it messed him up so much we almost didn't make it."

"Really?" I asked, a little shocked because they seemed so happy every time I saw them together.

She nodded as her eyes teared up. "Dammit." She gulped her wine, wiped her eyes, and laughed. "Sorry. It was a hard time, but we're good now."

"Thank goodness. And I'm going to take a wild guess that you and Ben are *not* good," Chloe said to me.

I blew out a shaky breath. "No. Kizzy called to cancel her visit. She and her wife were supposed to arrive last Friday."

"Nooo. If your kids are like Sutton, they couldn't wait to see their grandma."

I nodded. "I was looking forward to it too. And I've used her impending visit to soothe Skyler when she's been inconsolable about all the changes in our life. My mother-in-law's bailing on us totally triggered me," I said. "It brought back all the heartache of being left alone. Again."

"Yeah, I can see that," Chloe said.

"After Blake died, I promised myself I'd never have a serious relationship again." I swirled my glass, watching the wine circle inside. "You can't stop people from dying, but I could keep my heart safe."

Both girls watched me, waiting, as if they knew what I was going to say.

"I'm supposed to be deciding whether to put an offer in on a house tonight," I said instead, one hundred percent diverting.

"What?" Chloe said.

"You forgot to mention that little detail," Hayden scolded.

Chloe narrowed her eyes, looking pensive. "It's all connected somehow, isn't it?"

I squeezed my eyes shut, finding it even harder than I'd expected to talk about my feelings for Ben.

"You can tell us anything," Hayden said. "It doesn't go anywhere."

I swallowed, nodded, opened my eyes. Took in a deep, fortifying breath. "The house is perfect on paper, but something kept me from jumping on it. I went to Ben's afterward to get my kids, and as I drove up—" I sucked in air, tearing up again.

Hayden popped up off the sofa, came to my side, and put her arm around me. "You can let it out."

I covered my face and gave myself a pep talk. *Put your big-girl panties on and just say it. All of it.*

I sat up straighter. Hayden held my hand. Chloe refilled my glass. This was what girlfriends did, and I loved them for it.

"This strong, overwhelming feeling hit me, like...home. And then I saw Ben through the kitchen window, and I realized that...that...I fell in love with him." Tears gushed down my cheeks.

They were quiet for a few seconds. Then Hayden said, "Does he know?"

I shook my head.

"Has he given any signs that he feels the same way?" Chloe asked.

I lowered my lids and nodded. "He says he loves me."

Hayden hugged me tightly to her side. "So it would be perfect if you weren't scared."

I nodded again, and a sob escaped. "I feel sort of dumb because some people would be so happy but..."

"Fear sucks," Chloe said matter-of-factly. "So, so much."

Hayden hugged me while I cried. After a couple of minutes, my tears slowed. I wiped my eyes and sat up straighter. "I know I seem crazy."

"We all have our own special crazy," Hayden said.

"The question is, what are you going to do?" Chloe asked. "Are you going to let your fear prevent you from having a wonderful life with Ben and his kids?"

My mind flashed to Ben's home, with the fat Christmas tree and the cozy fireplace and the crazy rooster and the four-legged chaos...and the love.

I swallowed hard and squeezed my eyes shut. "I want Ben and all his crazy." Slowly I inhaled a deep breath and looked between my friends. "But I'm afraid I hurt him. I don't know if he wants *my* crazy."

"He wants your crazy and your sexy and your funny and your everything," Hayden said. "I'd bet a whole lot of money."

"But if you've hurt him, you might have to grovel a little," Chloe pointed out.

I thought about him yelling curses into the dark the other night. "Yeah. I'm going to need a plan. And it has to be really good, because I have to call Darius now."

Chapter Twenty-Five

Ben

Christmas Eve had arrived, and I wasn't proud to admit, by the time I closed the clinic at three, I was ready to tell the world to fa-la-la-la fuck off.

How many times over the past month had I envisioned how special this Christmas would be with Emerson and her kids under our roof? How harmonious and loud and full of laughter, with used wrapping paper covering the living room floor and hugs of gratitude overtaking the day?

She and her kids would be under our roof, but everyone's spirits had dimmed. The kids had no true idea what had happened between Emerson and me, but they could sense something was off. They saw how we interacted—stiffly and politely—every time we came into contact. Throw on top of it the still-present disappointment that Kizzy and her wife were missing the big day, and everything was just...off. Un-fucking-merry.

I trudged toward the house after my staff had left. The sky was heavy, the clouds low and dark with more impending snow, but not even a white Christmas was going to fix my mood.

The horses and llamas were tucked away in the barn. Evelyn had insisted the chickens needed some fresh air, so we'd left their house open, allowing the birds to roam in their pen while it was light out, but only Cayenne and Ginger were braving the cold air. The others had the right idea as far as I was concerned.

What I wouldn't give to burrow deep in my bed and sleep the afternoon away. I didn't want to dampen the kids' excitement, but I just couldn't act like everything was fine.

I wasn't fine. I wasn't in the same zip code as fine.

The more time that passed without Emerson wrangling her fears, the clearer it became: This had been my last chance with her, and my last chance was fizzling out in failure.

I went into the house, shed my coat, and inhaled the smell of recently popped popcorn. The washing machine was running in the laundry room, which told me Berty was doing a load of the kids' clothes even though I'd insisted I would take care of the chore.

I found Evelyn and Berty in the living room, Berty reading a paperback and my daughter doing a word search in an activity book, both with a bowl of popcorn at their side. Christmas music played quietly from a speaker.

When she saw me, Ev jumped up and gave me a hug. "Hi, Daddy! How was work?"

Her happiness coaxed a smile from me. "Work was good. Lots of cats in today, including five kittens from one litter."

"Can we get one?"

That pulled a genuine laugh out of me. "No room at the inn, dear daughter. The Holloway house is full up."

"But when Miss Emerson takes Nugget and Xavier and Sky and moves to a house, we'll have four spots open."

The truth of that hit me in the chest like a steel beam, but I did my best to hide it, instead sharing an amused look with Berty.

"We're not getting any new pets, vacancies or not."

"The humans are already outnumbered," Berty added.

"Kittens are so cute though."

"Maybe you could draw a picture of a cat family," Berty suggested.

Evelyn considered that. "Okay, I'll try it." She sat back down on the floor, pulled out a sketch pad from under the activity book, and started drawing.

"Are the others upstairs?" I asked.

"Last I knew they were building a blanket fort, hoping you'd let them sleep in it tonight," Berty said.

I headed upstairs.

"Wow. What alternate blanket universe have I walked into?" I asked when I stepped into Ruby's room. They must've absconded with every blanket in the house.

"Hey, Dad!" Ruby called from inside the fort.

"Hi, Dr. Ben! This is my room over here," Xavier said, his head popping up from between two blankets hanging on the far side of the room.

"Architects in training, huh?"

"We have a kitchen and two bedrooms and a living room and a game room," Ruby said, her voice getting closer as she presumably crawled through the tent. She popped out near me and hugged my legs.

"Where's Skyler?"

"She's not in here." My daughter stood and surveyed the fort from the outside.

"I think she's with Evelyn," Xavier said, poking his head out of a different space.

I frowned. "She wasn't with Ev. I'll check her room. Happy decorating."

Forty-five seconds later, I'd checked Evelyn and Skyler's room, the bathroom, and Emerson's room, which I needed to start thinking of as the guest room again, but found no Skyler.

With alarm beginning to pulse through me, I poked my head back in Ruby's room. "You're sure Sky's not in here hiding somewhere? I can't find her."

"Skyler!" Ruby called.

"She's not in my room or the game room," Xavier said, his voice moving under the blanket roof as he searched. "Not in our kitchen."

"Check under your real beds too," I said and went to do the same in the other two bedrooms. I looked behind the shower curtain and scanned all the closets. "Shit."

"She's not in there," Ruby said, exiting her room with a concerned look.

The three of us thundered down the stairs. "Check the laundry room and bathroom." I went into the living room. "We can't find Sky."

Berty shot up out of the chair quickly for her age. "Did you check Ev's room?"

"I checked everywhere upstairs. The kids are looking in the laundry room."

"What about the barn and the chicken house?" she asked.

"I'm on my way." I strode toward the mudroom.

Evelyn sped past me. "I'll go look in the chicken house, Dad."

"She's not anywhere," Ruby said, coming out of the

laundry room with Xavier behind her. "I'm worried, Daddy."

I summoned every ounce of confidence I could and said, "Let's not panic yet. You two get your coats on and check the workshop and the garage."

All four of us grabbed our coats and headed outside, scattering in different directions.

As I jogged to the barn, my panic crept higher. I didn't want Emerson to go through this fear again: the searching, the not knowing. I understood very well what it'd done to her last time.

The what-ifs and the worst-case scenarios were knocking on my brain, taunting me. Skyler might as well be my own daughter. I loved her as if she were. It was no longer just about her and Xavier being Blake's children. Not even just because they were Emerson's. They were part of our family, regardless of my relationship with their mom.

With my heart pounding, I slid the main barn door open and rushed in. The lights were low, and at first I didn't see anyone, but then I caught a glimpse of brown hair at the opposite end.

"Sky?"

Her head popped out from Esmerelda's stall—about four feet above the ground.

"Sweetie, *what* are you doing?" I jogged closer, not believing my eyes.

She was sitting in the llama's empty hay bin that attached to the half wall, smiling as big as day, Waylon the elephant next to her, Esmerelda's snout close by. Skyler had apparently shoved the large bin of cat food over to the wall, climbed up on it, then crawled over the shorter stall wall, plush elephant in tow.

"Sharing," she said proudly, holding up a half-eaten

rainbow-sprinkle cookie. Then with her other hand, she held out the zipper bag where the rest were stored.

Esmerelda chomped contentedly, her big eyes following the bag.

I rushed up to Sky on this side of the stall to ensure she wasn't in any danger, hugging her awkwardly over the wall. "You..." I couldn't help it. I laughed, feeling lightness in my chest that I hadn't felt in days, brought on by profound relief and the picture she made, sitting there in the feeding trough, happy as a...llama with a cookie.

I hugged her again. "We were worried about you, Sky Blue. You can't leave the house without telling an adult."

"Grandma Berty was busy doing laundry," she said matter-of-factly, and it was damn hard to muster any true annoyance. "And the llamas needed their Christmas presents."

"Cookies?"

She nodded once emphatically, looking pleased with herself.

I pulled out my phone and texted Berty.

> She's in the barn. All is well.

To prove my claim, and because you really needed to see this to believe it, I reassured myself the feed bin was secure, then stepped back a few feet, telling her, "Stay still and smile, silly goose."

We'd have a stern discussion later, when my relief leveled out.

As I went back to Sky's side, Emerson walked into the barn. "What's going on? Why's the door open?"

The sight of her punched me in the gut. She wore an oversized, fuzzy green sweater over leggings, knee-high boots, and a multicolored scarf around her neck. Her long hair was wind-tousled, her cheeks pink, her smile seeming a little more genuine than it had lately. Maybe she was actually feeling some holiday spirit.

"Your daughter's gotten into a little mischief," I said lightly.

Emerson's smile disappeared as she hurried toward us. "Skyler?" She craned her neck as she realized where Sky was. "*What* are you doing?"

"Eating cookies with Esmerelda," she said as if it was the most natural thing in the world and she hadn't been scared of the llama just a few weeks ago.

Emerson met my gaze with a questioning one.

"We couldn't find her for a few minutes. Luckily I looked here first. Everybody's fine." I hoisted Skyler and her elephant out of the feed bin and over the wall to our side, hugging her close. "We'll have a discussion about safety and rules later."

When I held Sky toward her mom, Emerson surprised me by putting her arms around both of us for a hug. Before now, she'd barely looked me in the eye since leaving last week.

I bit down on the questions that set off in my mind and soaked in the moment of being close to these two people I loved with all my heart.

———

Emerson, Xavier, and Skyler joined the four of us for our Christmas Eve dinner tradition of spaghetti and meatballs. We cleaned the kitchen as a group so we could take our annual drive around town to look at Christmas lights, with Berty claiming she needed to get home and to bed so she could join us early on Christmas morning. I'd suggested she stay at our place and sleep on the sofa, but she refused, saying her bones were too old for sofas. When Emerson had volunteered to give up her bed, Berty held to her determination to get to her own home.

During our holiday light tour, the snow had started falling in large, peaceful flakes that didn't stick to the pavement but quickly covered the grass and other surfaces in a white blanket.

Once we returned home, the kids raced out of the truck toward the house. Emerson and I walked more slowly from the garage to the door. She squeezed my forearm, smiled up at me, and said, "That was magical. Thank you."

I peered down at her, confused as hell. She'd been warmer toward me all evening. It made me wonder if she'd either decided to buy the house she'd toured or decided she needed to stay with us longer—or both. I knew she hadn't told the kids she was looking at a place, so I had to wait to ask her the status.

I wasn't sure how I felt about her staying longer just to leave in a few weeks as originally planned. Everything had changed. It was murkier now. I loved having her kids here, and I'd grown attached to her dog. But the tension between us, at least before today, made everything trickier. It made it hard to relax in my own home.

"What's going on?" I asked her quietly, so the kids wouldn't hear.

Her smile faded. "We need to talk." She glanced at the gang of kids clamoring at the door to the house. "Later."

Her expression seemed meaningful, but I couldn't figure out what the meaning might be. I was thankful for the warmth, whatever the cause. It was much better than the awkward politeness of the past few days. I couldn't help but wonder what had changed.

———

Finally, by nine o'clock, we had the kids in bed, convinced Santa might skip over our house if they weren't sound asleep.

Emerson was upstairs tucking in Skyler after reading *The Night Before Christmas* to all four of them, all of *us*—three times.

I'd come down after turning out the lights in Ruby's room, where she and Xavier were tucked into their beds after dismantling the giant fort. We'd helped them see reason by pointing out they wouldn't be able to play with anything new they might get for Christmas if they couldn't walk through their room.

I was antsy, curious, wondering what Emerson was going to say. I paced the living room, then stopped and tried to get out of my head and appreciate the moment, the quiet. The twinkling lights on the tree soothed me, and I looked at each ornament, some the kids had made, some we'd picked out together, all with memories and meanings.

Emerson came up to my side and aimed her attention at the tree as well.

"Everybody good up there?" I asked.

"They seem to be. The Santa threat works like a charm, doesn't it?"

"Every year. One of these years, Evelyn will be onto me if she's not already."

I wished I had a drink, something to hold on to. I considered offering her some wine or cocoa, but without knowing what she wanted to talk about or how it would go, a beverage seemed like a stall and a distraction.

"What did you want to talk about?" I asked, impatient.

She inhaled audibly, and I saw her chest rise with it out of the corner of my eye. I forced my focus back on the tree lights.

Emerson turned to face me, so I followed suit, feigning nonchalance while my pulse sped.

For a second, our gazes met, and I tried to read hers. She averted her eyes too quickly, seeming nervous. That did nothing to help my optimism.

She gripped her own arm at the elbow, which seemed only slightly less closed-off than if she'd crossed her arms over her chest. Or maybe that too was nerves. What the hell was she nervous about?

"I found the perfect house," she said, peering up at me again and holding eye contact.

Everything in me sank in disappointment, but at the same time, there was a little voice that reminded me I should be happy for her. This was what she'd wanted all along, what she thought would make her happy. I wanted Emerson to be happy.

"That's great, Ems," I said, maybe a second or two later than I should've. "Tell me about it."

She shook her head, lowered her gaze for a moment, then met mine again. "I decided not to put an offer in."

"What? Why?"

"There's"—she flashed a nervous smile—"not enough room for llamas."

I narrowed my eyes as I tried to decipher her meaning. "Are you...getting llamas?" As I said it, I had a flash of a thought that maybe she meant *my* llamas, but that didn't make sense.

She held out a hand palm up in an invitation for me to take it. I grasped her fingers, hope bubbling up like a hot spring.

"I realized the perfect house sometimes actually isn't perfect. That one was missing something I don't want to live without."

I didn't breathe, waiting for her to continue. When she didn't, I raised my brows in question, about to come out of my skin.

"There's this guy," she said, glancing down at our joined hands, her lips fluttering upward into a hint of a smile, "and these two little girls plus some dogs and cats and chickens and horses and"—she pierced me with those sage-green eyes again—"llamas." She shook her head and laughed. "And I realized I love the guy and the girls and the dogs. Maybe the cats. The chickens I'm not so sure I'd call it love, but the horses have potential, and apparently my daughter loves the llamas. And I'm pretty sure the entire herd comes with the guy, and I figured out...I want the whole herd almost as much as I want the guy."

I laughed, but it was more than just amusement. So much more. It was elation and disbelief that I could be this lucky. And love.

I stared into her eyes, assuring myself she meant it, that this was real. It wasn't every day that every dream you'd ever had was suddenly in reach.

"Really?" I said dumbly, aware on some level that a person wouldn't say all of that if it wasn't true. I laughed at myself.

Emerson went serious in an instant, and I wondered if I'd misinterpreted after all.

She let go of my hand, worrying me further, then

reached under her sweater from the hem and...adjusted her bra?

As she removed her hand, she fell to the floor, or rather, she kneeled. Make that went down on one knee. Gazing up at me with nervousness and love all over her beautiful face.

I caught my breath when I saw the men's ring she held between her thumb and index finger. "Holy shit, what are you doing, Ems?"

"Ben, I never, ever thought I wanted to get married again, but then you rescued me and my kids by taking us in. And then you rescued me again by loving me so patiently, wholeheartedly, purely, so I could finally, *finally* pull my head out and realize you're my other half, and I don't want to ever live without you. Will you marry me?"

"Get up here," I said, tugging her off the floor and into my arms, overcome with lightness and pure euphoria. "I'll marry you, Emerson," I said, laughing. "I'll marry you right fucking now if you want me to."

I pulled her into my arms and wrapped her up in my love as tight as I could, then lifted her off the floor and turned us in a circle. When I set her back down, I gazed into her eyes, my face splitting with an elated grin.

"I love you, Emerson. I can't believe you proposed. There's never been a better Christmas present."

"I love you too. Enough to propose. Phew, that was terrifying."

"As if I could ever turn you down."

"I'm so sorry I freaked out and ran away."

"I'm sorry Kizzy let you down again. I'll do everything I can not to. You and the kids are first in my life. All four of them."

"Same."

I pressed my palms to her cheeks, leaned down, and

kissed her, trying to infuse everything in my heart into that kiss. Her body melted into mine, making my need for her pound through me.

"Can we get married as soon as possible?" she asked.

"Like, courthouse soon?"

She nodded. "I want it official before I move into your room. Because of the kids."

"I'll marry you the minute the courthouse opens," I said with no hesitation. "Day after tomorrow. But I have my own condition."

"Yeah?"

"Going to need you naked in my bedroom to show you how I feel," I said, "in the next thirty seconds."

She laughed. "Then you better whisk me in there and rip my clothes off." She snapped her fingers. "I did the heavy lifting of proposing. Your turn for a little effort."

I had her in my arms before she finished her sentence.

Once we were in my room, I said, "We'll make this our new Christmas Eve tradition."

As I whipped her sweater off and peeled her leggings down, she laughed.

"You were right from the start," she said. "Traditions are the best. This one is my favorite."

Epilogue

One week later

Emerson

I held my husband's hand as we reached the door to the Honeysuckle Inn ballroom.

Ben had been my husband for nearly four glorious, chaotic, family-filled hours. It was still sinking in that I was his wife. This man was forever mine.

"You ready?" he asked, pausing to look down at me with his handsome, loving eyes.

"Let's do it," I said, grinning, thinking how we already *had* done it.

Ben tugged me up against him, his possessive hand at my waist, and bent to kiss me. He took his sweet time with my lips. When he finally ended the kiss, he said, "Come on, Mrs. Holloway. We have a lot to celebrate."

His words caused a fluttering in my chest.

We laced our fingers together again, and he opened the

door, unleashing a torrent of noise: an eighties cover group called Big Hair Band was playing "Living on a Prayer," and a couple hundred partygoers were dancing, talking, drinking, laughing, preparing to welcome in the New Year at midnight.

Cash Henry greeted us and asked for our tickets. He wore a black tee with the sleeves rolled once and black pants.

"*Dirty Dancing*?" I asked. "Johnny?"

He grinned. "You got it. You're one of the few who didn't have to ask."

"Ava's pale pink dress clued me in." She'd been at the check-in counter when we'd come through the lobby. Her pregnant belly took nothing away from the costume.

"Looking good," Ben said to him.

"*Princess Bride*, right?" Cash asked us.

"This is my Buttercup," Ben said, making me laugh and roll my eyes.

Embracing the eighties theme of the party, I wore a flowing red gown with a gold belt and a long blond wig. My handsome hero was dressed in black, with poufy sleeves and ornate boots he'd ordered online.

We stopped at one of the bars and ordered drinks, then did a private toast to us. I welcomed his mouth as he kissed me yet again. I didn't mind. I'd never mind his kisses. I hoped we'd still be stopping in our tracks to kiss when we were ninety.

"Look at West over there," Ben said to me, pointing.

I laughed. "A Rubik's Cube." The big, muscled guy was wearing what appeared to be a painted cardboard box. "I hope he doesn't want to slow dance with anyone tonight."

Next to West stood Chance, Max, Harper, and Knox.

Max noticed us and waved us over to their group, standing around a tall cocktail table.

We reached them and greeted them, and I hugged Harper.

"Who are you dressed as?" I asked, laughing at her poofed out, side-parted hair that hung to the side and her powder-blue, off-the-shoulders, giant-ruffled tea-length dress.

"Eighties prom couple, of course!" she said, tugging Max closer so I could appreciate his full suit with a matching powder-blue bow tie.

"You two look amazing," I said.

"So do you!" Harper snuggled into her fiancé's side as Max put his arm around her.

Anna, Olivia, and Maeve joined us as the band ended a song, making it easier to hear for a few seconds.

"Hey, newlyweds!" Anna said. "Happy New Year!" She wore an off-the-shoulders striped shirt and frizzed, tall eighties hair.

"Hello, rock n' roll girls," Ben said.

"Look at you guys," I said, taking in the other two costumes. "You make better Bangles than the Bangles themselves."

"Don't they?" Harper said. "Confession: I had to Google what they looked like."

"Such a young thing," Olivia said, side-hugging her.

"And yes, we're jealous," Maeve added.

"Where's your fourth?" I asked.

"Magnolia's floating around, seeing to details," Anna said. "She's the true rock star tonight."

"This place looks incredible," I said.

The entire ballroom was a neon explosion.

"Anna, Ava, and Magnolia knocked it out of the park,"

Olivia agreed. She leaned in closer. "You two were *fashionably* late." She directed the comment to me and raised a suggestive brow toward Ben.

Chance had pulled Ben aside and shook his hand, probably congratulating him.

"Yes, why were you late?" Maeve asked, trying to keep a smile off her face. "*Hmm?*"

Laughing again, I said, "Let's see, we got done at the courthouse just before they closed at four. Then we had to take the whole brood home. The kids were hyper, so we fed them dinner and tried to get them calmed down before leaving them with Berty all night. Then we had to check in to our room here and unpack and change into our costumes—"

"They're amazing, by the way," Anna said.

"Thanks. And here we are." I brushed my fake blond hair back over my shoulder, feeling a slight flush on my cheeks when I thought about the way we'd consummated our marriage with an earth-shattering quickie on the bathroom counter of our room.

We'd get down to the business of our official wedding night later. I'd make certain of it, not that I'd have to convince Ben. The only thing I'd had to convince him of was getting our costumes on and coming down to the party for a few hours before continuing naked time.

Our courthouse wedding had been a few days later than we'd hoped because the kids had passed around a cold in the days following Christmas, but the weeklong wait made it all the sweeter. I could say that now that it was over and we were married.

"Well, congratulations," Maeve said, hugging me. "I'm so happy for you, Em."

"Thank you." I felt lighter than air.

Anna and Olivia hugged me next. When the band started playing a Wham song, the girls dragged me out on the dance floor. I handed off my drink to my gorgeous husband, who pressed a kiss to my lips as I went. We spent the next dozen songs dancing to the admittedly good band.

Eventually, ready to take a break, I glanced around to find my husband. I left the others on the dance floor and made my way to Ben, who was still with his dad friends, only a few of whom were single now.

"Hey," I said as I sidled up to him.

"Hey, sexiest woman alive." Ben faced me, pulled me into him, and kissed me solidly, thoroughly, plunging his tongue into my mouth as if we'd been apart for two weeks instead of maybe an hour.

I didn't mind a bit.

I kissed him back, arching into him, loving the feel of his hard, solid body.

"Newlywed alert!" Knox bellowed, laughing.

Ben and I grinned into our kiss but didn't immediately pull apart.

"Get a room!" Chance called out.

"We've got one," Ben said, peering down at me with heat in his eyes before he looked at Chance. "Jealous?"

"He got you there," West said to Chance. Then West leaned in and said, "Lloyd here's been eyeing the mystery woman with Ava for the past fifteen minutes."

"Gotta admit she's hot," Chance said.

"Lloyd?" I asked.

"Dobler," Ben said. "From *Say Anything*. His boombox is on the table behind him."

I glanced behind Chance, who wore a trench coat over a T-shirt, cargo pants, and high-top sneakers, and spotted a huge boombox.

"I love it," I said, then turned my attention to the woman West had mentioned. "We don't know who the woman is?"

Cash, who'd been relieved of door duty, said, "She checked in alone this evening, so Ava insisted she come to the party. Not sure what her story is but she seemed a little out of sorts."

"Sounds like there *is* a story there," Max said.

"Why don't you go find out, Lloyd?" West said. "Maybe she could be your Diane."

"Maybe I will," Chance said.

Quincy, Harper, Piper, Dakota, and Cambria joined our group, and we all became absorbed in a discussion of our costumes and who we thought would win the contest.

Later, just a few minutes before midnight, Adrian Cormier, who was deejaying now that the band had finished, got on the mic.

"Hey, party people, the New Year's about nine minutes away. We're going to slow things down for a couple dances to get you in the mood for your New Year's kisses, so if you don't know who you'll be kissing yet, now's the time to figure it out. Don't be caught alone at the stroke of midnight!"

The first notes of Madonna's "Crazy for You" played, and my husband held out his hand.

"Care to dance, wife of mine?"

"We should probably warm up for that kiss too," I said.

"I love the way you think."

He led me out to the dance floor, and then we did kiss, but just a short few brushes of our lips. I, for one, was more than ready for naked time back in our room, but we'd agreed to hold out for midnight before making our escape.

We danced with our bodies pressed into each other, his erection apparent, telling me Ben was ready too.

The dance floor was filled, the tables throughout the place emptying as most people were taking Adrian's advice and coupling up.

The lights were dim enough and the dance floor crowded enough I couldn't see whether my single girlfriends had found someone to ring in the New Year with.

"Look at that," Ben said, nodding to the side of us.

I followed his nod to Chance, who was dancing with the mystery woman he'd been eyeing. Dancing *closely*. Body to body, just like my husband and me. The woman was peering up at Chance with a heated smile as they talked, inaudible to us. I couldn't see Chance's expression, but the woman, who was incidentally really pretty, seemed all on board with whatever was happening.

Interesting.

"Go, Chance," I said quietly.

"He could use a woman in his life," Ben said with a laugh.

"What about West?" I asked.

"He took off a few minutes ago, saying he wanted to relieve his babysitter."

"And avoid the New Year's kiss pressure?"

"That's my guess. His ex messed him up. Or rather, messed his girls up. He's gone cautious to an extreme."

"I guess that's not a bad thing. Good for him for putting his kids first."

The music segued into "Heaven" by Bryan Adams. I stopped thinking about all our single friends and nestled my head into my husband's chest, letting gratitude permeate every inch of me. I was so lucky to have this strong, loving, beautiful man. Tonight and for the rest of our lives.

Before the song was over, an army of servers scurried through, weaving around couples on the dance floor, passing out plastic flutes and filling them with champagne.

There were also people passing around noisemakers and horns, but with my drink in one hand and my attention focused on my husband, I had no need for anything extra. My celebrating this year was inside of me, in my heart and my soul.

"You ready?" Ben said, his empty hand at the small of my back, pulling me flush against him again.

"I'm so ready." I signaled my double meaning with my eyes.

He seemed to understand my message as he bowed his head close to my ear and growled.

"Here we go, folks," Adrian said into the microphone. "Ten, nine, eight..."

We joined him in the countdown, my gaze locked with Ben's as if making our second lifelong promise of the day to each other.

"Happy New Year!" everyone yelled as my lips locked with my husband's.

Our kiss went on for a good long while as we meshed our bodies together in the same way we'd meshed our lives together.

When we finally drew apart, I caught sight of Chance and his mystery girl out of the corner of my eye as they slipped out the ballroom entrance.

With a distracted smile, I peered up at my love. "Happy New Year," I said, running my palm over his bearded jaw.

"Happy New Year, love of my life."

We kissed again, this time a quick brush before he pulled back and added, "I've never felt so excited to dive into a new year as I do tonight. Because of you. I love you, Ems."

"I love you back."

"I love our life. Our chaotic, never-quiet, kid-filled, animal-filled, love-filled life."

"I do too," I said, my heart overflowing with love. "Like I never would've thought I could love the craziness. But I do one hundred percent. And Ben?"

"Mm-hmm?"

"If you take me upstairs right now, I'll show you *how much* I love it—and you."

With an irresistible smile as he peered down at me, he said, "As you wish."

Bonus Epilogue

July

Ben

The big day had finally arrived.

Our family had been looking forward to our boat rental since Xavier had won it back in December.

Evelyn couldn't wait to fish.

Xavier and Ruby were all about being pulled in a tube behind the boat.

And true to character, our Skyler was most excited about the food. She'd been guessing all week what kind of food would be included in our picnic lunch prize from the Country Market. Her delight at finding out we got to choose our dishes was priceless.

Emerson had enlisted our youngest daughter's help with all the picnic decision-making, and we had, in our cooler and picnic basket, ham and cheese pinwheels, fruit and cheese kabobs, chicken tenders, PB and J on a stick, ranch Goldfish snack mix, strawberry lemonade, and chips and salsa.

On top of all that, we'd stocked up on cookies from Sugar, more cookies than we should eat in a week, but I felt confident they'd be demolished by the end of the day. Emerson and I had agreed we'd let it happen. We'd also stashed a half-dozen for the llamas back home to ensure our furry princesses had what they believed was their God-given right.

As the six of us walked toward McNamara Marina, the kids skipped ahead, giving Emerson and me the semblance of twenty seconds alone.

"Are you excited?" I asked her, taking her hand in mine.

"I'm looking forward to it," she said. "The kids are wound up tighter than a tick."

"Are we crazy to trap ourselves on a small vessel with four hyped-up kids for several hours?"

"One hundred percent." She laughed. "Good thing they're cute."

"I can't wait to get out on the water. No phone calls, no appointments, no interruptions, no sick animals, no arguments over TV shows or who feeds which horse. Nothing can get to us out in the middle of the lake."

Emerson narrowed her eyes. "Almost sounds too good to be true."

"Bite your tongue."

Work had been extra insane for the past few months. What it came down to was that there were more pets in Dragonfly Lake than I could provide care for, so two months ago, I'd hired another vet and a third tech. In the long run, it would work out well, but getting the new people trained and used to the way we did things took extra effort on top of an already overfull work week.

I gazed out at the lake as we headed to the entrance. It was calm, dappled with sunlight, dotted with boats, but it was a large lake. We'd find our piece of serenity.

Twenty minutes later, we headed out from the dock in our mid-size pontoon. Our family would've fit on a small one, but Cade had arranged for the medium one as the prize, so that's what we got. The kids were all in the front, the bow. I wasn't too fluent in nautical speak, but I did know how to drive a boat.

Emerson was in the seat next to my captain's seat as we set off to find a spot where the kids could swim before we ate. Cade had offered a couple of tips, places we might find some relative privacy and good swimming spots.

I increased our speed at the kids' urging—"Go faster, Daddy, go faster!"—and headed to the eastern half of the lake.

All four kids were Holloways as of two weeks ago, but Skyler and Xavier had started calling me Dad from the day I married their mother. My girls, too, called Emerson Mom. Evelyn insisted on referring to Leeann as Mama to distinguish between the two, which I thought was a touching idea.

"How does this look?" I asked Emerson as I slowed the pontoon in an area where there were no other boats.

"I'm no expert but this looks swimmable."

We dropped the anchor with the kids buzzing with excitement. Emerson stood and shed her cover-up, revealing a modest blue and purple bikini that made me wish we were alone. Before she could join the kids at the stern, where there was a small deck, I pulled her close.

"You're fucking gorgeous," I said so the kids couldn't hear.

She kissed me quickly with a heated look in her eyes

that I knew was a promise for tonight. I turned my thoughts to practical things like our children's safety in an effort to cool my jets.

After coating them with sunscreen and double-checking their life jackets, we helped them jump off the back of the boat with noodles, a raft, a tube, and a floating ball.

I took my shirt off, thinking I'd need a dip in the water to cool off soon.

Emerson and I stood watching them for a few minutes. Once we were sure the kids were comfortable and safe, we went to the bench seats at the bow and each stretched out our legs on them.

"Ahh," she said as she re-secured her hair in a scrunchy. "Can you hear that?"

I glanced at her pretty, relaxed face as she leaned back against the end cushion, and it hit me. "Relative quiet?"

The kids were talking but at low volumes for the time being. Their voices were like white noise to us anyway, so it seemed peaceful.

Our home hadn't been peaceful for five weeks, as we'd contracted with Levi Dawson's construction company to add on to the house. The addition would enlarge our master bedroom and add a master bath on the main level and a fourth and fifth bedroom on the second floor, so each kid would have their own space and Berty could stay with us any time as well.

It was going to be perfect for all of us, and it was almost finished. That couldn't happen fast enough.

I reclined, keeping one eye on the kids, and let out my breath, feeling as if I hadn't for...months.

Five seconds later, Emerson shot upright.

"Did you hear that?" she asked, more curious than alarmed.

"Hear what?" I heard water sounds, the kids' voices, the creak of the boat as it rocked.

She listened for a few seconds, then relaxed a degree, shaking her head. "I'm not sure. Something super high-pitched, I thought, but I don't hear it now. Maybe it was my imagination or my ears reacting to low decibels."

I laughed. "We're pretty programmed for all loud, all the time, huh?"

As she stretched her legs out again on the bench seat, I fought not to think about them wrapping around me as I pounded into her. I swallowed hard, stood, went to the cooler, and grabbed myself a bottled water. "Want a drink?"

"Iced tea, please."

I grabbed a bottle for her, watched the kids playing some kind of game with their noodles, then went back to sit with my wife, whose eyes were on the kids too.

"Thank you, Dr. Holloway," she said oh-so-properly, knowing exactly how that made me want to mess her right up. A few seconds later, she sat up again. "There's that sound."

I strained my ears but didn't hear anything different. Eventually my wife relaxed again.

"It was bound to happen," I teased her. "Just seven months in the Holloway household and you're losing it."

"I was losing it after one night and that crazy cock—the one in the chicken house—woke me up."

"And still you married me."

"Thank God," she said, taking my hand across the small space between our benches.

"Thank God," I repeated, meaning it times a hundred.

After about twenty minutes of relaxing, watching the kids, I stood. "I'm going in. Care to join me?" I held my hand out to Emerson.

She took it, stood, and kissed me. I caught her with my arm and pulled her in again, kissing her for more than a peck. She moaned low, which did nothing to make me want to let go of her, but the kids were right there.

That was the story of our life. It wasn't easy to find alone time with my gorgeous wife, but we managed to as often as possible.

After swimming, we were famished. The kids' enthusiasm didn't wane at all as they climbed out, dried off, and gathered around the picnic basket. Skyler took pride in her job of distributing the food, and then she filled her plate to overflowing, making me grin.

The six of us were sitting in the back half of the pontoon, eating our lunches, discussing which food was the best, when I heard something faint and high-pitched. My gaze went to Emerson, who stopped chewing and raised her brows, telling me she'd heard it too.

"What was that?" Xavier asked, glancing around. "It sounded like an animal."

"We're in the middle of a giant lake," Evelyn told him. "All the animals are far away except fish and birds."

The sound came again. It definitely came from a living thing. Something on the boat.

I jumped up at the same time Emerson did, both of us eyeing the bench seat under Xavier and Ruby.

"Stand up, kids," I said.

Emerson took a step back as the sound came again. Whatever was in that storage bin was small and unlikely to hurt us. I wasn't going to be careless though.

Standing to the side, I removed the cushion, then eased the storage lid up. My jaw fell open.

Before I could get any words out, Evelyn said, "A mama cat and kittens!"

Ruby peeked over the edge and squealed and jumped up and down. "Daddy, can we keep them?"

Emerson's hand shot over her mouth to catch a laugh, then she sent me a wide-eyed look of disbelief. "Too good to be true," she muttered, repeating her earlier suspicion.

I bent down to get a closer look. "Those are newborns," I said.

The mother eyed me warily, tiredly, and I took a step back, respecting her need to protect her babies. With my mind spinning, I gently closed the storage lid.

"Let's give them some space," I told the kids. "Those babies can't be more than a few hours old."

"Ooh, Daddy, I want to hold them!" Ruby said, dancing from one foot to the other.

"We can't," Evelyn told her. "The mom needs to bond with them. We'll need to take them home, Daddy."

Emerson and I exchanged a glance that said, *Not so fast*.

"There's a good chance the cat belongs to Cade or one of the McNamaras," I said optimistically.

"Can you call them and see?" Ev asked.

I picked my phone up from the console where I'd left it and saw, unsurprised, I didn't have a signal out here. "I'll have to ask when we take the boat back. Or as soon as we get a signal."

"Can we look again, Daddy?" Skyler asked. "I didn't get to see them."

I knew it was too much to ask for the kids to just move to the bow and go on their way, pretending there weren't stowaway kittens in our midst.

"Okay, here's what we're going to do. I'm going to open it again, and you can each get one good look. I want to make sure they all seem like they're nursing okay and that nobody's in distress. Then we have to let them rest."

Emerson sidled up next to me. "You can take the vet out of the clinic but you can't get the vet out of the man."

I put one arm around her, then eased the lid up again. "Shh. Everyone be quiet and move slowly when you look. No touching."

As the kids checked out the cat nest, I did a visual check. There were four kittens, and all four were nursing from the short-hair white and gray mother. I didn't see anything that alarmed me.

"Adorable," Emerson whispered beside me.

Once I'd closed the lid softly again, the kids grabbed their remaining food and pranced to the front bench seats to finish eating, talking about the kittens.

Emerson stayed back with me. "They look okay?"

I nodded and blew out a breath. "I didn't see a collar on the mom."

Her brows went up. "You think she's a stray?"

"I'm a little worried."

She pressed her lips together against a grin. "More souls for the Holloways to save, Doctor?"

I growled at her, then nodded to the captain's and first mate's seats. "Shall we finish our lunch and try to pretend we don't have stowaways?"

With a laugh, she sat down with her plate. "It's killing you not to examine them closer, isn't it?"

I shook my head. "I don't want to mess with them unless I need to."

"We're going to need to get them out when we get back, aren't we?"

"They can't stay on the boat," I agreed. "In fact, maybe we should head back early and find them a safe place. It can't be easy on them to ride around on a speeding boat."

After we finished eating, we broke the news to the kids

that tubing would have to wait so we could make a special delivery and get the McNamara cats back where they belonged. They embraced our new transport mission importantly, and I pointed the boat back toward the marina.

Unfortunately, it turned out to be more than a transport mission.

"I haven't seen her before," Cade said. "Neither have my brothers or my mom. She isn't ours."

"Do one of you want to take them?" I asked.

Emerson was outside with the kids, walking along the docks with them.

Cade leveled a look at me. "My dog would likely eat those babies for an afternoon snack."

"That's fair." I chuckled. I knew Diesel, his Great Dane, well. He was a gentle dog but had toenails the size of those newborn kittens. "I'll find a home for them."

When I rejoined my family a few minutes later, I told the kids Cade had given us an extra gift certificate so we could go out another day, when we didn't need to save a litter of kittens. I wasn't sure how they'd take that news, but they were so into the cat rescue that they cheered at having a second day on the lake.

Evelyn asked, "Whose kitty is the mama, Dad?"

With a glance at Emerson, I admitted, "She appears to be a stray. No collar. No one's seen her before. I'll have to check her for a chip before we know for sure, but I'd be surprised if she has one."

"Ooh, can we have the kittens, Dad?" Ruby asked, bouncing up and down. "Pleeease?"

"Yeah, please, Dad?" Xavier pleaded.

"And the mommy?" Skyler said, concerned.

"The mom can't be separated from her babies," Evelyn said.

271

When I looked at Emerson, she was watching me with a subdued but amused expression. She raised her brows as if to ask, *What are you going to do?*

"Kids, your mother and I need to talk." I went over to the picnic basket and took out the cookie container. "Each of you take a cookie and go over to that picnic table to eat it."

Once the kids skipped off with their snacks, I moved closer to Emerson. "We're a team now," I said quietly. "This isn't just my decision."

She faced me, weaving our fingers together. "Do you want me to save you from yourself here? Or do we want five new mouths to feed?"

I frowned.

"You can say no," she gently reminded me.

"They'll need to be fostered for several weeks regardless."

"Which you're thinking of doing," she said, reading me accurately. That or knowing me well.

"I am."

"And you're worried the kids will get attached in that time anyway," she said, grinning.

With a sigh, I said, "You know they would."

"They would. So you're thinking we might as well just adopt them now and avert a foster failure."

Chuckling, I admitted, "I might be. It's possible you know me too well."

"It's possible I know you inside and out, and I love every bit of you."

"I'm so damn thankful for that," I said, "and I love you too." I ran my hands up her arms and gazed into her pretty green eyes. "Would you be okay with it?"

"Adopting the cats? They *are* adorable, and there's one kitten for each kid."

"It's like fate."

"The number of kittens *and* the mother choosing the boat the local veterinarian animal lover rented for the afternoon. We kind of didn't stand a chance."

"We kind of didn't. Kids," I called out, "start thinking of kitten names."

The joyful uproar at the picnic table sounded more like twenty people than four. Then it moved as one big, swarming gang of excitement and ended with all four of them circling Emerson and me, hugging us, and cheering.

"We might be crazy," I said to my wife.

"But it's a happy, love-filled crazy, and I wouldn't change a single thing."

"Neither would I."

Note from the Author

Thanks for reading *Single All the Way*! I hope you loved Ben and Emerson.

Next up is *Single Chance*, Chance and Rowan's story. Watch for it in early 2025!

If you missed the Henry Brothers series, you can dive into book one, *Unraveled*! Find out how a marriage of convenience can test even the best of friends!

Find *Unraveled* in ebook, audiobook, and paperback in my author store at amyknuppbooks.com!

――――

If you liked *Single All the Way*, I hope you'll consider leaving a review for it. Reviews help other readers find books and can be as short (or long) as you feel comfortable with. Just a couple sentences is all it takes. I appreciate all honest reviews.

――――

Note from the Author

Single All the Way is part of the Single Dads of Dragonfly Lake series, which includes:

- Singled Out
- Single All the Way
- Single Chance
- Single-Minded

Also by Amy Knupp

North Brothers Books 4-5

North Brothers: The Complete Series

Or binge the North Brothers in audio:

North Brothers Audiobooks

<u>Hale Street Series</u>:

Sweet Spot

Sweet Dreams

Soft Spot

One and Only

Last First Kiss

Heartstrings

<u>Hale Street Box Sets:</u>

Meet Me at Clayborne's

Clayborne's After Hours

It Happened on Hale Street

<u>Island Fire Series</u>:

Playing with Fire

Heat of the Night

Fully Involved

Firestorm

Afterburn

Up in Flames

Flash Point

Fire Within

Impulse

Slow Burn

Island Fire Box Sets:

Sparked (books 1-3)

Ignited (books 4-6)

Enflamed (books 7-10)

OR

Island Fire: The Complete Series

Themed Bundles

Single Dad

Opposites Attract

Grumpy-Sunshine

Cinnamon Roll Heroes

Childhood Crush

Forbidden Love

Friends to Lovers

Coming Home

Musicians

Second Chance

Workplace Romance

Heroines Finding Their Path

About the Author

Amy Knupp is a *USA Today* Best-Selling author of contemporary romance. She loves words and grammar and meaty, engrossing stories with complex characters.

Amy lives in Wisconsin with her husband and has two adult children, two cats, and a box turtle. She graduated from the University of Kansas with degrees in French and journalism. In her spare time, she enjoys traveling, breaking up cat fights, watching college hoops, and annoying her family by correcting their grammar.

For more information:
https://www.amyknuppbooks.com